Secrets, Lies, and Online Dating

By Sylvia McDaniel

Books by Sylvia McDaniel

Contemporary Romance

Standalones
The Reluctant Santa
My Sister's Boyfriend
The Wanted Bride
The Relationship Coach
Her Christmas Lie
Secrets, Lies, and Online Dating
Paying for the Past
Cupid's Revenge

Anthologies
Kisses, Laughter & Love
Christmas with you

Collaborative Series

Magic, New Mexico
Touch of Decadence

Western Historicals

Standalones
A Hero's Heart
A Scarlet Bride
Second Chance Cowboy

The Cuvier Women
Wronged
Betrayed
Beguiled

Lipstick and Lead
Desperate
Deadly
Dangerous
Daring
Determined
Deceived

Scandalous Suffragettes
Abigail
Bella
Callie
Faith

The Burnett Brides
The Rancher Takes a Bride
The Outlaw Takes a Bride
The Marshal Takes a Bride
The Christmas Bride

Anthologies
Wild Western Women
Courting the West
Wild Western Women Ride Again

Collaborative Series

The Surprise Brides
Ethan

American Mail Order Brides
Katie

Secrets, Lies, and Online Dating
Published by Virtual Bookseller

Cover Design by Rogenna Brewer
http://sweettoheat.blogspot.com/

Editing and Formatting by Laurelle Procter
laurelleprocter@gmail.com

Short Description: Can three generations recreate their lives, and
learn that the bond between them is stronger than secrets, lies,
and thrilling new loves?

ISBN: 978-1-942608-14-1 (paperback)
ISBN: 978-1-942608-15-8 (e-book)

{Contemporary Romance – Fiction}
{Romantic Comedy – Fiction}
{Romance – Fiction}

www.SylviaMcDaniel.com

Synopsis

One lie changes the course of three lives…

When Marianne Larson uncovers a truth about her marriage, she sets out to change the course of her life, finding herself along the way. But that journey doesn't come easy as her mother and daughter decide to take a ride of their own–a ride that just might change all of their lives.

While discovering secrets, lies, and the truth about men & dating, three generations and three very different personalities recreate their lives and strengthen their female bond. But what they find might just be what they knew all along…

Table of Contents

Chapter One

Marianne Larson stood before the apartment door of her husband's latest fling with his two suitcases in hand, determined, scared, and mad as hell. Birds twittered happy songs in the early spring afternoon in North Dallas, but it could have been a death dirge for all she cared.

Like an overcooked steak, she felt fried, burnt to a crisp —she was emotionally done. She had finally let go of the idea that marriage is forever. Each breath she took felt like a fifty-pound bowling ball resting on her chest.

Marianne dropped the two bulging suitcases onto the concrete walk and waited for the constable to step out of sight. She shoved her blonde hair away from her face, yanked back her shoulders, and lifted her shaking fingers to the doorbell.

Her new life was about to begin.

A shadow filled the peephole, and hushed, panicked voices echoed from inside the apartment. She recognized her adulterous, soon-to-be ex-husband's voice. The door opened as far as the security chain allowed.

A blonde woman peeked through the gap with a too-wide, fake smile. Marianne blinked in disbelief at the girl's thigh high boots, clinging thong, and bustier. A leather whip was still in her hand, the perfect accessory to her dominatrix outfit.

"Marianne! What a surprise."

For a moment, Marianne stared, stunned, before hysterical laughter bubbled up from deep within her. She recognized the girl from the company picnic, but leather? Whips?

At her laughter, the girl's russet eyes darkened.

"Yes, a surprise for both of us. I never knew Daniel was into…" Marianne stumbled over the word "…games." She gathered her wits. "I brought Daniel his clothes."

The woman's dark eyes widened. "Here? Whatever for?"

"Look, I know Daniel is inside. His BMW is in the parking lot. You're not the first one to climb on top of him while earning a promotion, though I see you have a unique way of securing your advancement."

Daniel's reddened face appeared in the doorway, his body hidden by his dominatrix. "Marianne, what are you doing here?"

"Bringing you your clothes."

Marianne gazed upon her college sweetheart, her heart void of the love it once held. Daniel shoved his lover aside, slid back the security chain, and yanked the door open.

"Honey, you know this means nothing."

The view of her husband with a leather choke collar around his neck and a leather thong clinging to his loins brought uncontrollable laughter spewing from her like a fountain. How could she not have known that he was into sexual games?

The constable standing to the side muffled his snicker.

"You're right. Your cheating means nothing anymore." Daniel flinched.

She handed the bulging suitcases to the man she'd once loved.

"Here are your things," Marianne said, trembling from nerves, though she'd never felt more certain in her life. "And Constable Warren has something for you."

The constable stepped into the breezeway. "Are you Daniel Larson?"

"Yes?"

The officer shoved the paperwork into Daniel's hand. "Consider yourself served."

"Marianne?" Daniel questioned, his voice rising as he tore open the envelope. "What the hell is this?"

"It's called a divorce. You've cheated on me for the last

time."

His dark eyes widened as he scanned the contents of the document.

Daniel lifted his shocked gaze to her. "You can't be serious! You locked me out of our home?"

"Yes. I'll see you in court," she said, wanting to escape before the scene turned ugly.

His tone became cajoling. "Marianne, honey, we've been married a long time. Because of me, you live a comfortable life. You *need* me to take care of you."

God, no wonder Daniel was top salesman year after year. "You know, that line worked the first hundred times you used it, but not any longer. I'm done, Daniel."

Marianne walked off, certain they'd said everything.

Daniel followed her, barefoot, his dog chain clinking on the ground. At noon, most people were at work, but a few stopped to stare.

"Don't do this, Marianne. Think of our daughter."

She kept marching, each determined step finishing what she should have ended years ago.

"I'll end the affair. I'll change," Daniel promised.

Marianne whirled around to face him. "Why?"

He stopped, his chain rattling, his expression perplexed by her question. "Because – because you want me to."

"Do I?" She paused, considering his remark for a few seconds. "And that would last until the next pretty blonde in your office offered you a little booty, and then you'd cheat again."

Daniel stood half-naked in the open parking lot, a baffled expression on his handsome face. He didn't seem to know how to react.

"Don't do this," Daniel begged. "I won't give you a divorce."

"Fine. I wanted to make this quick and to protect our daughter from knowing the truth about her father, but we can do this the hard way. A long, drawn-out legal trial will force me to parade your extra-marital affairs through the courtroom. In the end, I'll be entitled to sixty percent of our assets instead of the normal fifty. And our daughter will know what a douche bag her father is."

His dark eyes burned her. "You wouldn't dare."

"And this little escapade will make for interesting viewing in the courtroom. Wave at the camera, darling."

The detective she'd hired moved from behind the van and waved at him, the red light of the video camera beamed as it recorded his stunned expression. Part of her felt despicable for being so brutal, but the rational part knew he deserved this and more. This time he would not brainwash her into believing she had no choice but to stay.

"You planned this," he said in awe.

"Yes, I did," she admitted, proud that she had pushed aside her fears and done what should have happened years ago.

Daniel gave her a pleading look that reached inside, igniting all the fear locked away. Never again would she return to being the same wife who had tolerated his cheating for at least three years.

"Marianne," his voice changed to the sweet seductive tone that normally convinced her to see things his way. "We've been married a long time, baby. You don't play these kinds of games with me. We have a good life together. We have a daughter."

"I want out."

"You've spent the last eighteen years a stay-at-home mom. Are you going to get a job?" He tried to take her hand, but she stepped out of his reach. "Who's going to hire an older woman with no skills?"

He'd gone for the jugular, and for a moment, her breath lodged in her lungs as bitter bile filled her throat. Wasn't this how he always lured her back? Reminding her of her faults, how she couldn't take care of herself, how she depended on him for her easy life.

The constable cleared his throat, reminding her he was still there.

"You got pregnant so that you wouldn't have to finish college. You need me, honey," he said, his voice soft and persuasive, like a preacher trying to coax a sinner to return to his faithful flock. The words left her feeling like a giant lizard had just licked her, leaving behind a coating of slime.

Was it true? Had she been afraid of flunking out and deliberately gotten pregnant to keep from finishing college? Maybe she couldn't take care of herself and Katie. Maybe she…

"Stop!" Marianne commanded as much for herself as for him. She drew a deep calming breath, and her nostrils filled with the sweet scent of roses. Slowly she released the frozen air in her lungs, her armor once again firmly in place. "I deserve a man who is faithful to me."

"You *need* someone to take care of you," Daniel corrected. "And I need to have a little fun every now and then." He waved his arm toward the blonde's apartment. "This isn't serious. You'll come back to me, you'll see," he said with enough confidence to rattle her.

Marianne gave a strained smile and dug deep within herself to find a well of resources to bolster her courage. "If you don't want our daughter to know the truth about her father, you'll give me a divorce."

Marianne walked away with the constable following her. Underneath the pain, she felt stronger than she had in decades. Until today, she'd had no plan for what to do with her life once Daniel was gone. Now she would go back to college and finish what she'd started years ago. Now she had a plan.

~

Brenda Jones glanced around the country club pool, gazing at the rich old cows that bobbed in the water, waiting for class to start. Steam rose from the heated pool, and the scent of chlorine saturated the air, like the constant prickliness that permeated Brenda. Damn George for dying and leaving her alone!

Since the death of her husband, Brenda's life appeared as empty and alone as that old house she rattled around in. Thirty minutes, three times a week at the pool, was hardly time to reconnect to the outside world.

And these women were like trying to connect to a dead battery. No sizzle, no spark, and no battery operated bouncing bunny.

Brenda shoved her morbid thoughts aside as her friend Liz entered the pool.

"Hi," Brenda called and jumped into the warm water, eager to visit with Liz.

A month had passed since she'd seen Liz at water aerobics, and every time Brenda phoned her, she only spoke to the answering machine.

Brenda made her way to the woman who had once been her best friend. "How have you been? I haven't seen you lately."

Her long-time friend turned to her, a small smile lifting the corners of her mouth, her bottled hair color 70B Plum Brown hairdo outshining her fake grin. "Dean and I just returned from France with Jane and her husband Fred."

Liz had seemed distant since George's death, as if she'd drawn up the bridge over the moat to keep Brenda at bay. But then, nothing had been the same since George died.

"That sounds like fun. I remember when we all went to France that year. We had a great time."

The couples had been close, the very best of friends, until George's heart attack. Then they'd disappeared along with her husband, leaving Brenda alone in her darkest hour.

Liz gave her a guilty little smile. "Yes. So what have you been doing with yourself?"

"Trying to stay busy. I don't see many of our friends anymore. It almost feels like my friends are avoiding me."

Liz pursed her lips and fidgeted.

"It's true," Brenda said, realizing her suspicions were correct. Her stomach clenched at the unfairness of their rejection.

Her friend shifted nervously in the water and refused to look at Brenda. "People are uncomfortable with George gone. It's just not the same."

A ripple of unease scattered through Brenda. "George didn't want to die. We had so many plans, and none of them included a heart attack." She paused, understanding dawning. "This is why I never see you and Dean anymore?"

"Maybe you should join that widows group at the club. The one where they all go to dances and out to dinner together," Liz said.

The ugly truth that her best friends no longer sought her companionship, when Brenda needed their friendship the most, left her reeling with shock. The warm water turned cold, giving her a chill.

"So who do you play cards with on Friday nights?" Brenda asked, and like lightening it dawned on her. "It's Jane and Fred, isn't it? You hate Jane."

"She's all right," Liz defended.

A woman that Liz had often called an old hag had replaced her. Brenda clenched her fists, anger skipping along her spine and slamming into her gut. She'd lost her best friend, George. Did she have to lose her other friends as well?

"We've been friends since grade school," Brenda said.

"Yes."

"But, because I'm no longer part of a couple, I'm being

excluded?" Brenda asked in disbelief, the realization leaving a bitter taste in her mouth.

Liz released a heavy sigh, rolled her eyes, and faced Brenda for the first time. "Not really *excluded*. At dinner parties, it's always hard to sit a single. And I just can't bring myself to place you with another man. I mean, you and George were together for so many years."

"Yes, but I'm not dead, and I miss my friends," Brenda said, her voice rising with resentment that rose like a thermometer on a hot summer day.

"Brenda, it's not the same anymore," Liz said, growing agitated.

"So I should buy a gun and shoot myself," Brenda responded, beyond annoyed at the insensitivity of the person she'd considered her best friend. "Or could it be, I shouldn't inconvenience my friends by reminding them that their husbands might die and leave them alone?"

Liz's body stiffened. Her shoulders drew together in a rigid manner, horror frozen on her face, and Brenda knew she'd connected with the truth. "That's it. You're afraid. If my George could die suddenly, so could Dean. You could be left alone with no one."

"Dear, you're overreacting and drawing attention," Liz said, glancing around at the other women in the pool.

Brenda realized the ladies were gawking at them with interest, but she couldn't seem to care. "Excuse me, I'm being kicked out of the married friends club."

Several women gave nervous twitters.

"Let me give you a piece of advice," Brenda told them all. "Don't outlive your husband because, if you do, your supposed friends will have to face their own mortality and they will kick you to the curb."

Brenda noticed Liz quietly moving away from her, and she followed, determined to get the last word in before she left this geriatric pool party. "And Liz, one more thing about our Friday evening get-togethers. The positives are I don't have to eat your awful crab salad. I don't have to listen to how wonderful your bratty children are. But best of all, I don't have to dodge Dean's sneaky hands patting my ass."

"Brenda!" Liz said, her mouth open in shock. "You've gone over the edge."

"You're damn right I've gone over the edge. Today, I learned who my real friends are. I'm dumbfounded that it's taken me fifty years to realize you're not one of them."

Brenda made her way to the ladder, the other women in class silently watching her. She climbed out of the pool, turned, and faced the ladies with their mouths hanging open. "Ta-ta, ladies. There has to be more to life than water aerobics and I'm off to discover it without my married friends."

~

Marianne was surprised to see her mother drive up later that afternoon and realized the For Sale sign in the yard would end her peaceful interlude. It wouldn't take long for the fireworks to prevail.

"You did what?" Brenda asked, her maple-colored eyes wide with shock.

"I kicked Daniel out, Mom. I caught him cheating on me," Marianne said, quietly standing at the sink in the kitchen of her Highland Park home.

Cinnamon wafted through the kitchen from a burning candle on the granite countertop.

Two weeks had passed, and Marianne's life hadn't gotten any easier. Katie hated her, and today, her mother had shown up unexpectedly. Her mother's forehead wrinkled in a frown, her gray hair framing her oval face.

"Please tell me you cut his balls off, so his cheating is no longer an issue," her mother said in her commanding voice.

Marianne smiled. Maybe her Mom was going to be okay with the divorce. "He's still Katie's father."

"His only accomplishment in life," her mother acknowledged in her graveled sarcastic tone. "How are you going to take care of yourself and Katie? You've never worked."

"We'll get by," Marianne said. She'd balanced the checkbook that afternoon and knew that without Daniel's salary, her share of their bank accounts and home sale would not support her forever. The time to return to college was now. She required a career.

Marianne watched her mother draw a deep breath and release it slowly. Brenda walked to the kitchen table, sat down, and pointed to a chair. "Sit, Marianne. We need to talk."

Tears welled up in Marianne's eyes, but she obediently sank onto the nearest chair, feeling ten instead of forty.

"I understand you're hurt. I understand you're angry, but being alone is never easy. Starting over is hard. Single mothers live in poverty. Single men at this age are like forgotten leftovers in the fridge – cold, stinky, and rotten to the core."

Marianne had always known her mother was opinionated and judgmental, but today she'd expected comfort, outrage, and her mother to take her side. Disappointment ripped through Marianne at her mother's attitude. "A minute ago, you wanted me to cut his balls off."

"Yes. Serve them for dinner and make his life hell." Brenda pointed to the well-appointed kitchen with stainless appliances and granite countertops. "Daniel provides very well for you."

"So staying with Daniel and getting the clap would be better than getting a divorce?"

Her mother frowned, and Marianne decided that she needed to know the truth. "This is not the first time he's cheated on me. I have tolerated it for years for all the reasons you mentioned, but Katie's grown now, and I deserve someone who loves and wants only me."

"Good luck finding him," her mother stated. "You're not as young as you once were and men your age want young trophy wives."

"Mom!" With sudden clarity Marianne remembered why she never confided her problems to her mother. Right now she sought comfort, not a lecture on the lack of good single men at her age.

"What? It's true."

Marianne stiffened and briefly imagined a lifetime of never finding a man better than her horrible husband. She imagined herself always lonely, always empty, and it was tempting to crumble and retreat back to her safe, miserable marriage, but enough was enough. She had to do this.

"Then maybe I'm meant to be alone," Marianne sighed with a bitter twist to her lips. She reached out and grabbed her mother's hand, needing her approval, her reassurance.

Brenda bit her lip. "Marianne, I'm not disapproving of your decision. I just want to make sure you're aware of the hard facts of being single. You're still young enough to need companionship. Men my age want someone younger, and men your age will too."

"Not a problem, Mom," Marianne said. Living alone would be easy compared to her life with Daniel.

Brenda took a deep breath. "Soon you'll realize that women you deemed friends are nervous with a single woman coming around their husbands."

Her mother's maple eyes had a distant gaze to them, and with sudden realization, Marianne knew her mother spoke about her own life.

"Mom, this is about me, not you. This is about Daniel

fucking a skinny blonde with a…" she paused, the image startling her yet again. The DVD in her mind automatically switched on, replaying the horror show while shudders rippled like water through her. "Oh, Mom, if only you'd seen him."

Marianne buried her head in her hands, both embarrassed for Daniel and trying not to burst out laughing again.

"Oh honey, I'm sorry. You must be hurting something awful," her mother said, touching the top of her head and running her hand through Marianne's hair in a comforting gesture.

Marianne raised her head and stared at her mother. Had she understood anything she'd said? Why did they always seem to talk to each other, but never connect? "No, I'm not hurting. I fell out of love with him years ago. I feel embarrassed for him...and kind of creeped out at catching him in a dog collar and leather."

Her mother gasped, her eyes wide in disbelief. "Oh God, you didn't."

"Yes, Mom, I did," Marianne said, wanting her mother to get the full image. "His dominatrix answered the door. Daniel wore a leather thong with a dog collar around his neck. Now do you understand why I'm divorcing him?"

Her mother laughed, the sound easing the strain in the room, and even Marianne chuckled. In so many ways she was glad that she had a video of Daniel parading around in his collar. He still didn't want the divorce, but at least he was working on the settlement. Without the video, she didn't know if he would have been quite so cooperative.

"That's an image I'll take to the grave. Seems fitting for the bastard. He deserved to get whacked across the butt hard. I want you to be happy," her mother said adamantly. She squeezed Marianne's hand. "My own recent experiences have made me realize what I lost."

"You still miss Dad?" Marianne asked, pushing back her blonde hair, knowing how difficult life was without her father.

"Every day. I never imagined I would spend my retirement years alone," her mother said sadly.

Marianne missed her father and the stability he'd brought to their family. The way he tempered her mother and kept her calm.

"What about Katie?" her mother asked. "How is she handling the divorce?"

Marianne sighed. Her daughter didn't understand what had happened to her loving family. Marianne and Daniel had created a happy family atmosphere for their daughter. Now that lie was working against her.

"Katie is angry at me. She doesn't know the truth about her father's indiscretions. She should never have to know."

"Like hell. Katie deserves to know what happened between her parents," Brenda replied. "She should know her father enjoys a good spanking with someone other than his wife."

"Certainly not, Mother," Marianne responded, a trickle of alarm skittering along her spine. "He's still her father. Katie will not learn the truth from me, and you won't tell her either."

Her mother frowned. "What if I just hinted a little bit that he cheated?"

"Nothing, Mother. Don't make me regret telling you. Promise me you won't say anything."

Brenda sighed and reluctantly agreed. "I promise I won't tell Katie. But I think you're making a huge mistake by not being honest with her."

"Maybe, but that's my decision."

Brenda's response seemed less than sincere, and Marianne worried she'd said too much.

"So what are you going to do now?" her mother asked.

"I was shocked at the For Sale sign in the yard."

Marianne wanted to keep the atmosphere chummy, and she knew the news of the move would send her mother into a nuclear meltdown. She didn't like Paige. Yet Marianne had delayed her own life for so long that she refused to wait any longer.

"Do you remember my good friend, Paige, from college?" Marianne said glancing at the clock, knowing Katie would walk in any moment.

"That trashy girl on her third marriage?"

"That's the one. I'm selling the house and moving to Fort Collins, Colorado to go to school. Paige lives there. Plus I'll be closer to Katie while she's at college."

Her mother sat with a stunned expression on her face, her body tensing. For the longest time, she didn't say anything and an uneasy nervousness fluttered in Marianne's stomach. Silence this long wasn't good! It could only mean her anger was building.

Brenda's maple eyes flashed, and her face looked pinched, like someone had stapled her lips shut. She took a deep breath, and Marianne recognized the danger signals of an impending meltdown.

The kitchen door burst open, and her innocent, blonde-haired Katie rushed in from school. Marianne's heart swelled at the sight of her beautiful daughter. Katie dropped her backpack on the kitchen floor, giving Marianne a momentary reprieve.

"Hi Nana," she said and hugged her grandmother. She kept her back to Marianne, deliberately ignoring her.

Sadness slapped Marianne, like a blow to the heart. No matter how hard she tried, she couldn't connect with her daughter or her mother. And now the divorce had left a rift between them larger than the Grand Canyon.

"Did Mom tell you she kicked Dad out?" Katie said with a dramatic flip of her hair.

"Yes, she just told me," Brenda said, as if they were talking about the weather, not a life-changing event. Brenda's anger simmered in the air, like a gathering thunderstorm.

Katie snuck a glance at Marianne. "Did you convince her that this is some kind of mid-life crisis, and someday she will regret kicking out Daddy?"

Marianne glared. "I may be at mid-life, I may even be going through a life crisis, but it's my crisis, thank you."

Katie marched to the sink and leaned against the counter and glowered. "Well he's my father, and you're dissolving our family. I mean, what more can you freakin' want from him, Mother? He's given you everything."

Marianne glanced at her mother, fearful of her revealing the truth. Brenda was all but eating her lips to keep from talking. Marianne was tempted to tell her daughter exactly what she expected from Daniel, but she had vowed to stick to the high road, no matter how much she was provoked. Katie loved her father, and Marianne was going to protect her daughter from Daniel's indiscretions.

"I have explained myself once, twice, three times to you, and I'm done. I'm sorry you're hurt, but this is between your father and me."

Katie's eyes were as green as her father's and spewed emerald fire as she faced her grandmother, her hands on her hips. "Convince her she's making the biggest mistake of her life, leaving Dad, selling the house, and moving to Colorado. Tell her not to throw away eighteen perfectly good years of marriage—"

"Katie, you're old enough to realize that sometimes things are not as they seem," Brenda hesitated, glancing between them. "But moving to Colorado…did either of you stop to consider me? I've not only lost my husband, but now my daughter and granddaughter are moving over a thousand miles away?"

Seconds could be heard ticking slowly by in the quiet of the room. Her mother stood, and threw back her head in a way that elongated the length of her neck, giving her a regal appearance.

"I'm sixty years old, lonely, and bored out of my mind. My married friends act like I have the plague of death on me, and if they get too close, they might become the next widow on the block." Her voice climbed steadily higher. "And now my daughter and granddaughter are moving away. Leaving me more alone than ever."

Marianne had known this was coming, but she'd never considered that her mother had lost everything and now it sounded like everyone. But for once she had to lead her own life.

"Mom," Marianne tried to interrupt.

"Oh, sure, you'll come home for Christmas and holidays. There will be the once a week phone call and occasional birthday visit. In the meantime, what am I supposed to do?"

Brenda walked towards the door, her body stiff like a queen making her grand exit. At the door, she turned and gave them one last parting glare. "I'm not ready for the nursing home. I'm not ready for the grave. Damn George! I didn't want to be a widow."

"Mom," Marianne jumped up, her voice rising, not wanting her mother to drive in this agitated state. "Don't go. You know you can always visit us."

"No! I'm sixty years old and alone. Maybe my mid-life crisis is just twenty years late in arriving. Maybe it's my turn to act a little crazy."

Running behind her like a small kid chases after its mother, Marianne followed her to the door.

"Mom, you're overreacting!" Marianne resisted the urge to say, 'like you always do.'

"No, Marianne, I'm not. When do I get to run away and act crazy? When do I get to do something besides sit in front of the TV and wait for a phone call?"

"Nana, you're scaring me," Katie said, softly, her voice quivering.

"No, Katie, I'm making you stronger, so that you'll know what to do when your daughter and granddaughter abandon you."

Marianne gasped. God, her mother had a way with words that plunged a dagger into your heart. Between her mother and daughter there was always a lot of drama. Now more than ever.

Brenda stormed out the door, slamming it shut before Marianne could stop her.

Marianne met the icy green of her daughter's glare.

"Well, Mom, you certainly handled that well. I think you've just about run off everyone who loves you – except for your friend, Paige. Call up that home-wrecker."

Did no one ever think she could do something without being influenced by someone she knew? She'd made this decision after Daniel chased her in the parking lot. It was time for her to create her own life.

"Katie, stop it. Paige didn't cause your father and me to end our marriage. And you know how your grandmother can act."

"Yeah, a lot like you. Go call Paige so she can convince you, even more, that the single life is so much better. You two deserve each other."

Katie whirled around and ran up the stairs.

"You're acting like your grandmother!" Marianne yelled. The resounding slam of Katie's bedroom door her only response.

Marianne sank down onto the kitchen chair. She hadn't been the one to cheat, yet she bore the brunt of everyone's anger. Without Katie knowing the truth, Daniel escaped all the drama.

The phone rang, and as she picked up the receiver, she recognized the number. Daniel. Just what she didn't need. Another promise-the-world, sucking-up, begging call.

Katie answered the call and then opened her door to yell, "It's Dad, and he wants to talk to you."

God, Marianne couldn't escape Daniel. She hit the button on the phone. "What do you want?"

"Dinner and a movie tonight?' he said, his voice cajoling. "Or I could get away from work for a few days, and we could fly to Cabos San Lucas. You loved it there."

"Why do you think today's answer will be any different from yesterday's when you called? The answer is still the same. No. No. No."

"I'm not giving up on us."

"You gave up a long time ago, when you cheated. It's over." She took a deep breath, relishing the news she had to tell him. "By the way, I have a buyer for the house."

"Damn it, Marianne. I don't want to sell the house. You're fucking everything up!"

"Goodbye Daniel."

She hung up the phone and sighed. She should call her mother and make sure the older woman made it home safely, but right now she didn't have the energy.

The phone rang again. She glanced at the caller I.D. It was Katie's boyfriend, Matt. Marianne laid the receiver down. The kid was nice, but hormones exuded from him, and she could see that he so wanted in Katie's pants.

Marianne couldn't move them to Colorado quick enough.

<u>Chapter Two</u>

Matt's lips locked around Katie's like they were glued together. His hand slipped beneath her shirt and bra to caress her breast. Forbidden pleasure had her blood racing through her veins to her pounding heart. Music played from her phone, and candles flickered, creating the perfect romantic set-up. It was a great day to lose her virginity.

Doubts fluttered through her mind like nervous butterflies and she batted them aside and tried to relax. Today was the day she became a woman.

Desire spiraled through her as he kneaded her nipple, causing her to moan. His mouth trailed down her neck and he laid her against her bed and raised her shirt.

With a click, his fingers unhooked her bra and pushed the material out of the way. His mouth covered her nipple and she groaned from the pleasure of his touch.

They had been experimenting for the last month, fondling each other through their clothes, but they'd never had the luxury of being alone like they did today.

"Did you bring the condom?" she asked him between kisses.

"You're certain your mom isn't going to come home soon?" he asked, his voice low, his breath spreading goose bumps across her skin.

"Yes," she gasped as his fingers traced a path across her breasts. "She and my Dad will spend hours arguing while they sign the papers on the house. We have at least an hour."

Katie needed this diversion. She needed this time with Matt to forget all the changes in her life. Graduating and going to college were more than enough to deal with, but her family breaking up and her mother's determination to move to Colorado had her completely freaked.

"Great," he said sitting up. He shucked his shirt, his

chest smooth, and his abs tight and rippled. He rose to remove his pants, while Katie removed her clothing a little slower. She'd chosen tall, dark Matt for her first lover, and when she left for college, they would call each other every day. Their life together started now.

The gorgeous, blue-eyed prom-king stood naked before her. She smiled. Today, he was all hers. She lay back on the bed, her body shaking as she waited for him to join her.

Matt sank onto the bed. His lips covered hers as their naked skin met for the first time, catapulting desire through her. An intense ache built between her legs, needing, wanting something she had yet to experience.

Wouldn't her mother be surprised when she learned she was no longer a virgin?

His fingers trailed down her thighs as he gently spread her legs, his gaze lingering on her, melting her overheated skin.

"Condom?" she gasped.

"Baby, we don't need it," he said, positioning himself between her legs.

Her breathing sounded raspy to her ears and for a second she was tempted to just let him. The chances of her getting pregnant were slim, but a spark of fear swept through her. Since she was a child, her mother had preached about the dangers of unprotected sex.

"Stop. You've got to put a condom on," she said, not wanting to spoil the mood, but fearful just the same.

His lips thinned into a frown, but he hopped off the bed. With the rip of the foil wrapper, she breathed a sigh of relief.

She watched him endure several attempts before he rolled the condom down his penis. When finished, he turned and hurried back to bed. He crawled over her, his lips pausing at her neck, his touch reigniting the desire that held her captive. She moaned and slid her hands down his back, preparing herself for the shock of his entry.

The door to her bedroom swung open and her mother shrieked, "Aghhhhh…Katie! What the hell is going on here?"

Matt jumped off the bed, his hand covered his privates as he faced her mother, his erection wilting.

"Shut the door!" she yelled.

"Oh, my God! Damn it, Katie! You two have exactly one minute to get dressed and downstairs."

Her mother slammed the door.

"Fuck," Matt exclaimed. "I am not talking to your mother," he said, jerking off the rubber and tossing it onto the floor. He yanked on his jeans and t-shirt.

"So, you're going to just leave and let me face her alone?" Katie asked, jumping from the bed and pulling on her underwear.

"She's your mother!"

"But she caught the two of us," Katie said, a wave of disappointment and disbelief rocketing through her. A shaft of pain pierced her heart at the realization this was the boy who promised to make it good for her. Who she thought would be by her side forever.

"I don't have to deal with her," Matt said picking up his jacket. "I'm out of here."

"Thanks a lot," Katie said, not liking his attitude. A true boyfriend would have faced her mother's ire with her. "You're a coward."

"For not staying? I don't need this crap," he said. "You promised she wouldn't be home for hours."

"How was I supposed to know she'd get home early?"

"Well, she did."

"Just get the hell out. And don't bother calling me. I can't believe you are such a jerk!"

Matt gazed at her. "No problem. You are not worth the hassle."

"Just go," Katie insisted, opening her bedroom door for him. As he hurried down the stairs, she followed him. "And don't let the door hit you in the ass on the way out!"

The door slammed, and Katie whirled to face her mother who stood in the hallway. "Don't worry, I'm still a virgin."

"What the hell were you thinking? Has nothing I've said to you over the years gotten through? Do you want to get pregnant?"

"We had a condom," Katie said, crossing her arms across her chest. She couldn't look her mother in the eyes for fear of what she'd see there. Humiliation spread through her, rising up to flush her cheeks. She'd just learned her supposed boyfriend was nothing but a pansy, all because her mother came home early. Thank God she was out of school. This would have been so much more embarrassing.

"Condoms break!" her mother exclaimed. She paused in the doorway to the family room, gazing at Katie. "Look, we both know you're going to lose your virginity someday. But this is not the time, and definitely not in my house. That kid didn't even care enough about you to speak to me."

Katie bit her lip until she could taste blood as she battled the tears that threatened to spill. Furious, she squeezed her eyes shut. Never had she been so angry and downright embarrassed. How much more mortifying could it get than her mother walking in when they were naked and about to have sex? This was so humiliating.

"I'm eighteen," Katie said, defiantly giving her hair a shake to reign in the explosion she knew lay just below the surface.

"I know," her mother said calmly. "I was there for your birth. You're out of high school; you're on your way to college. You'll soon be on your own."

"So why did you barge in?"

If she knew she was an adult, why hadn't her mother just let them finish before she'd gone all postal on them?

"You're still living under my roof. I don't want to know when you have sex. I don't want to hear it and, God, I definitely don't want to see it."

"So, it's okay for me and Matt to have sex as long as we don't have it here?"

Her mother's face scrunched up into the expression she always got when Katie goaded her too far. Her voice came out sharp. "No. I'd like to be naïve and think my daughter would remain a virgin until she married."

There was no way she was going to wait until she was married. Over half of the girls in her class were not virgins. She was not going to be the last one to experience what everyone was talking about. But she didn't want a baby right now either.

"It's my decision," Katie said calmly, liking the way she'd managed to rile her mother.

"Yes, it is." Her mother inhaled sharply and Katie steeled herself for the coming lecture.

Mother Lecture #929 about the virtues of going to college and how not to get pregnant. That your first time should be with the man you love and not just a boy who wants sex. She steeled herself to hear the words again.

"Look, Katie, we're both going through a lot of changes right now. I've told you since you were little that I got pregnant in college with you. I don't regret having you. I love you with all my heart and I'm so glad you're in my life, but I want more for you. I want you to get your college degree before you're forty. You deserve someone who loves you and makes that first time special."

Katie's stomach clenched in pain and she blinked back the tears. This was not what she'd expected, and inside she rebelled against liking her mother right now. She refused to accept that her mother was right.

Katie wanted to hate her for what she was doing to their family. She wanted to lash out at her and make her hurt like Katie was hurting.

"I'm going to have sex before I leave for college and there is nothing you can do to stop me."

The pain that crossed her mother's face didn't bring the satisfaction Katie wanted. It only made her feel worse.

She watched her mother take a deep breath. "You're at a turning point in your life. You're in charge of decisions about your future. The mistakes you make will be yours to live with."

"I know, Mother. I know all about your unwanted pregnancy. How it kept you from finishing school. How you had to marry my father. How it ruined your life."

"You're wrong. I loved your father. I wanted to marry him. I wanted you with all my heart."

"I'm supposed to believe this when you're divorcing him?"

She'd known kids whose parents had divorced, but she'd never expected it to happen to their family. Her mother was single-handedly *destroying* all of their lives!

"Yes. When I married your father, I loved him fiercely. But people change. He changed. I changed, and now it's not possible for us to remain together. So as much as you may dislike this divorce, you're going to have to accept it."

Katie felt like her heart was being shredded. She loved her parents, but she didn't understand why it had come to this. "I'm moving in with daddy until I go to school. You can start your single life with Paige a little early."

Again, her mother's eyes darkened with pain and disappointment. Katie knew she'd hurt her, but she wanted her mother to experience the misery that racked Katie over her parents' divorce.

"If that's your decision, I understand. But don't close

the door on our relationship. I will always love you and be here for you."

Katie didn't need her mother. And she'd severed their mother-daughter closeness. They wouldn't have a relationship until her mom realized the mistake she'd made and begged to return. Katie and her dad would be fine without her until then.

~

A week passed and though Marianne left several messages for her mother, Brenda hadn't returned her phone calls. This was so typical of her.

Did she think that Marianne needed more stress in her life? Her daughter hated her, and her mother was angry, and Daniel…well, his incessant phone calls were driving her crazy.

Marianne turned her clunker car down her mother's street and wondered at the number of parked cars that lined the cul-de-sac. Panic seized her as she saw crowds of people at her mom's home, until she noticed a large sign in the yard. 'Estate Sale.'

She parked in front of old man McKinley's house and all but ran to the yard. Her mother's furniture, house wares, everything was piled on the lawn. What the hell was she doing? It appeared that everything she owned was on display. What had enamored her to sell her possessions?

Her mother's gray hair bobbed as she meandered through the crowd, a carpenter's apron around her waist. She stopped to argue with a customer. "No, I will not take less for that lamp. It's a Tiffany that I bought years ago. Three hundred, firm. Take it or leave it."

The man placed the lamp on the table and walked away while Brenda made a hrmph sound. She whirled around, and when she saw Marianne, a frown creased Brenda's forehead.

"Mom, what are you doing?"

"What does it look like? I'm having an estate sale."

Marianne swallowed the lump that filled her throat, preparing for battle. "But why?"

"I won't need this anymore." She took money from a lady and counted out change. "Enjoy."

Her mother strolled to a table, her resistance obvious. Marianne hurried after her, like she was once again a child chasing her mother.

"What do you mean you won't need all this anymore? What have you done, Mother?"

"I've sold the house and now I'm selling the furniture. I didn't think you'd want any of it, since you're moving."

Brenda began to refold shirts on a table that Marianne recognized were her father's. After a year, her mother was finally getting rid of his things. That was progress, but her prized blender? Had she finally flipped and gone off the deep-end?

"Then what?"

"I'm joining the Peace Corp," Brenda smarted back and hurried towards a man with a coffee pot in his hand.

Marianne hurried after her. "Not funny, Mother."

"Really, I tried, but they rejected me. I thought about becoming a missionary, but that just seemed depressing. Plus one curse word and I'd be gone. And we both know I like to curse."

"Mother, that's ridiculous." Why couldn't Marianne ever get a straight answer from her? She was up to something that couldn't be good and she would make Marianne suffer before she told her. That was just Brenda's way of doing things.

"Why? I refuse to sit here alone and grow older, while you and Katie are off in a different part of the world. I decided to follow the dream I shared with your father, God rest his soul."

Her mother made the sign of the cross.

"What dream?" Marianne asked, afraid.

"See that shiny new beast parked in the driveway?"

Marianne glanced to the rear entrance along the drive. Her heart skipped a beat and raced to catch up, signaling to Marianne her stress level was now on overload.

A new gleaming motor home sat parked in the drive.

"Oh God, no. Mother, you didn't."

Her mother planned on going out on the open road alone in an RV? Oh no.

"Yes, I did. Don't worry. Old man McKinley has turned me in to the homeowners association for parking an RV in the drive. Screw the bastard!"

"Mom, you're acting crazy."

Brenda stopped straightening the items on her kitchen table and glanced at her daughter. "Not any more than you are."

"I know it looks like I abruptly made the decision to leave Daniel, but I've been thinking about this for years," Marianne said her voice low, her head close to her mother's.

"And your point is…"

"You don't make decisions that completely change your life in just a few days."

"Why?" Brenda asked surprised. "I could be dead tomorrow."

Oh no, here we go with the death threats, Marianne thought, wanting to jump back in her car and just drive. Between her mother and her daughter, it was time to leave town.

"Mother!"

"At my age, you make your decisions based on days, not years."

"Mom, you're a sixty-year-old woman. You can't drive that motor home. It's a gas-guzzler. You have no business camping alone."

"Who says I'll be alone? *Sexy Grandpa 99* wants to go with me."

"Sexy Grandpa?"

"Yeah, I met him online a couple of nights ago."

Dear God! Marianne hadn't even ventured into the dating world yet and her mother was meeting men online. Why couldn't she have an ordinary retired mother who played bingo and knitted?

"You're doing online dating?"

"Why not? It's the new way to meet that special someone," she said, straightening a table of pillows.

"What happens when you get tired of traveling? Where will you go?" Marianne asked, trying for a different approach.

"The nursing home," Brenda smarted off. One glance at Marianne and she sighed. "Oh, I don't know. I'll cross that stretch of highway when I come to it."

Frustrated beyond belief, Marianne gave in to the hurt and the annoyance, releasing the valve on her pent-up stress. "Mother, you're doing this to get back at me."

"For what?" her mother asked, her eyes wide, her hands on her hips.

"Why is it that I can't have a midlife crisis without sharing it with you? You've done this to me all my life. The year I got pregnant, you had an emergency hysterectomy. When Katie started school, you went on anti-depressants."

Her mother's skin went from pale to flushed in mere seconds. The pupils of her eyes dilated, her mouth tightened, and Marianne recognized the signals. She'd pissed her off royally.

"Excuse me! I'm sorry I don't plan my crises better. I didn't plan on your father dying or being kicked out of the country club last week for being a widow." Her mother placed her hands on her hips, her voice loud enough to draw attention. "As for the emergency hysterectomy…take your complaints to my ovaries. And after listening to you moan about your only child starting school, I needed that happy pill."

Marianne groaned. Her mother should have been an actress.

"We should be part of a scientific study. Mother and daughter's life crisis always coincide like two asteroids on a deadly course," her mother spouted.

Brenda hurried over to a piece of furniture to straighten the pillows, her motions jerky with anger.

Marianne was convinced aliens had invaded her mother's body, as they never spoke the same language. Left alone for long, they could argue over the simplest things. Surely, there was some rational part of her she could reach.

"What about your friends? You're willing to just drive off and leave them?"

Brenda didn't even turn around, but threw up her palm in the universal stop sign.

"Country club," she repeated for Marianne. "This way they won't catch the widow's disease."

"Widow's disease?"

She whirled around and faced Marianne. "Dead husband disease."

"Oh good grief, Mom. Dad is probably cursing St. Peter right now for not letting him return to straighten you out."

"Maybe so. But I've joined a camping club and on Saturday, the "Gypsy Coach" and I are on our way to Florida for some sun, sand, and bikinis. Male bikinis, that is."

The visual made Marianne cringe. "Mom, that's just gross!"

"Look, Marianne, I understand why you're changing

your life. But I'm not going to sit here and wait to die. I've always wanted to do this and nothing short of a heart attack or a stroke will stop me."

"Mine or yours?" Marianne smarted at her mother.

Brenda gave her a long look. "Funny," she said, sarcasm stretching the word.

Right now, the heart attack option almost sounded good. "Mom…"

"Thanks for stopping by, but I need to get back to my sale. If you see anything you want, take it."

"Mom…"

"A moving van is picking up the few things I decided to put in storage. I'm leaving town Saturday and I'll be stopping in Baton Rouge to meet up with Naughty Nana."

"Who?"

"That's her online name. Kind of reminds me of the 70's when CB handles were the rage."

Marianne held up her hand, "I don't want to know this."

"I thought of going with Bedroom Brenda, but I feared I'd give some eighty-year old a heart attack. I considered Brenda Ball Buster – that had such a nice rhythm – but I settled for Broadway Brenda."

Marianne gave a sigh of relief, for a moment she'd been concerned. She'd always known her father tamed her mother, but now, Mom had lost her mind. "And what are you and 'Naughty Nana' going to do?"

"She's meeting me in Baton Rouge and we're driving to Florida."

Marianne didn't know what to say. One moment, her mother had sat in her kitchen semi-calm and now she had sold the furniture and became an RV gypsy.

No way was she going to win this skirmish. Better to wave the white flag and walk away unscathed.

"Be careful, Mom. There are predators out there."

"I may be sixty, but I'm not stupid. Besides, I keep a Colt 45 real close and I'm not afraid to use it."

"Call me at least twice a week to let me know you're okay."

"I'll try, but I may be too busy."

"Let me rephrase that. I'll send the state police looking for you if I don't receive a call once a week," Marianne warned. No matter how much they argued, she still loved her mother.

A lady strolled up her hands full of Brenda's knick-knacks.

"All right, I'll call you," Brenda said reluctantly before she turned her attention to her customer.

Marianne stared at her mother, not knowing whether to wish her well or commit her to a mental hospital. What could she do?

Slowly she walked to the car. All these years and still the two of them were like oil and water, never mixing well, never communicating like a normal mother and daughter, and now that problem included her own daughter. Funny, how history repeated itself.

~

A month later, Katie lay out at the pool near her father's apartment in her pink string bikini, working on her summer tan.

Her best friend, Emily, lay on the chair next to her.

"Hey, what if we go to that new club on sixth street tonight?" she asked Emily.

"We have a slight problem," her friend said, without moving in her chair. "We're slightly underage."

The only good thing about her parents' divorce had been her father's willingness to give her anything she wanted. Shopping had become her past-time and you'd think she was training for an Olympic Competition. A closet full of new clothes, a new Jeep, and all the money she needed to hang with her friends, but no father and no mother.

"Yeah, I know, but we could give it a try, you know slip in somehow. I'm bored. All I've done all summer is lay around by the pool and shop."

"What a life. I'm working my ass off at the supermarket every day and you have the awful privilege of lying out by the pool and spending your father's money. Gee, what a problem."

Sure it sounded like a fun life, but every night, her father worked late, which was a big disappointment. She had imagined when it was just the two of them, he would come home early and they would cook dinner together. It was what she'd done with her mother for years. But his job was important and the hours long.

During the day, she pretty much did whatever she wanted. She'd never experienced this kind of freedom and yet she hated it. She felt more alone than if she'd been drifting on the ocean on a life raft.

"It gets monotonous after a while. I'm so bored I even considered calling Matt to see if he wants to try again."

"Give up trying to lose your virginity already!"

"Don't you want to lose yours? I bet we're the only two girls going to college with our hymens intact."

"Gross," Emily drawled. "I bet we're one of the few who don't have HPV."

"Gross," Katie echoed.

"But honest."

Katie was bored, unhappy, and impatient for classes to start. Her mother called her at least once a day, but Katie didn't answer the phone. She wanted her mother to realize what she'd lost and come home. She'd been in Colorado for weeks and while Katie would never admit it, she missed her mom.

Katie gazed up at the hot Texas sun. Her life was slipping away and she was stuck bored out of her mind in this apartment complex with nothing to do. Having sex would at least be taking a step to becoming a woman and an adult. Yet, Emily didn't seem eager to jump into bed with a guy.

"Are you still planning on waiting until you're married before you have sex?" Katie asked with disbelief. "That just seems so yesterday."

"I'm not making any promises, but I'm not searching for some guy to give it away to, either."

"I just feel so restless."

Emily sat up and glanced over at her. "You know since your parents' divorce you've gone from being this girl who knew what she wanted and how to get it, to someone who seems so lost." She paused. "You're not the first kid whose parents have gotten divorced."

Her family had been happy right up until her mother decided that being a single woman, going to clubs, and hanging with her divorced friend was more fun. Yes, she said she was going to college, but Katie doubted she'd make it all the way.

"My parents were in love," Katie shot back, a little too vehemently even to her own ears. "Divorce was not supposed to happen to our family."

Emily shrugged. "It never is, but that doesn't mean it doesn't happen."

"How would you react if your mother just up and decided to leave your father?"

Emily held up her hand. "You're talking to the girl whose mother already left her father."

"Yeah, but you were two years old."

She shrugged. "At least your father is still around. Mine barely remembers to send me a birthday and Christmas card. He only telephones when someone on his side of the family dies or to let me know he's being transferred. I haven't spent time with him since he remarried when I was ten."

Katie paused for a moment. She'd forgotten that Emily's father figure was really her step-dad. What if *her* mother or father got married again? What if one of her parents no longer wanted her in their lives?

She sat up, needing to do something besides bake in the hot Texas sun. She picked up her sunscreen and towel. "Come on, let's go in the house and make margaritas. We can raid my father's liquor cabinet. He won't be home for hours. You could spend the night."

"I have to go to work at seven."

"Call in sick. Say you have the cramps."

Emily considered it for a moment. "We haven't had a party all summer…what if we called some of the crowd from school?"

Katie thought about it for about ten seconds. "Sure, maybe I'll get lucky."

Emily shook her head. "You're obsessed with losing your virginity. Why?"

"Why not?"

Until a month ago, she'd known what path her life was going to take, but now suddenly nothing felt right. At this age, if she were to get married and have children, her mother would be so disappointed in her. But was that what she wanted? At this time everything was changing and nothing felt stable. Nothing.

"And maybe your father would catch you this time. He wouldn't have been nearly as understanding as your mother."

"God, no, he wouldn't. But he's not going to be home for hours. Pizza, margaritas, and video games. I bought that new game Blaster."

"And you're sure your Dad won't come home?"

Most of her days were spent by the pool and her evenings were spent alone. She tried to remember if he worked this much when they were all together and didn't know. Had her mother been alone this much?

"Last night, it was after midnight."

Emily frowned. "Did your father come in this late when he was married to your mother?"

Katie shrugged, not wanting to doubt her father. He was a good man. If he was to blame for her parents' divorce then everything she'd believed was true about their relationship would be a lie. It couldn't be true. "He works hard. I was usually in bed before he got home."

"Have you ever considered that your father might have been cheating on your mother and that's why they split up?"

Katie felt a rush of anger so intense, she gripped the bottle of the tanning lotion tightly in her trembling hand to keep from hurling it at her friend.

"My father is not a cheater. He would never have stepped out on my mother. He loved her. He was devastated by the divorce and begged my mother not to leave him."

"That doesn't mean he's not an adulterer. Maybe she caught him."

Katie's gut tightened and she raised her voice. "My father did not cheat on my mother!" She grabbed her towel from the chair. "Forget the party. I'm not in the mood. It was a sucky idea anyway."

Emily started packing away her stuff. "I need to go to work. Look, I didn't mean to make you mad. My mother caught my father with someone else and that's why she left him. I'm sure your Dad isn't like mine."

"I know he's not like yours."

Katie turned from her friend. "I'll call you."

"Sure."

She returned to the empty apartment alone. She couldn't be that wrong about her father, could she? Her mother would have told her if she'd caught him with another woman. But what if she hadn't?

<u>**Chapter Three**</u>

Marianne sat in her friend's apartment in Fort Collins, Colorado. She'd been there a week, sharing Paige's small, cramped apartment.

"To your new life," Paige McLane exclaimed, clinking her glass of wine against Marianne's. "Without the dominatrix and Daniel!"

In some ways, she felt relieved that her daughter had remained in Texas with her dad until she went to college, though Marianne had made Daniel promise no girlfriends around Katie. Not yet. Not until their daughter accepted their divorce. Of course, he'd looked her straight in the eye and told her there was no one but Marianne. Right, and she'd just won the Nigerian Lottery.

"Yeah, well my ex-husband could act out his wild fantasies with other women, just not me. Not that I would paddle him, but…" Marianne took a sip of wine. "Am I really that dull, Paige? I've been so focused on raising Katie that now I feel older than dirt and about as interesting. Even my mother is more exciting than me."

Marianne couldn't repress a smile. The pain of the divorce had eased with time, though Daniel still called, trying to woo her home. He considered this her rebellious period and assumed she would soon beg to come home. The man indulged in a great fantasy life, not to mention an ego. Marianne was holding tight to her divorce papers.

"Oh, Marianne, honey, you're just you. You've always had that down home, Betty Crocker look going. Daniel has no idea what he's losing."

"Betty Crocker?" Marianne exclaimed making a face. "You're not making me feel younger, Paige. If you'd said Rachel Ray, at least I would have felt young and attractive."

Paige, with her blonde hair, blue eyes, killer smile, and

Barbie doll figure had men practically dripping from her fingers, instead of diamonds. A year after her third marriage ended, Paige was once again in the game, acquiring marks on her bedposts.

They were polar opposites, yet they'd been friends since college.

"Rachael knows how to make even the most boring dish look scrumptious."

"How about sexy or attractive?" Marianne asked, desperate to hear that a wife and mother could somehow be sexy.

"Rachael? Definitely."

Well duh, what about me? Marianne wanted to shout as her ego plummeted like the Dow. She pursed her lips and kept her wounded feelings to herself.

"Now, Marianne, nobody is saying that you aren't sexy." She paused for a moment, studying Marianne. "It's just that you've got more of a soccer mom appearance."

"My daughter is enrolled in college."

"See, you still look young enough to be a soccer mom," Paige declared, like she was giving her a compliment.

"Right. And the next thing you're going to recommend is that I get some 'work' done."

"Well…not yet."

"Paige!" Marianne exclaimed. Her friend looked like she'd stepped out of the pages of a woman's magazine that catered to young, hip women, while Marianne looked like she should drive a mini-van and had for several years.

"I think you need to expand your horizons. Change your looks. Get a new style and dive into the dating pool."

"Are you crazy? I haven't dated for almost twenty years. I wouldn't know where to begin." The thought sent a shiver down her spine and almost left her nauseous.

Paige sipped from her wine glass. "You're a quick learner."

"My mother is meeting men online," Marianne confessed, still shocked that she'd been trolling for men to meet and was now traveling across country. The very thought of her mother dating curled her toes. Why, all three of them would be dating, and that made her shiver.

Paige laughed. "Your Mom was always way cooler than most women her age. You could be meeting men online too."

"No. Tell me how *else* you meet men in today's world."

Marianne really wasn't interested in dating, but knew her friend thought she was teaching her the single life, so she'd let her for now. But that didn't mean she was going to seriously pursue a relationship. Her focus had to be on college, her daughter, and her mother – if she could *find* her mother.

"They're everywhere."

In disbelief, Marianne stared at Paige. "I just walk up to a man on the street who isn't wearing a wedding ring, and say, 'How about it? Would you like to go out sometime?'"

This new world of college and dating scared Marianne. She really wanted to crawl back into her shell and just focus on learning.

"Yes, women ask men out these days."

"No, thank you. Besides, I'm just not ready."

The idea of dating was frightening. Dating meant sex. She'd rather hunt rattlesnakes than show her body to another man, right now.

"Like I said, you need to jump into the dating pool." Paige raised her brows like a schoolteacher advising a student.

"I know I didn't help my marriage by focusing more on raising my daughter and not enough on Daniel. Now that she's eighteen, maybe I do need to add some excitement to my life. To get out and see how the rest of the world lives. I always imagined I would do that with Daniel, but now..."

Damn him for screwing the plan. She'd done the 'mommy thing' and had anticipated the two of them traveling when Katie attended college. She'd imagined cruises, with the two of them dancing in the wee hours of the morning, lingering in bed, and exploring the world together. Instead…he was getting a beating from his dominatrix. And she was starting her life over.

Her daughter was going to college, her mother was traveling the highway, and she felt lost. She had a path, but until school started, she didn't know what to do with herself.

"Maybe I need to make this time of my life all about me."

"That's the spirit," said Paige, raising her glass of wine in the air. "You need to let yourself go wild."

Marianne laughed, the three glasses of wine she'd consumed leaving her woozy. "Right," she drawled. "I'm going to college to learn how to support myself. Somehow it doesn't sound wild."

"No, Sweetie. That's not wild. You need excitement. A night life. Dancing 'til dawn. Champagne breakfasts and naked daylight."

A giggle escaped Marianne. Isn't that what she'd wanted with her husband? Now Paige concluded she should share it with some man she'd yet to meet.

"Let me show you how to experience the single life. Let me put some pizzazz in your style. Just like when we were in college. Carousing the town, searching for men, wild and single."

"I don't remember those days."

"That's because Daniel and you were too busy checking out the backseat of his Mustang."

This was a new town, a new day, and a new beginning.

Excitement filled her with the possibilities of the future she could create. From this day forward, she could achieve a new life. Maybe her friend was right. Maybe she should start with an updated look. "Okay, Paige, I'm open for some lifestyle changes, a makeover and maybe even a little partying. Just don't expect me to have sex with a stranger."

"Oh honey, you'll soon be begging for sex and then you'll wear out some poor man."

"Yeah, right." Marianne knew that wasn't going to happen. Sex was not on the agenda. Not for a long time. She lifted her wine glass to Paige's. "To new beginnings."

~

Brenda drove the big RV through the park, searching for campground number fifteen with a scenic view of the ocean. She glanced at Naughty Nana, aka Sandy Baker, sitting beside her, whose nose was buried in the latest issue of a Hollywood gossip rag, her mouth thankfully silent.

They'd been on the road together for over a month, and so far, Sandy's only contribution was her constant yammering at Brenda about her desire to get remarried.

The only time the woman's jaw wasn't yapping was when she slept or read the latest trash magazine. Eight hours a day of non-stop lip-smacking, whether it made sense or not, had left Brenda with a case of selective hearing. Only so much time could be devoted to talking about men before you repeated yourself. Sandy yammered on like a stuck recording, repeating herself over and over.

Brenda had learned all the details of Sandy's two husbands and how they had died, leaving her barely enough money to survive. How their children didn't want her living with them. How she'd given up everything to come with Brenda on this journey to find husband number three. And God love her, Brenda hoped she found him soon.

The distance between Texas and Florida had not eased Brenda's longing for George, and she'd come to realize that maybe she was only meant to have one true love in life. Maybe, when George died, part of her had gone with him. Maybe she would spend the rest of her days alone, but Lord, she knew she didn't talk non-stop about his death.

"Oh, look at that, would ya? You can see the ocean from the campsites. Which one is ours?" Sandy asked, the magazine momentarily forgotten.

"Number fifteen."

"Oh, I can't wait. As soon as you park this big rig, I'm going to slip on my bathing suit and check out the beach for men and shells."

Nothing like seeing a sixty-five year old grandma, size sixteen, bleach blonde hair, and saggy wrinkles in a bathing suit, strutting around the campground, a drink in one hand and a cigarette in the other. The sight was guaranteed to make you diet.

One thing for sure, Sandy wouldn't be around to help set up camp. In the month they'd traveled together, she'd done little more than pay her portion of the gas and groceries. No help with the cooking or cleaning.

Instead, she flitted like a lovesick bee from one RV camp to the next, meeting people and searching for nectar.

Before they left Baton Rouge, Sandy had made the announcement that on this trip she would find love once again. More power to her, but so far her search had only yielded lust. As long as it was male and they were breathing, she was interested.

"There is number fifteen and would you look at the scenery right next door."

Two gray-haired gentlemen in walking shorts sat outside their trailer, a can of beer in one hand.

"I don't see any women's bathing suits hanging on their clothes line. I bet those boys are in need of some female companionship." Sandy clapped her hands like an excited child. "This is it, I feel the vibes. We're going to get lucky."

Lucky at what? Brenda thought with a sigh. Syphilis? Gonorrhea?

Brenda drove past the concrete slab of the campsite and backed the big rig into the small space, lining up the camper with the water and electrical connections. She pulled the parking brake and gazed out at the scenery.

"We've arrived," she said, turning off the engine and watching Sandy's ass exit the camper. Brenda sighed, glad to see the woman go.

Oh God, I promise I'll never choose a traveling companion online again!

Brenda opened the door and slid out. With keys in hand, she unlocked the side panel and grabbed the chocks that blocked the wheels so the camper couldn't roll. The routine of making camp took over as she hooked up the water and electricity.

Sandy had blazed a trail over to the men sitting in the camping space next to them.

"Hello," she called. "I'm Sandy Baker. My friend, Brenda Jones, and I are traveling together."

Her shrill voice traveled across the area, competing with the pounding of the ocean against the beach.

Brenda stopped and drew in a deep breath as memories washed over her like the surf, threatening to pull her under. George on the beach with their children laughing as he chased after them in the water.

Damn him for dying before her.

The pounding of the waves soothed her, and she focused on breathing air in and out, remembering George's hands on her, the memory bittersweet. She missed that old man. Yet, the ocean never failed to give her peace.

No, this wasn't the perfect situation, but in the last month she'd felt more alive than she ever had sitting in that empty house. Like her daughter, she had to move on with her life. George was gone and somehow she had to learn to live without him. Leaving all her friends behind had been tough, but change never came easy. Sometimes you had to jump into the surf of life, even if that meant you got slammed into the sand.

At the crunch of gravel, she whirled around to see the two men in their late sixties following Sandy into camp like obedient puppies. God, men were easy.

"Brenda, come meet Dick and James. They're retired and traveling together, just like you and me."

Brenda gazed at the tallest of the men, James. Big brown eyes twinkled with merriment, and his wrinkled face had an infectious smile.

"I'm James," he said to Brenda. "Nice to meet you."

"Nice to meet you," she replied, wishing they would leave, so she could finish setting up camp.

"Nice camper."

"Thanks, it's courtesy of my dead husband."

One thing she could say about George, he'd left her well taken care of and for that she was grateful, though she would rather he was by her side.

"Oh," he said taking a sip of beer from the can in his hand.

"Yeah, we were supposed to travel together, but unfortunately, he couldn't make it."

He gave her a compassionate glance. "I'm sorry to hear that."

"Yeah, me too," she said, not really knowing why she had told him about George, but James had a kind face and a sympathetic gaze. She just hoped he was smart enough to stay out of Sandy's clutches.

"Can I help you set up your camp? Maybe hook up your electricity?"

"Thanks," she said, "I have the power and water done. All I need to finish is roll out the awning and string the lights before dark. Then I have to cook something for us to eat."

It was nice to have help setting up the camp. And James obviously knew what needed to be done.

"Don't worry about cooking. We have fish on the grill that are almost ready. Why don't you girls come over in fifteen minutes and we'll have dinner together," Dick offered.

Brenda shook her head. "Oh no, we couldn't impose."

"We'd love to," Sandy responded, giving Brenda a quick glance of disapproval. "Let us freshen up a bit and we'll bring a salad. That'll be our contribution to the meal."

Oh, no. Sandy had thrown out her bait and looked like she was about to hook a sucker.

"Sounds great," Dick said.

"In the meantime, I'll finish setting up camp," Brenda replied, dreading the evening after a long day of driving.

"Here, let me help you with the awning," James offered, stepping forward and taking the crank handle from her.

He rolled out the awning, pulled out the poles and snapped them into place. He made it look so easy. She wanted to curse George all over again. Why couldn't a woman have the strength of a man?

"Well, damn, you did that in no time. It takes me thirty minutes."

"And sometimes it rolls back up all by itself, because she didn't do it right," Sandy informed them, throwing her two cents into the conversation.

Brenda resisted the urge to strangle her. It wasn't like she helped pull the awning out or even held the poles for her.

"Me, I don't do manual labor," Sandy announced. "I gave up that nonsense when I received my first Social Security check."

"You can say that again," Brenda said, beneath her

breath, her teeth clenched.

Brenda figured Sandy had given up manual labor years before she received her social security. The woman thought work was something you convinced other people to do for you. And right now she had Brenda. But that wouldn't last forever. Soon she would either find a husband or Brenda would decide to head the RV back to Baton Rouge. And that could happen *very* soon the way things were going.

"I'm going to go get ready. See you soon," Sandy said, climbing into the camper.

"I need to go check on the fish," Dick said, and left James and Brenda alone.

"What else can I do to help you?" James asked her, an easy smile on his lips.

Brenda opened the box on the side of the camper and pulled out a string of stars that, when plugged in, would light up the camping area. They shed enough light that she could walk around at night without a flashlight.

"All I have left are these lights to hang."

He grabbed the string from her. "Where do you want them?"

Uneasiness settled over her as she gazed at him, wondering about his intentions. "I'm not used to men offering to help me. What is it you want?"

He grinned. "Talking to Dick all day and night gets kind of boring. A little female companionship over dinner is something that I would do back flips for, if I still could."

"What do you mean by 'female companionship'?"

She wanted to make certain he knew right up front that there would be no hanky-panky with her. She couldn't vouch for Sandy, but Brenda wasn't playing that game.

"Dinner and conversation," he said, raising his hands. "That's all."

"You'll get plenty of conversation from Sandy."

Stringing the lights around the awning, he said,

"Someone to sit around the campfire, listen to the surf pound the beach, sip wine, and talk with would be nice."

That sounded way more than nice. How could she say no? "Okay, dinner with someone other than Sandy sounds great. I think I can do that."

"Good. Now I have the lights strung. What else?"

"I'm done."

"We'll see you at six-thirty," he said, with a wave as he left camp.

"Yeah, we'll see you then," Brenda said, for the first time actually anticipating the dinner Sandy had charmed their way into.

It sure beat the shortcut Sandy had suggested on the road in Louisiana. Nothing like driving a gas-guzzling tank of a camper down a muddy dirt road.

Brenda was certain they were going to meet Jesus on that road, and Sandy almost had, because Brenda had been ready to dump her out of the moving vehicle.

Brenda watched James stroll back to his camp. She had come on this trip to meet new people, experience new things, and have fun. Maybe, the time had come to start doing just that.

~

Katie trudged up the stairs to her dorm room, not knowing what to expect and wishing that one of her parents were with her to experience her first day at college. Why had it seemed like her father had been relieved to see her leave. All her dreams of leaving for college had never been like the reality. She'd thought her parents would deliver her to school and they would have the tearful goodbye.

Instead, she was alone and questioning everything she'd come to believe in the last eighteen years.

Nervous, she opened the dorm door to see a big bouquet of flowers on a desk. With a quick glance around the room she realized she'd arrived before her roommate.

Walking over to the flowers, she saw her name on the card. She imagined they were from Matt and quickly tore open the card. Disappointment filled her as she read the message. *I'm so proud of you. Love you with all my heart, Mom.*

A gigantic lump formed in her throat. She clenched her eyes shut to keep the tears from spilling onto her cheeks. She refused to cry.

Two months had passed since she'd seen her mother and she missed her. All summer she'd tried not to think of how, in summers past, they would have spent time together, even going on girl trips. But no matter what, Katy ached for her mother.

If she'd learned anything this summer, it was that her mother was the better parent. Her father loved her, but her mother was always there for her. Her father was absent most of the time, and she couldn't stop wondering if he'd been this absent in the marriage to her mother.

She glanced around the dorm room, her home for the next semester on the campus of the University of Colorado.

Nowhere felt like home anymore. She sighed and returned to her car to haul up her suitcase. Her Mom had wanted to help her, but she'd refused. Her Dad hadn't even offered, just kissed her on the cheek and told her to drive safely. All alone, she'd driven from Texas to Colorado.

She wondered if he was as relieved to see her go as he'd appeared.

He'd not participated in the shopping for her dorm room, but handed her his credit card and told her to get what she needed. A thousand dollars later, she'd bought stuff just to spend his money and punish him for not making dorm decorating fun.

Staying the summer with him had been a huge mistake.

She hauled up the last box of her things, feeling like an

outsider as boys and girls called to one another. What was she doing? Why hadn't she let her Mom come with her? At least her mother would have helped her get settled and made the experience fun.

But no, she told her Mom she could do this on her own. Now, as she watched families helping their kids get settled, carting boxes and having teary farewells, loneliness settled over her like a suffocating blanket.

Katie closed the door to her room and sank onto a bed on the far side of the wall. Maybe she should grab her stuff and haul ass. Jump in the car and drive as far away as possible and not tell anyone. Would her parents care if she never showed up for college?

The door swung open and a skinny, blonde, geeky girl entered the room.

"Hi," she said awkwardly. "I'm Crystal. You must be Katie."

"Yeah," Katie replied, thinking they couldn't have picked two people more dissimilar.

Crystal's mom and dad rushed in and dumped boxes and suitcases. The small room felt cramped as they all exchanged names and information.

As she watched them help their daughter unpack, loneliness swamped Katie, leaving her nauseous. She wanted to go home. But where? Not like she had a home anymore.

Soon, they stopped and glanced at each other, knowing the time had come to say goodbye. Katie just wished they would end it and leave. She didn't need to witness this gushy, emotional family moment that she'd not experienced and wanted so badly.

Previously she'd been the girl with the family bond. Now she had nothing.

Crystal's mom tried to smile at her daughter, but her eyes filled with tears. "Now, if you need anything, call, and when you want to come home, you're always welcome."

"Yes, Mom. You've already told me a thousand times," Crystal said as her mother crushed her against her chest.

Katie's stomach cramped fiercely. She wanted her mother worse than a baby would. She wanted her family back. She wanted them the way they were before the divorce.

Or had that all just been a front for the child they'd created together?

Her dad squeezed Crystal affectionately. "Do us proud honey."

"I'll call you," Crystal promised, walking them to the door.

Her parents stood in the hallway, gazing at their daughter, and finally, with tears in their eyes, they turned and left. Crystal closed the portal and turned to Katie.

"Okay, give me the scoop. Have you checked out the boys yet?"

Katie gazed at the girl, startled by her question. Maybe she wasn't as big a geek as she'd originally thought. "No. Maybe we should cruise the hall and see what we can find."

"Let me fix my lipstick and let's go. I'm so excited. College! Parties!"

Katie smiled. Maybe things would be okay.

Still, she'd call her mother later. She wanted to thank her for the flowers. She wanted to see her. She needed one of her hugs.

~

Marianne drove her car slowly along the tree-lined street of older Victorian homes, searching the house numbers. From her college advisor she'd learned of a last minute cancellation that made a small garage apartment available. The rent was affordable, and if the apartment was nice, she'd live alone in her own space for the first time in her life.

The fear of living alone tinged the excitement to find the perfect place, yet she couldn't wait.

Spending the last month with her friend, Paige, had gotten old. After years of living in a house, a boxy apartment seemed sterile and suffocating. She needed a yard with flowers and trees, even if they would soon be snow-covered.

She pulled up in front of a yellow Victorian home with a wide sweeping porch surrounding the warm and inviting house. The wind scattered dried foliage along the sidewalk, while a huge oak tree sprinkled the lawn with orange and gold leaves. The neighborhood reeked of old money and antiques. It was a place she would like to live. She put the car in park and switched off the engine.

Eager, she reached for the door handle of her old, beat-up mini-van. She cringed when the car door emitted a painful creak as she stepped out of the car. Daniel had promised her a new car when he received his bonus two years ago, but instead he'd bought himself a BMW. For appearances, he'd told her.

The roar of a motorcycle engine distracted her and broke the historic ambiance.

Following the driveway, she walked around the corner of the house to the back. A muscular man was bent over a Harley-Davidson, tightening a bolt. He twisted the handles, causing the engine to sputter an unhealthy cough.

A leather jacket encompassed his broad shoulders and a baseball cap turned backwards covered his head. This Easy Rider wannabe looked out of place here and for a moment she doubted she had the right address. Yet behind a vine-covered trellis, she could see a stairway leading to an apartment nestled over the garage. The professor's son, possibly?

She cleared her throat to gain the man's attention, but he didn't respond. She didn't know if he'd heard her over the sputtering engine.

"Excuse me," she said, raising her voice over the crackle and pop of the engine.

The man held up one hand. "Hang on, lady. I've almost got this baby fixed."

Baby? Oh, please. It was a motorcycle, not a child.

He twisted the throttle one more time, gunning the engine. A nice healthy growl filled the driveway, and even she could hear the difference in the motor.

Pleased, he smiled at the engine, and she wondered if he'd forgotten she stood waiting.

"That's better," he said, talking to himself and the motorcycle. He killed the engine and slowly straightened his six-foot frame. Emerald eyes gazed at her with interest as he wiped his hands on a nearby rag. Tiny creases lined the edge of his eyes and she realized he was older than she'd first thought.

"I'm looking for Professor Russell."

He hesitated, his eyes gazing at her with interest. "You found him."

A ripple of shock spiraled through her, causing her to take a second glance. This man owned this house and was a professor of philosophy at the college?

The corners of his mouth turned up as if he could read her mind, his green eyes twinkled in amusement.

"Are you here to see the apartment?" he asked.

"Yes," she stammered. None of her professors looked like him. Maybe she was taking the wrong classes.

"The student who was going to rent it decided not to return to CSU this year. The rent is five hundred a month. I don't allow any parties or drugs on my property. So if your son or daughter is into partying, they'll need to find someplace else."

She lifted her brows, pleased that she could shock him in return. "The apartment is for me. I'm a sophomore at CSU this year."

He nodded, his eyes seeming to reassess her as he slowly grinned. "Come on and I'll show you the apartment."

"Thank you," she said, wondering at the silent communication she could read so easily with him.

He led the way up the stairs and opened the door, allowing her to go first.

She brushed past him, and his large body overshadowed hers. A nice masculine scent teased her as she passed him. Since she'd been separated from her ex-husband, she'd forgotten how a man smelled. Did Professor Russell just smell nice?

She stepped into the apartment and noticed the living room kitchen arrangement was cozy with a large bay window overlooking the backyard. Empty oak bookshelves lined the opposite wall, along with a built in desk. Cream-colored tile and wooden floors gave the room a homey appearance. What little furniture she'd kept would fit in the small room.

When she walked into the kitchen, she knew as long as the bathroom was clean and the bedroom a decent size, she'd take the apartment.

Turning, she went through the only open doorway. The bedroom had windows that overlooked the backyard, where a gazebo sat nestled in the corner of the yard. She gazed into the freshly painted bathroom and walked into the large closet. The place was perfect. Her insides gave a little happy dance at the idea of moving here.

"I remodeled the bathroom over the summer and put in all new tile and cabinets. If you take the apartment, you'll be the first one to use it since the renovation."

She gazed at the big man who stood just inside the

bedroom staring at her. His face had nice features with high cheekbones and dark brows. Short brown sideburns graced his face, but she couldn't see his hair because of the backwards baseball cap.

More than anything, she sensed a kind gentleness about him that put her at ease. Something she didn't experience with most men.

"Does the apartment have washer/dryer hookups?" she asked, trying not to stare, yet oddly curious about this man.

A chuckle escaped him and she noticed how expressive his green eyes were. "No. Most of my renters don't own their own appliances."

"No, I guess they wouldn't."

"There is a hookup down in the garage. It hasn't been used since my grandmother lived here. I don't know if it still works, but we can give it a try."

"Five hundred a month?" she asked knowing that the price fit her budget, knowing she'd found her new home.

"Just want to let you know, I've got another student who will come by later today."

She gazed out the bedroom window one more time and faced him. "I think you better call that student and tell them to keep looking. When can I move in?"

Her first adult apartment and she loved that it was not in a fancy complex. This fit her lifestyle and she loved the view of the backyard and the gazebo. In the spring she would be sitting out there studying.

"As soon as you sign the lease and give me the first month's rent." He smiled. "Understand that I'm serious about no wild parties or drugs."

"Professor Russell, I'll confess to being a little crazy right now, but I've never done drugs and I'm here to get my education."

He gave her a sympathetic glance. "Divorced?"

She nodded. The word still oddly pierced her, though

she'd long ago given up loving her husband. The word labeled her a quitter and she hated the connotation.

"Welcome to CSU and the Bentley House."

"Bentley House?"

"Yes, it belonged to my Grandmother Bentley."

The old house had a family history and that made it even more special for her. She'd always dreamed of owning a Victorian home. This was perfect.

"It looks lovely."

"Thanks. Sometimes, old houses are more work than they're worth. But I can't imagine living anywhere else."

"The house and yard are beautiful. Your wife's done a great job," she told him, taking another look at the back yard.

He shook his head. "I'm not married. Divorced three years ago."

"Oh." Though he'd offered the information casually, there was an awkward silence. Finally unable to bear it a moment longer, she asked, "When can I get the key and start moving in?"

"I'll run the credit report this afternoon and if everything is fine, you can move in tomorrow. I'll need you to sign the lease agreement and give me a check." He walked over to the desk and pulled out the document and handed it to her to complete.

She read the lease agreement and reached in her purse for her checkbook and wrote him a check. Handing him the signed lease, a rush of giddiness put a smile on her face. Her own place.

"The mailing address is the same as the house, but with an A. You can park your car in the garage and when it snows, I have a kid who clears the drive."

He glanced at her brand new checks and smiled. "Nice to meet you, Marianne."

"Oh my gosh! I never even introduced myself."

She'd been so enthralled with gazing at this big handsome man and his bike that she'd never told him her name!

"That's okay. You were too busy admiring my bike. Please call me Luke Bentley."

She liked his name. It was an old, solid, biblical name and she knew it meant strong and loyal. Not that she'd be testing the waters to find out if that was accurate.

"Okay, Luke. I've never been around a motorcycle before. My ex thought only thugs rode them, and my mother would have had a coronary if I'd ridden on one," she responded before realizing she'd just called him a thug. "Not that I believe all motorcycle riders are thugs. I've never been around anyone who rides a motorcycle."

What was she doing? Rambling like a complete idiot spouting off about thugs and her mother and her ex-husband. She just needed to shut up before he refused to rent to her.

His green eyes twinkled in amusement.

"Maybe someday I'll take you for a ride and you'll see that not everyone who rides a motorcycle is a thug. Of course, we won't tell your mother."

She smiled. She liked this guy. He was funny and kind of interesting.

"Oh God, I'm not getting off to a very good start with my landlord."

He shrugged. "As long as you pay the rent and are quiet, we'll have no problems."

"I think I better go and begin packing my things before you change your mind."

Luke shoved her check in his pocket and walked out the door. At the bottom of the steps, he paused. "Let me know if there's anything you need."

His gaze sent the blood rushing to her face, sending sudden warmth through her. Oh, there were a lot of things that a good-looking man like him could do to fulfill her needs, but she wasn't about to ask for any of them. She didn't need the kind of trouble a man like him was sure to provide.

Years ago, she let a man get in the way of her college education, but not this time.

<u>**Chapter Four**</u>

Marianne looked around the Monkey's Library, a popular club in town, and told herself she was going to have a good time. Sure, she was probably the oldest person in the club besides Paige, but you didn't outgrow fun.

Paige placed her margarita glass on the table. "Come on Marianne. Everyone is on the dance floor. Let's go."

Young girls in low cut, tight-fitting jeans swayed to the music on the dance floor.

"Oh no, you're not getting me out there."

Paige frowned. "If you don't dance, you can't enter the contest."

A blizzard in South Texas was more likely than Marianne showing off her underwear in a dance club.

"You're senile and crazy if you think I'm going to enter that underwear contest." Marianne took a gulp of her frozen drink.

Paige shook her head. "Come on silly, you dance and guys guess what kind of underwear you're wearing."

"I prefer for my underwear to remain anonymous."

"You said you wanted to act wild. Your attitude is not that of a wild-woman, Marianne. You're acting the same as you've always done. If you want to be different, you have to step out and let go of your inhibitions. Now come on, you big chicken, let's go play."

Oh crap! She did want to change from soccer mom to someone who was at least interesting...She didn't want to be the same old Marianne. The nearly forty, divorced mother whose ex-husband didn't find her attractive any longer.

But what about other men? Was she just an aging woman whose choice of underwear was irrelevant to the barely-legal members of the opposite sex?

It wasn't like she had to show anyone. What were the

odds that a young college boy would pick her?

Marianne glanced at the crowded dance floor where women danced, while the men looked on. When the music stopped, the crowd would choose from the women and guess the women's color, cut, and style of underwear.

Twenty women, including her friend Paige, danced to the beat of a sexy song. Marianne took a deep breath. If she wanted to change, she needed to experience new things. She needed to see if any man still found her attractive or whether she should just retire to the Past-Their-Prime old women's home. There were few men in the bar her age, and most of them were chasing younger women. She was safe. No one would choose her.

Heart pounding, she took a step up onto the dance floor and joined the other gyrating women. Paige gave her a thumb up and moved her pelvis in a suggestive motion.

The other women used their bodies in ways that encouraged the men. Self-conscious, Marianne mimicked their motions and tried to blot out the noise of the crowd. Awkward and unsure of herself, she danced, wondering what the big deal was about a woman's underwear. As the alcohol flowed through her veins, she relaxed.

No one would choose her, so she let the music flow and surround her. She blocked the sound of cheering men standing around the dance floor. Only the pounding rhythm of the music and the need to move her body existed. Closing her eyes, she let the years slip away and danced like she was eighteen, young and beautiful once more.

The music stopped and the men roared, yanking her back to the present. Paige came to stand beside her. "Pretty fun, huh?"

"Yeah, I'd forgotten how much I like to dance," Marianne said, confident she would not be one of the women chosen. "Let's sit down."

She started to walk off the dance floor, when she heard

her name. "Marianne Larson, table two wants to guess your underwear."

Her heart leaped into her throat and she turned and glared at Paige. "You gave them my name?"

Paige scrunched up her face in an awkward smile. "Don't be mad. It seemed like a good idea at the time…"

Marianne faced the disc jockey, wanting to strangle her friend, determined not to look like a complete idiot in front of this crowd of college students. Someone from her classes could be here.

She glanced over at the men at table two, barely older than her daughter. Part of her just wanted to walk out the door, but the new Marianne said stay.

The disc jockey strolled to the table, microphone in hand. "Now gentlemen, as you know this is for charity. If you guess the correct style and color of Marianne's underwear she must donate thirty dollars to Delta Phi's charity of choice, Toys for Tots. But if you're wrong, you get to donate the money to our charity. Marianne, are you willing to show us your underwear?"

The entire club focused their eyes on her, chanting 'raise your skirt, raise your skirt'. Nausea rose and she feared she'd puke right there on the dance floor. She wanted to back out, but it was for charity and she did want to live a different kind of lifestyle. She didn't want to be afraid to experience life. Yet this wasn't exactly on her list of new experiences to try.

God if Katie found out, she would just die.

"We're waiting, Marianne. The sorority sisters are counting on you to help them raise money for the children for Christmas. So will you show us your underwear?"

Closing her eyes, she took a deep breath and released it slowly.

"All right," she said, praying she never saw any of these people ever again.

The disc jockey turned to the young men sitting at table two. "What kind of underwear is Marianne Larson wearing?"

They put their heads together, and the spokesman for the table said, "White, granny style."

The disc jockey looked at the man like he was nuts. "Now why would a woman wearing granny panties get out here and dance?"

"Because she didn't think anyone would choose her," the man replied lamely.

Oh great, not only was she unattractive, but they thought she wore granny panties. Well, damn if she wouldn't make them pay. She smiled in their direction.

"Okay, Marianne who is going to pay?"

She shook her fingers at the young men, turned, and lifted her skirt to show her red silk boy cut panties, thanking God she'd thrown away every granny pair she owned when she moved.

Wolf whistles filled the air and her face flamed with embarrassment and quickly she dropped her skirt.

"Thank you, Marianne. And the Delta Phi sorority thanks table two for your generous donation. Now, who's next?"

The disc jockey moved on, and Marianne stepped off the stage wishing the floor would open up and swallow her. Paige stood waiting for her with a drink in her hand.

"Hey, you did great!" She handed her a margarita. "Here, you look like you need it."

Marianne took the frozen alcohol from her friend, and downed a huge gulp of the ice-cold margarita. "You are so going to pay for that little stunt."

Paige lived life on the edge. Marianne would never go to the extremes like she did and that was okay. Tonight she'd crossed a boundary she'd never imagined going over and realized she didn't need to show people her underwear just to prove she was beautiful.

"It wasn't that bad. I mean…you helped the children. You did it for charity. And that's definitely not something the old Marianne would never do."

"The next thing you'll be asking me to do is screw for charity. At least I'd get some satisfaction out of the deal."

"I bet we'd raise a lot of money, too."

Marianne stopped and stared at her friend, shaking her head. "There are limitations to how wild I'm willing to become."

Tonight she'd reached that limit. She would never be like her friend.

Paige smiled. "You're always talking about doing something crazy. I thought this could be a small, not totally outlandish, stunt." She shrugged her shoulders and grimaced. "You're not mad, are you?"

'Furious' was her first thought, but now…it had been kind of titillating to show a crowd of people her underwear. Something she would never have done a year ago. She felt stronger, more alive for taking the risk. A small baby step in her new life that reminded her she had boundaries for a reason. And it was okay to be Marianne.

"Next time give me some warning and let *me* decide if I want to humiliate myself in public."

Paige smiled. "Nah, you shouldn't be embarrassed. You totally shocked them. That's what they get for assuming you wore grandma panties. We're not part of the Depends crowd yet."

Marianne laughed. Paige was right, the young punks deserved to get spanked for thinking she was ready for the retirement home. She clanked her glass against Paige's.

"To older women."

"Sexy, single, and experienced. You can't beat the combination," Paige said, finishing the toast.

Marianne finished her drink and set it on the table. "It's

after midnight and I'm moving tomorrow. I think I'm going to call it a night."

While Paige enjoyed the club scene, Marianne found hanging out in a bar was just not what she enjoyed doing. Somehow the thought of relaxing in front of a fire sounded so much more enticing.

Paige smiled. "Okay. Don't wait up for me. There is this really good-looking guy that has been making eyes at me all night. I'm going to flash my baby blues at him and see if he takes the bait."

"Be careful," Marianne said, hating that she sounded like a mother. "See you later."

She grabbed her purse and strolled toward the exit, proud of herself. The old Marianne would never have gone into or left a club by herself, not to mention shown her underwear.

The bouncer opened the door for her. "Good night."

She turned to thank him and cold dread flooded her. Following her through the door was none other than her sexy landlord, Professor Russell.

Her cheeks flamed like a barbecue grill as she realized her landlord had seen her panty display.

He grinned at her. "Red happens to be my favorite color. See you tomorrow, Marianne."

~

"Hey, Mom, where do you want this box to go?" Her daughter called out to Marianne as she entered the small garage apartment.

Marianne's heart gave a little squeeze. When Katie called this morning and said she wanted to visit her, her heart had swelled with love and relief.

Maybe the summer apart had helped her daughter get over the divorce. All she knew was the sight of her gorgeous daughter driving up and offering to help her move had thrilled her. She'd missed her so much.

"There are only three rooms. Just sit the boxes down wherever."

Katie dumped the box in the middle of the living room. "Only three rooms?" she asked, standing in the middle of the living room, looking around. "Wow, you've really come down in the world, Mom."

Marianne shook her head. Her daughter didn't understand. Sure the place was small, but it was *her* place and she already loved it for that reason. But she wanted to mend her relationship with Katie. "Depends on what side of the world you're looking from. This is all the room that I need."

Tonight she'd spend her first night alone in her very own place and she was excited. Paige had not returned home until this morning and Marianne had felt like she cramped her friend's style.

"Yeah, but it's so small. Dad's new place has a hot tub and a pool."

And no lack of pool bunnies, she wanted to retort.

"Your father is not a full-time student either," Marianne responded, checking the kitchen cabinets to make sure that they were lined with paper.

"You know he would take you back," her daughter said softly.

Marianne glanced over at Katie, her stomach tight with apprehension. She didn't want to spend the day arguing with her daughter, but she had to remain firm. "But that's not what I want."

Katie frowned and opened a box of dishes. "So what if I want to stay the night? Where am I going to sleep? And what about next summer? Where will I go?"

"We'll make do. You can sleep with me or take the couch. You're always welcome here, but I thought you would want to go back to Texas to see your Dad."

She doubted that Katie would ever want to move in with her, but she had a place if wanted to stay here.

"I don't know. Dad's not home very much. It was kind of lonely being there all by myself. Has he always worked a lot?"

Marianne stared at her daughter, unsure how much to tell her, and decided to be honest. "Not when we were first married. When you were about ten, things started to change. He got a big promotion at work. He began to travel a lot and worked late a lot of nights."

Even then she'd had suspicions that he was cheating on her, but just never sought out the truth. Not until she came down with the first STD.

"Remind me when I get married to make sure the guy is going to be around."

What could she say? Most marriages started out happy until life and work intruded.

"Were you terribly disappointed your Dad didn't come up with you to college?"

Katie didn't say anything for a moment. Finally, she frowned. "Yeah, I was. Everyone's family was there but mine."

"Oh, Katie, I'm sorry. I would have come if you asked me to."

Marianne felt bad, but she'd waited until her daughter reached out to her. She would always be here for Katie, but Marianne knew she'd needed time to heal from the divorce. She'd tried to give her some space.

"I know, but Dad's coming to visit me for parent's day. That's coming up in two weeks. I thought that maybe we could all go to dinner."

Marianne's insides tightened. The thought of sitting across the table from Daniel was enough to make her lose her appetite. She had to put a stop to Katie's manipulation to get her parents back together.

"No, thanks. I think you should spend that time with your Dad."

Katie looked disappointed at her mother's rejection of her offer, but said nothing.

"Are you still thinking about marketing as your major?"

She shrugged. "I don't know. I don't even know if I like college."

"You've had a traumatic year. We both have. Please don't make any life changing decisions for a while. Just get through the next six months and then look around and see what you want to do."

Katie frowned. "You made this a traumatic year. Part of me just wants to jump into my Jeep and drive as far as it will take me."

Sighing Marianne put her arm around her daughter wanting to comfort her. "I'm sorry. But I couldn't stay married to your father any longer."

She walked out of her hug. "What if I just got married and had a family of my own?"

Marianne's heart skipped a beat and she tried not to panic. "You could do that. You're old enough to make that decision. But you would have a really tough time. No college degree. You'd have to find a menial paying job and put the child in daycare. Is that what you want?"

"Right now, I don't know what I want. Nothing feels right."

Maybe it would have been better if she'd stayed with Daniel, if only so her daughter wouldn't be going through this, but how could Marianne put up with more of his cheating? And sooner or later Katie would have learned the truth. At least this way, she was protecting her from discovering her father was a loser. Or at least she hoped she was.

"It will get better, Katie. I'm sorry, but the marriage had to end."

"Why?" Katie asked.

"We'd grown apart. We had different interests and we no longer fit each other's needs."

Katie frowned and shook her head. "That's not the way I remember our family."

That was because Marianne had sheltered her for years from the way her father was, and now that was coming back to haunt her.

Marianne hurriedly changed the subject. "Come on, let's get another load of boxes from the car."

They hurried down the stairs and were standing at the trunk when her landlord roared into the driveway on his sleek Harley. He gave a quick wave and drove the bike into the garage. Katie's eyes widened at the man on the Harley.

Marianne dove into the trunk of her car, lifting a box and handing it to her daughter. She knew the time would come when she'd have to face her landlord again, but not now, not here with her daughter. Not with her panty display at the club last night unspoken between them.

"Cool bike." Katie said, eyeing the professor.

"That's my landlord, Professor Russell."

And yes, he was hot. Very hot, but she didn't want to think of him in that way. Her focus was on finishing school, not finding a man.

"Your landlord drives a motorcycle? Way cool, Mom. Can I ask him for a ride?"

"Not today. We've got at least two more loads of boxes to get out of storage and then we have to wait for the furniture to be delivered."

Luke took off his helmet and ran his hand through his dark brown hair. His shirt stretched across his chest, outlining his six-pack. He dropped the keys to the bike in his pocket.

"Wow! I wish my professors were hunks like him."

God, her daughter was saying the thoughts that filled

Marianne's mind. "Why don't you take that box up and I'll bring this big one."

"Okay." Katie lifted the smaller box and headed toward the stairs.

Marianne heard his boots before she saw him.

"Hi. Let me get that for you," Luke took the oversized box out of her hands.

"Thanks." She glanced at him an awkward silence. This big, hunky, good-looking guy had seen her underwear. She pulled one silly stunt in a bar and he witnessed her bizarre behavior.

"Did you have a good time last night at the Monkey Library?"

"Yes," she said, in a clipped voice. Why did she feel ashamed? She had enjoyed herself, she'd wanted to try new experiences, and it wasn't like anyone had seen her naked. She took a deep breath, resolved to squelch that unwanted feeling.

"Good," he laughed. "I admit I would never have guessed red panties. I figured you more of a pink lady."

At least he didn't say white granny underwear. They walked up the stairs. "Pink is Friday's color."

She swung open the door to the apartment for him and they stepped in. A quick glance at Katie confirmed her worst fear.

Katie stared at her mother, her mouth open, and her eyes wide in stunned disbelief. Marianne noticed the open window and realized…she'd heard every word.

Luke dropped the box in the living room. "I hope this is where you wanted it."

"That's fine. Professor Russell, I'd like to introduce you to my daughter, Katie. She's attending the University of Colorado at Boulder this semester."

"Nice to meet you. Boulder has a great university."

Katie shook his hand politely, but gazed at him like he

was the evil archangel about to steal her mother away. She stared at Marianne like she was seeing her for the first time as a woman and not just a mom.

"How many more boxes do you have?" Luke asked, ignoring Katie's cold reception.

"I think there is one more load this trip."

"I'll help you bring them up."

Marianne dropped her box down to the floor and hurried out the front door, careful to avoid looking at Katie. She didn't want to deal with her right now. Later, once the professor was gone, she would explain.

Luke followed her out to the car. "Did I say something to offend your daughter?"

Marianne laughed the sound anxious to her own ears. "She's still dealing with the divorce."

And now the fact that she'd shown her underwear in a bar. That was an image a daughter didn't want to have of her mother.

"Divorce is tough on kids of any age. I was fortunate that I didn't have any children during my marriage. I would have liked to have had kids, but we could never find the right time."

She handed him one of the last boxes out of the trunk of the car. "I only have Katie, and she hasn't given up on getting her parents back together, though a snowstorm in hell has a better chance."

There were so many issues with Katie, and now she'd just added two more: her gorgeous landlord and exposing her underwear. How could she explain to her daughter that neither were life threatening when everything at Katie's age seemed so final and dramatic?

Luke smiled knowingly and headed toward the apartment. He walked into the space and set the box on the floor.

"If you need help unloading the next carload, just

knock on the door. I should be home the rest of the day." He glanced at Katie who leaned against the kitchen counter with her arms crossed and a mutinous expression on her face. "Nice to meet you Katie, and good luck at school."

"Thanks," she replied, her voice cold.

What happened to the young girl who had been commenting on the professor's good looks? Who wanted to ride his bike?

Marianne walked him to the door. "Thanks for your help."

"No problem." He shut the portal and she could hear his footsteps on the stairs.

A long moment of silence stretched in the apartment. Marianne decided she was not going to bring up the elephant in the room. If Katie had heard anything, she was going to have to start this conversation.

"You're sleeping with your landlord?"

"What? Of course not!"

Why in the world did Katie think her mother was having sex with her landlord? Sure he was a gorgeous temptation, but ice cream was her only temptation at night.

"Then how did he know the color of your underwear?" her daughter demanded.

Marianne took a deep breath. How did you explain this to your teenage daughter and then encourage her not to follow your example?

"Paige and I went to the bar everyone on campus goes to and they had a contest where people guessed the color of your underwear. If they were wrong, then they had to donate money to a local charity. Professor Russell happened to be there."

Marianne refused to feel guilty. She should have told her it was none of her business.

"Mom, I can't believe you would show your underwear to a bunch of drunk college boys. Paige put you up to it didn't she?" Katie remarked, anger in her voice.

"Paige was with me, but I'm quite capable of making my own decisions." Did her daughter see her as spineless? But then again, didn't her father and even Marianne's own mother see her as weak?

"Dad said she would get you into trouble, but I told him not to worry. After everything that you've taught me, you would never do anything silly. Boy, was I wrong."

At eighteen Katie, could win an Oscar for best dramatic performance.

Marianne stopped and stared at her daughter. "I made the decision, and honestly, I didn't think anyone would choose me. I was quite surprised when they did."

"You were an easy mark, mother. The guys probably thought they could guess your underwear with no problem and I'm sure they did."

A sliver of annoyance shivered down Marianne's spine. Even her daughter thought, like her ex-husband, that she was predictable and boring. Did anyone realize that she was a loving human being who enjoyed a sexual side? Just because she was forty didn't mean she'd dried up.

"As a matter of fact, they had to donate money to the charity." Marianne declared to her daughter.

"Were you drunk?"

"Of course not!" Marianne exclaimed. "I left and drove home not long after the contest."

Katie didn't say anything, though her brow was furrowed deep in thought.

"Is Dad the only man you've ever slept with?" she asked, shocking Marianne.

"Katie!"

"Well, I just wondered. I mean you're divorced. You're going to college. You're showing guys your underwear. I'm worried that you're having some kind of mid-life crisis."

Yes, Marianne was having a crisis. One that should have happened years ago after the first time that Daniel brought her home a disease.

"I'm not having a mid-life crisis and who I've slept with is none of your business."

"Maybe not. But college life is different from when you attended. Everyone is sleeping with everyone else. Girls aren't waiting any longer until they're married. It's not like when you were younger, Mom."

Why did every generation think they were different? When she'd gone to college, some of the girls were having sex and some were not. When would it become about personal choice and not what you were being told was happening?

"Just because everyone else is sleeping around, doesn't mean that you and I have to sleep around," Marianne said, placing dishes in the cupboard.

"No, but look at your life. With Dad, you had a nice house, you didn't work, and you didn't have to worry about catching an STD from someone."

It was all Marianne could do to keep from laughing. She didn't have to worry about catching an STD! Damn it, he'd given her one. She'd worried every time she had sex with Daniel that she was subjecting herself to catching something. In fact, the last time she found out he was cheating on her, she'd quit sleeping with him and gone to the doctor.

But she couldn't tell her daughter and ruin Katie's image of her father. Even if she wanted to tell Katie the facts, now was not the time. Her daughter might hate her for being the one to destroy Katie's beliefs about her father. It was best to wait. Daniel would eventually reveal his true nature to his daughter and then Marianne would be there for Katie when she learned the truth.

Marianne looked at the daughter she loved with all her

heart and decided maybe she needed to try a new approach. "What about you? You're a young, beautiful woman just entering college. Are you going to give it away?"

"Mom! That is none of your business."

"Ditto, kid."

Silent, Katie stared at her and then slowly nodded her head. "Okay, Mom, but be careful. Dad would not understand if he found out you slept with someone besides him."

Marianne didn't know when her daughter was going to get a clue, but she was going to have to start being blunt.

"Katie, honey, it doesn't matter what your father thinks. We're not getting back together. This is not a phase I'm going through. I'm not going to wake up and change my mind. Listen carefully. Your father and I are done."

Her daughter frowned and shook her head as if she couldn't comprehend the idea of her mother without her father. "Just watch out for Professor Russell. If he likes your underwear, then he may want to try to get into them."

Marianne picked up a small pillow and threw it at her daughter, who caught it with a giggle. "Please. I'm almost forty, and as for the professor, he's not my type."

"Yeah, well if he's not your type and daddy's not your type, what kind of man are you looking for?"

Marianne thought for a moment. She had no idea what kind of man she wanted to marry. Only that she required he be faithful. "I don't know. But I have years to find out. Now come on, Katie-bug, let's go get another load of boxes before it gets dark."

~

"Damn," Brenda said as she burned the end of her finger on a log she was pushing into the flames of the campfire. She could cook the steaks inside on the stove, but nothing tasted better than grilled steaks over a fire.

Sandy had gone to Dick's camp to invite the boys to dinner.

Florida was great this time of year and she had enjoyed the trip from Texas to Florida with stops along the way, but she was beginning to get homesick. Only she no longer had a home. She wanted to see Marianne and Katie. Sure, she and Marianne had cryptic phone conversations at least once a week, but so far neither one was backing down.

If George had been alive, he would have told her she was acting crazy and maybe she was. Marianne was her only daughter and yet the hurt of her decision to leave had barely dimmed. In years past, Brenda knew she'd let life come between them, choosing the Bridge Club and her friends over Marianne and Katie.

Now she ached to see her daughter and granddaughter. She longed to go by the cemetery and check on George.

The sound of Sandy's giggles echoed in the campground as she walked through the trees in the darkness. Following along behind her were the two men they had met when they first arrived last week. A couple of widowers from New York, trolling the RV Camps, looking to pick up women.

This is what her life had become, one senior citizen swinging camp ground after another. People searching for the last love of their life, desperate to "hook up" as the young people called it.

"Brenda," Sandy called, "Look who's coming for dinner. And they're bringing two bottles of wine and a bag of salad."

Brenda looked at the three. "It appears to me that the three of you have already been doing a little wine tasting."

"Just a sip." Sandy acknowledged with an inebriated giggle.

They strolled into the camp area that Brenda had spent the better part of the afternoon cleaning up after last night's poker party.

"Dick says that he doesn't want to play poker with you anymore. He thinks you cheat."

Brenda turned and looked at him, "Well, good. I was going to recommend that tonight we play strip poker, but I guess that's off the table."

She would never have suggested the game, but she liked to tease and Dick deserved being picked on. The man was on a quest to get Sandy and she was leading him on a merry chase. Brenda expected his camper to start rocking any night now.

"Wait a minute. I'd consider playing strip poker, I just can't afford to lose any more money. Hell, five hundred in one night is a lot to lose."

"Or a lot to win," she retorted. "Too bad you're not up to playing again."

"Don't count me out. I'm up for strip poker," James said.

Brenda glanced at James. He was a big strapping man who liked women, lots of women, and was still playing the game at seventy.

"Settle down, big boy, I was only teasing."

"Damn teasing women. Always getting your hopes up," he said dejectedly.

Yeah well, he could get his hopes and anything else up that he wanted, but she wasn't going to fulfill his dreams. Not this granny.

After dinner, Sandy went inside the camper and turned on the stereo until Perry Como crooned through the campground.

"I think we should dance," Sandy said. "Some soft music, twinkle lights, and a little wine certainly sets the mood."

Oh dear, Brenda recognized that look. One of the two gentlemen was about to get lucky. Probably Dick. She just hoped that if he took heart meds, he had them handy. Sandy could wear a man down quickly.

Dick walked over to Sandy. "I'm up for dancing."

He grabbed her and started dirty dancing. Brenda had to turn away, while Sandy broke out in giggles.

James came over and took her by the hand. "May I have this dance?"

Why not? A man hadn't danced with her since before her George died. "I'd love to."

Music continued to play and Brenda let herself relax in James' arms. His strong arms entwined her and she sighed at the secure hold around her. It felt good to feel a man's body, to breathe in his masculine scent and, for a moment, she closed her eyes and just held on. Only in her mind, it was George's arms around her again.

God, she missed the bastard.

When the music stopped, she looked over to see Sandy and Dick in a full-fledged lip lock. She glanced away, her cheeks flaming. It looked like the chase had just ended and Dick was about to be caught.

"I think we've lost them for the night," James said.

Brenda peaked over his shoulder to see the two of them quietly sneaking away.

"Sorry," James said. "I think you're stuck with me for a while. Any moment now, that camper is going to start rocking."

"I don't mind," Brenda said. "Sit down and open up that bottle of wine."

She threw another log onto the fire and watched as sparks swirled into the night sky, like lightning bugs all aflutter. Loneliness crept through her soul like a familiar blanket. Why couldn't she just jump into another man's arms, forget her husband?

Because she had loved George. Loved him heart and soul, missed the rhythm of his heartbeat close to her at night, missed his throaty laughter, and his smiling eyes.

"So, James, how long have you been traveling with Dick?" she asked to bring herself back to the present and push the loneliness aside.

"Over a year. My wife's been dead since April a year ago and Dick's been divorced for five years. We decided to spend our retirement money on the road. And here we are."

Two gentleman trolling campgrounds looking for widows? She'd never thought about finding your next mate at the state parks.

"My George died a little over a year ago. This is my first trip without him."

Her chest ached with the memory and she felt kind of lost. He'd been her everything.

"The first one is the hardest. After that it gets easier."

"How long were you married?"

"Forty years," he said, his hands nervously twisting the stem of the glass. "How about yourself?"

"Forty-two," she said. "Any kids? Grandkids?"

"Yeah, two kids and five grandchildren. Another one on the way."

"Wow."

"Yeah," he said, his voice trailing off. "You want to dance again?"

The man really wanted to get lucky like Dick, but she didn't have the heart to lead him on. It just wasn't going to happen. He was a nice man, but she loved her husband, whether he was living or dead.

"No," she said, watching his Adam's apple bob nervously. "Are you okay?"

His face was ghostly white with a sheen of perspiration.

"Yeah, it's just a little warm," he said, wiping his forehead with a handkerchief.

"Can I get you some water?"

"No, I'll just sip a little more wine," he said, gulping

the liquid.

She watched his hands shake.

"Do I make you nervous?" she asked.

"No," he responded quickly, his breath coming out in a rush.

He grasped his left arm. His eyes widened with pain, and she knew immediately. Fear had her jumping up from her chair and running to his side.

"Oh my God, you're having a heart attack."

"No, I'm fine. I just took one of Dick's Viagra and… it seems to have caused me chest pains."

"No. You're not supposed to take Viagra with alcohol. In some men, it can trigger a heart attack."

His eyes widened and she could see the panic on his face. "Oh, shit."

"I'm calling 911."

"No! That's not necessary," he said, wincing as he massaged his arm. "I'm feeling better."

Another man was not going to die while she was here. She'd watched George slip away from her and she couldn't go through that again.

"You old fool, it's very necessary if you want to live."

She ran inside the trailer and found her purse. She picked up her cell phone from inside and ran back outside.

James had slumped to the ground. She kneeled down beside him.

"My friend is having a heart attack!" she said frantically when the operator answered.

"What's your location?"

She gave the woman the address and the operator stayed on the line with her.

She leaned over James as he lay there. He was conscious, but she could see the pain reflected from his eyes, even in the semi-darkness.

"An ambulance is on the way." She told him. "Try to

stay conscious."

"Don't tell them," he whispered.

"About the Viagra?" she asked, astonished at his request. "I have to. Did you really think you were going to get lucky with me tonight?"

He gave her a small smile. "I hoped."

She picked up his hand squeezed it. "I don't know whether to thank you or yell at you. Don't you die on me."

"I won't."

"Good," she said. Sirens could be heard screaming their way toward them. She stood and waved her arms to get their attention. When she glanced back, she noticed his eyes were no longer open. James had slipped into unconsciousness.

~

Marianne glanced in the mirror again. She gazed at her short, cropped, totally blonde hair, wondering if she'd made a serious error. She'd wanted a new look, but this seemed…short and bleached.

"Relax, Marianne. It looks gorgeous," Paige insisted, watching her from the spa chair where the nail technician was busy giving her a pedicure.

"Hmm…but my hair has always been shoulder length. I've never worn it this short. And never this blonde."

She missed the sway of her hair against her neck. Her neck seemed naked and vulnerable, just like she feared she would soon be here at the Sanctuary, a day spa that Paige had dragged her to for a makeover and pampering.

"Out with the old and in with the new," Paige said, her eyes lingering over a young man dressed in Egyptian attire who walked through carrying an armload of towels.

"Paige. Behave yourself," Marianne said, giggling at her friend's naughty behavior.

"Not a chance." Paige sipped from the glass of wine

and leaned back in the chair while the technician scrubbed her feet in the soapy water. "This is your first divorce, but it's my third, and this time…this time I'm going to do things differently. This time, I'm going to be the one breaking hearts and having multiple orgasms in the process."

Paige seemed to enjoy her bohemian lifestyle, while Marianne just couldn't seem to get into it. How could she tell her daughter not to live this way, and then turn around and do it herself? It just didn't feel like she was being herself.

"What are you talking about? Paige, you've been breaking hearts since college. And I'm not going to comment on the orgasms."

Paige laughed, the sound sarcastic. "Why not? You need to experience a few more big O's."

"Not open for discussion," Marianne interjected quickly.

Marianne's nail technician took the file and moved it swiftly over her nails while her tocnails dried a passionate pink. She'd chosen the color because it was the only passion in her life right now.

"Look, I've had my share of men, but in the past, I let my emotions get involved. Not anymore. At forty, I don't need a man for anything but pleasure."

The male nail technician gazed adoringly at Paige and smiled. Marianne watched in disbelief as she winked at the barely legal, young man massaging her legs.

"Miss McLane, you have very nice calves," the young man said as he massaged her legs. "Do you work out?"

She smiled. "All the time, and I barely break a sweat."

Marianne shook her head at her friend. Since college she'd wanted to be like Paige, but never had the courage to be outspoken and so sophisticated. Paige was a career woman who had the balls to run corporations, yet appear sexy and feminine with a will of steel.

"I told our dates, Brad and John, that we would meet them at Sophie's tonight at six. That gives us just enough time for our massage, a quick shower, and we'll still have time for drinks."

Marianne frowned. "I can't believe you found us two men online."

"Why not? Everyone's doing it these days."

Shaking her head, Marianne wondered why she'd agreed to spend the day and evening with Paige. But she'd felt guilty that she hadn't spent much time lately with her friend.

"I'm not everyone. I've never done it before."

"Just like you didn't think a day at the spa was necessary. Just go with the flow Marianne and enjoy."

Call her uptight, old-fashioned, or even plain, but Marianne liked who she was and was slowly coming to the realization that she didn't want to be wild and different. She didn't know what she wanted.

"I can't wait for my massage."

Uncomfortable Marianne glanced at her friend. "Is a massage really necessary?"

Paige gazed at her in amazement. "You've never experienced one before, have you?"

"No," Marianne admitted.

The technician, a very good-looking young man, stared at her and smiled. "You will be hooked after our masseuse finishes with you. You're going to absolutely love it."

She could only manage a feeble smile at the very hunky young man. She would love it? What man described a massage this way, unless he was gay, a gigolo, or both?

"Paul, my favorite masseuse is going to work on you," Paige said as the chair vibrator relaxed her.

"Okay," Marianne said meekly, knowing there was no escape. So she had a phobia of appearing naked or even near naked before a good-looking, young man.

"Remember you wanted to try new things," Paige reminded her.

"And I am," Marianne said with determination she didn't quite feel. "It's just that no other man besides my ex-husband has seen me naked."

Paige jerked into an up-right position, laughing out loud. She almost kicked the technician at her feet. "You're kidding me."

"Nope," Marianne said, noticing that her own technician had ducked his head, a smile on his face. "Okay, so I'm not a woman of the twenty-first century. Remember I've been married for most of my adult life."

"Well, after today, more than one man will have seen parts of your body. And Paul will most certainly get all your kinks worked out and not even care that you are a naked massage virgin."

Twenty minutes later, Marianne would have preferred to dance around a bar in her underwear rather than lie here and wait for the masseuse. Maybe some women didn't mind getting naked with just anyone, but let's face it, she no longer had the body of a twenty-one year old. Age had left subtle reminders that forty-one was rushing at her like a freight train.

A knock on the door startled her. "Mrs. Larson, are you ready?"

She swallowed, and made sure that the sheet was firmly wrapped around her naked body.

"Come in," she called weakly.

The door opened and her heart slammed in her throat and her jaw clenched like a trap door. Standing before her, looking like a male dancer, was her masseuse in his Egyptian costume, his pecs standing at attention, his blue eyes gleaming in amusement.

"I will make certain that the sheet covers you

everywhere but where I'm working. Would you like a happy ending with your massage?"

What in the world was a happy ending? It sounded nice. She was here, she should just experience it.

"Sure," she said.

"I promise you'll leave here feeling completely relaxed. Let's begin."

It was all she could do to keep from squinting her eyes closed. At the feel of his touch, she jumped, and he made clucking noises. "Relax, you are too tight."

Yeah, she was way tight. Whatever Paige was paying him, he was going to more than earn his money if he could get her to relax.

His large, warm hands gently, but firmly, began to massage her neck and shoulders, his fingers kneading tightened muscles. When was the last time a man's hands had caressed her body? When was the last time someone had given her skin and muscles this much attention?

When was the last time a man's touch was so focused on her and her pleasure? Only her?

She sighed and the tension slowly left her body. She soon forgot about the dimples in her butt, and the unease regarding her biology test on Monday and the English paper due next week disappeared.

All that mattered was the way his hands were working out all the kinks in her neck. Slowly his fingers wound down her back and by the time he got to her buttocks, she felt like a limp noodle that didn't care what he was doing as long as he continued.

Very carefully he spread a sheet over her legs and pulled the first sheet up to cover her back and shoulders. He was kind to think about her modesty while he continued working his magic on her muscles. And when he bent over her, she could smell the sweet scent of oil that lingered around the two of them.

As the masseuse kneaded her slick oiled skin, her mind turned to her good-looking landlord and she couldn't help but wonder how his big hands would feel on her flesh. Could he make her feel this good? A small moan slipped through her lips.

"Am I hurting you?" the masseuse asked.

"Oh, no," she sighed. She would never tell the man that small moan was the source of a much larger pent-up emotion. The lack of sex and a really good orgasm had caused enough pressure to build inside her to solve the energy crisis.

Not to mention the man's touch on her skin. How could she have forgotten the simple pleasure of touch? Her insides were beginning to turn into a warm liquid mush as Paul's hands moved down her legs, touching her in ways that left her hungering for more.

"If you will roll over onto your back, I will finish."

With the sheet covering her, she rolled over onto her back and dreamed of tossing the sheet aside and pulling him down on top of her. She imagined his shock, and the feel of his body crushing hers.

She wanted to leave her eyes open and watch the way his hands stroked her, but something about gazing into his eyes while he touched her frightened her. What if he realized the feel of his hands excited her? What if he realized that only a slight touch in the right spot would have her spiraling over the edge with the best orgasm she'd experienced in a year? Correction. The only orgasm she'd come close to in a year.

She squinted her eyes shut, trying not to think about climaxing. Trying to remain calm and keep her breathing from making that raspy noise that was present during lovemaking, she focused on math problems, hoping they would keep her from spiraling out of control.

She thought of her biology class and the textbook she'd

recently read. Not working. A grocery list? Nope, lettuce and tomatoes had never been sexier.

And then his hands skimmed her pelvic area, his fingers lightly touching her sex and she sat straight up on the table. Moist heat flamed between her legs, like a warning siren. Another touch and she would be crying out his name and moaning like a banshee.

She could barely breathe. "Excuse me, I think I'm done."

The man looked at her in shock. "But I'm not finished. You said you wanted a happy ending?"

"What is a happy ending?"

He smiled. "An orgasm."

"Oh no. I've had enough. Thank you."

She'd had no idea what she'd requested! Her cheeks flamed in embarrassment.

She grabbed the sheet and hopped off the table. Under the hands of a masseuse, she'd all but had an orgasm right there on the table. Oh my God!

<u>Chapter Five</u>

"Wasn't the massage heavenly?" Paige asked as they sat at the bar drinking martinis, waiting on their dates.

Marianne closed her eyes and didn't know how to respond. It was the best of times, it was the worst of times. She'd come so close to experiencing one of the best orgasms of her life with a stranger. On the upside, her skin and muscles had never felt better.

"Hmmm…it was nice," she finally muttered, not willing to discuss her embarrassment, hoping that Paige would let the subject drop.

"Well since this is sort of your kick-off into singledom, I wanted to give you this."

Paige reached into her tote bag and pulled out a small gift.

"From me to you," she said, handing Marianne the sack.

Marianne took the bag, unease creeping down her spine. She loved Paige, but the phrase *kick-off into singledom* set off tremors of alarms.

"Paige, I've been divorced for almost three months. There's no need for a gift."

"Well, this is your official Colorado sexy and single kickoff." She smiled. "Open it. It won't bite."

Marianne laughed and peeked into the bag. A box of condoms, a little black book and…. "Oh my God."

She shut the bag quickly, a rush of warmth spreading across her cheeks. "That wasn't necessary."

Paige laughed. "Every woman needs one. It's called Mr. Big."

"I don't name imitation body parts."

"Relax. As long as the batteries are working, you won't care what you call it."

Marianne took a deep breath and knew even if she tried

to give the gift back, Paige would refuse. It would also hurt her feelings. The less attention she gave this gift the better.

"Just promise me that if I die, you will come to my apartment and remove this thing before my daughter finds this monster in my drawer."

"Maybe I should have bought one for Katie, too."

"Don't you dare. I'd like to remain in parental fantasyland that my daughter is still a virgin and doesn't even know these exist."

One thing for certain, Paige always managed to expand her sensibilities even when she didn't want to know.

Paige shrugged. "I'm glad that I didn't have children. Too much responsibility."

"But so much joy and love." Marianne smiled, thinking of her daughter. "Promise me."

Maybe she shouldn't have asked Paige to promise her. She should just throw the thing in the trash when she got home. That way she wouldn't hurt Paige's feelings and yet she would also not have that thing laying around for someone to find.

"Whatever. I promise."

Paige raised her brows and glanced across the room, searching for their dates.

Marianne quickly put the bag of goodies in her gym bag. "Thanks, Paige. I'm sure I must sound ungrateful, but you've been very good to me during this whole experience. I appreciate our friendship."

Her friend had been good to her, it's just they were on different paths in life right now. Paige was out expanding her horizons and living it up, while Marianne was studying biology and cramming for math tests.

"Oh girl, it's nothing. I've enjoyed helping out. And tonight, we're going to have some real fun. Here come the boys, now."

Marianne's stomach tightened as nervous butterflies

skittered across her body at the sight of two much younger men walking toward them.

"Them?" she asked as two handsome, hunky men made their way through the crowd.

"That's our boys."

"You really meant it when you use the word *boys*. Why they can't be—"

"Brad is thirty-two and John is thirty-six and he's mine."

Marianne groaned and just wanted to go home. Why did she continue to torture herself by going out with Paige? They were different and she just needed to accept that she would never be like her friend.

"Great! My first date and it's with a man almost ten years my junior."

"That's not that much difference in age."

"It seems young. He's probably going to call me 'mother'."

Paige laughed. "Who cares, as long as it's not when you're climaxing."

Oh, that wasn't happening. Not tonight. Not on the first date. Sure, it was okay for anyone who wanted to, but she felt like a newborn toddler learning its way around the world.

"Please!! I haven't even met the guy and you're talking sex."

"Well…it does happen. People do sleep together on the first date."

Marianne gazed at her friend. "It's my first date in almost twenty years. It's not going to happen."

"Suit yourself. You know, they say when you fall off a horse, the best thing to do is jump back on and go for a ride."

Marianne took a long, deep, steadying breath. Maybe for other people, but she didn't know what kind of saddle she wanted.

"Well my horse has been out to pasture for a while. I'd like to walk her around the yard to make sure she likes the feel of the saddle on her back and the bit in her mouth is not too tight."

"You do that, but I'm going to jump on and ride this stallion."

The two men reached the bar where they were seated. She tried to relax and smile, knowing that this was just her first time out of the chute and there was no hurry. Tonight was about having fun.

"Hi, I'm Brad," he said putting his palm in her hand.

"Marianne," she said, noting his blue eyes were checking her out. Would he realize their age difference? Would he care?

"I'm John," the older man said, shaking her hand. "Have you been here before?"

"No," Marianne said.

"Good, you're in for a treat! They serve food until nine and then they turn down the lights and a jazz band plays."

"Do you dance, Marianne?" Brad asked.

"Yes."

"Italian food and dancing. Tonight is going to be fun," Brad said smiling at her like she was dessert.

While they waited for dinner, they talked and laughed, the men telling of a deep-sea fishing trip they'd just returned from. Marianne found herself relaxing and enjoying Brad's companionship.

Besides her fellow classmates, her only male interaction had been with Luke, her landlord. There was something about Luke that warned her she'd be playing with fire if she got too close.

She needed to test her engines. After twenty years of sitting in dry dock, she wasn't sure she knew how to play the dating game any longer.

At nine o'clock, the lights dimmed and the soft sweet sounds of a jazz quartet begin to play.

"Would you like to dance, Marianne?" Brad asked.

"Yes, thank you."

They walked to the dance floor and he pulled her into his arms. They danced slowly to the swish of a drum and the moan of the saxophone.

"So do you miss Texas?" Brad said, next to her ear.

Marianne leaned back in his arms and gazed into his face.

"Not really. In Texas, the changing of the seasons is hot one day and cold the next. Here the mornings are crisp and the leaves are such brilliant burst of colors. It's beautiful." It felt good to be on the dance floor in the arms of a man, and that surprised her. "So what do you do for a living, Brad?"

He smiled. "Paige didn't tell you?"

"No."

"I work for an escort service."

Marianne's jaw dropped. She turned and glared at Paige who was busy talking to John, their heads bent together. That would be the absolute last straw if Paige hired them men of the evening. She wasn't that desperate.

"What kind of escort service? Please tell me it's not the kind that women call and get…Paige didn't hire you, did she?"

Brad threw back his head, laughing, and missed a step, treading on Marianne's toes. "No, Paige didn't hire me, and it's not that kind of escort service. But I have to tell you, your reaction is the best one I've had to that line."

He went on, "I work for a company that escorts security risks. My job is to make sure that the person or the cargo gets to its destination without any incidents."

Marianne breathed a big sigh of relief. "Sorry, for a minute there, I thought Paige had hired me a date."

How embarrassing for someone to think they had to hire her a man. She would have just died if Paige had contacted an escort service.

"Would that have been bad?"

"Well, yes. I'm not desperate."

He grinned and she relaxed in his arms. "If it makes you feel better, I've never accepted money to date someone. And with your looks, I don't think you have to worry about lack of dates."

"Thanks. It's amazing what a day at the spa will do for you." She was tempted to question him why he thought she didn't have to worry about dates, but wanted to just enjoy the feelings his words evoked for a little longer. "So do you travel with this escort business?"

"Yes, I'm gone quite a bit. What do you do?" he asked.

"I'm a full-time college student and I work part-time in the library. I've returned to school for the first time in eighteen years. Oops," she said. "That kind of lets you know how old I am, and I didn't intend to tell you that.

He laughed. "Why not?"

"Well, because obviously, I'm older than you."

"Age doesn't matter as long as there's chemistry. And I don't know about you, but I felt a sizzle as soon as I walked in the door."

Oh God! She tried to smile, but somehow she felt like her cheeks were burning. Did men really say these kinds of things on first dates with perfect strangers? Didn't chemistry come after you got to know the person?

"I think you're just hearing the sound of the band," she said, trying to deflect his obvious attempt at seduction.

The song ended and they returned to the table, where Brad pulled his chair up against hers. He reached over and took her hand, caressing her palm with his fingers. Should she tell him she felt no sizzle? That somehow, he hadn't lit her Bunsen burner and his chemistry experiment had failed?

She glanced over at Paige. She and John were sipping from the same wine glass, and she was all but in his lap. The phrase 'get a room' came to mind, but Marianne feared being left alone with Brad, the sizzle man. He was young and attractive, but…

She felt his mouth on her hand and then his tongue on the inside of her palm. A shudder of revulsion shimmied along her spine, and she wanted to yank back her hand. She had to resist the childish notion of cooties.

"John and Paige seemed to be getting along very well," Brad said.

"Yeah, maybe a little too well."

The band started another song and this time, Paige and John took the floor. Their sensuous tango left little doubt they would finish their dance in the bedroom.

When they returned to the table, John took Paige in his arms and kissed her deep and long. Marianne looked away, embarrassed at her friend's display.

"I think it's time to take this party to the next level," Brad whispered in her ear, his eyes on John and Paige. "We should retire to my apartment where I can show you photos of some of my 'escort services'."

Marianne all but laughed right in his face. She reached for her bag and purse. She stood and Brad jumped up, eager to follow her. Maybe this would be better handled outside.

She turned to Paige and John to say goodnight, but once again they were lip-locked and would soon need life support if they didn't come up for air.

Frustration filled Marianne. Was this dating in the twenty-first century? She walked out of the restaurant with Brad eagerly following, obviously assuming they were going to his apartment.

"What are you driving? You can just follow me."

Outside, the cool night air strengthened her resolve. She stopped at her clunker car and took a hold of Brad's hand.

"You know, I really enjoyed tonight. You're a nice man, but tonight was my first date since my divorce. I think we should say goodbye here."

He frowned, his shoulders sagging. "Come on, I want you to see my place." He wrapped his arms around her and pulled her into a hug. "I'm not ready for the night to end. I want to spend more time getting to know you."

Marianne opened her mouth to reply and his lips came crushing down on hers. He pressed his body against hers, letting her feel his erection, moving his mouth over hers as he kissed her deeply.

Somehow his seductive moves seemed desperate and Marianne felt nothing except the need to get in her car as quickly as possible.

Finally, she pushed him away. "Brad, it's not working for me. You're a really nice man, but I'm just not capable of having any kind of relationship right now."

"Come on baby, I'm not asking for a lifetime. I'll make it fun for you. I'll give you the best orgasm of your life."

She placed her gym bag in front of her body, reached into her purse for her keys and opened the car door. She got in the car and sank down on the cold leather seat. "No, thanks. Not tonight, Brad."

Quickly, she closed the door and he leaned on the car. "You don't know what you'll be missing."

She put the key in the ignition, praying it would start. With a grinding noise, the engine hummed and she breathed a sigh of relief. She smiled and waved at Brad through the window.

Brad still leaned on the door and she put the car in reverse before he finally moved.

"Welcome to the world of dating," she said to herself, as she pulled out of the parking lot.

~

Brenda sat in the hospital waiting room and wondered for the hundredth time what the hell she was doing. She barely knew this man. They had been friends for only a couple of weeks and yet here she sat, waiting to find out if he would survive.

She'd called his daughter. She'd called and left a message on Sandy's phone, but so far she sat all alone. Just like when George died. She couldn't help but remember that awful day. It was the beginning of the loneliness that gripped her now.

She picked up a magazine and tried to read the pages, her eyes blurring. God, she was tired. She had ridden in the ambulance with James and somehow she had to find a way back to the campground. It was two am and nothing good happened at this time of day. She could be back in her bed, sleeping, but instead she felt obligated to wait. The man was alone and possibly dying. Someone should be here.

"Mrs. Conner?"

"No, I'm just a friend. I think Mrs. Conner passed away a year ago."

He was just another lonely, single, senior citizen and she didn't want to leave him alone in the hospital.

"Oh. We moved him into ICU and he's on a heart monitor. As long as nothing unexpected happens, he should be okay."

"Thank God."

"Did you contact his next of kin?'

"I called and left a message with his daughter," she paused, suddenly wanting to make sure he was okay. "Can I see him for just a moment?

The nurse glanced at her watch. "Since he just came out of the ER, I'll let you have five minutes with him."

"Thanks," Brenda said, and headed towards his room.

She paused in the doorway and gazed at all the machines hooked up to him, probably monitoring even his farts. She gave an inward shudder. This was no way to die.

She stepped to the side of the bed and lifted his limp hand. He opened his eyes and tried to smile at her.

"Hell of a way to end a party," Brenda said, grinning at him. "I've never had this kind of effect on men before."

"Too much excitement," James said in a ragged whisper.

"I can only stay a couple of minutes," Brenda said, knowing she needed to tell him what she'd done. "I've contacted your daughter and I left a message for Sandy. Who knows when they may come up for air?"

He grinned. "I guess this is the price we pay when we're older."

His words made her heart clench with pain. In some ways she felt envious of the dead. They weren't left behind, alone and unsure where to go from here.

"Speak for yourself. I'm still sixteen at heart. It's just the body that matured."

He smiled and his eyes drifted closed. She squeezed his hand.

"I'm leaving. I'll try to come back and see you in the morning."

He nodded, his strength completely gone.

She released his hand and started toward the door. She glanced back and he waved at her, his hand barely rising before he let it fall onto the bed.

Sadness overwhelmed her. Another man knocked down to his knees by age and wanting to be young. Walking down the empty halls of the hospital, she remembered again the night George died. Loneliness swept over her.

As she hurried down the hall, she saw Dick and Sandy whose short, worn out legs were moving as quick as they could toward her.

"Oh my God!" Sandy said with empathy. "I heard your message about twenty minutes ago. I didn't know where you'd gone to." She glanced at Dick and smiled. "We were kind of occupied before that.

Dick grinned from ear to ear like a clown's lips on steroids. "How is he?"

"They're keeping him in ICU, but they think he will be okay once they get all the Viagra out of his system. He mixed Viagra with alcohol. He could have died."

Dick shrugged. "What a way to go."

"Hardly," Brenda said, put out with the callousness of his attitude. "I thought he was going to die before the ambulance arrived."

Sandy twisted her hands nervously. "Hmmm, Brenda there's a reason why we didn't hear those sirens at the campsite tonight."

"I wondered why the two of you didn't come out of that trailer to see what was going on."

She thought they were probably naked as the day they were born and too busy rocking the trailer to come check on them.

Dick wrapped his arm around Sandy protectively. "We snuck off this evening and got married."

"Married!" Brenda said, loud enough to draw the attention of the nurses at the nursing station. They hardly knew each other and they had committed spending their last days together? "Are you nuts? You've known each other less than a month! You don't even know if he wears clean underwear!"

"Oh, I know," Sandy said, giving Brenda a sly wink.

Gross! That was information overload.

"She's everything I've been looking for in a woman."

"And he's so wonderful," Sandy said, gazing at him adoringly. "Besides, at our age you never know how much time you have left."

"Yeah, but there's plenty of time to be miserable," Brenda said in disbelief.

Dick bristled. "I've picked them right each and every time."

There was a plural sound to that statement that frightened Brenda.

"How many times have you been married?" Brenda couldn't resist asking.

"Sandy is wife number four."

If he'd had that many wives die on him, there was a reason and it couldn't be good.

"Where are the others?" Brenda asked.

"Two died and one ran off."

"Anyway, we're married," Sandy, said, holding up her hand and showing off her new gold wedding band. "So I won't be traveling with you anymore."

"But what about James?"

"We were going to tell both of you tonight when we got back, but when we returned, you were gone."

Sandy stepped over to Brenda and laid her hand on her arm. "I hope you don't mind that I'm no longer traveling with you, but I told you that I had a good feeling about this location. All my dreams came true."

Brenda didn't know what to say. The night had been overwhelming, to say the least. First James damn near died and now Sandy and Dick were married. But losing Sandy as a traveling companion, that deserved a celebration.

Relief spread through her and she wanted to dance a jig, but knew that would be frowned upon. She wouldn't have to put up with Sandy and her man-crazy ways anymore. She'd snared her a man, hook line and sinker.

"I'll be okay," Brenda said, knowing she really would be. "But what about James? When will you tell him?"

Dick stepped up, "Don't worry about him. He told me this week, if it hadn't been for you, he would have already flown home. Now, I'm sure he'll want to fly home."

Almost by mutual agreement, they begin to walk towards the door. "Can I get a ride back to the camper with you guys? I hate to interrupt your wedding night, but cabs scare me at this time of night."

"Don't worry about our wedding night," Sandy said with a smile. "We still have plenty of time to celebrate."

Brenda couldn't help but shudder at the look Dick gave Sandy and she grinned at him. Ugh, just the thought was enough to make her want to invest in a vat of anti-wrinkle cream.

~

The autumn morning air was crisp as Marianne threw her backpack into her battered old car. Fifteen minutes until the class she dreaded, her anatomy class. She put the key into the ignition and turned it.

Click. Click. Click.

"No!" she exclaimed, knowing this was not the morning to be late. She turned it again.

Click. Click. Click. She kept turning the key hoping that something would give and the car would start.

"Damn!" she cried hitting the steering wheel. She wanted to get out and kick the stupid car.

She would have to go upstairs and call the auto club and have them either tow this god-awful car or try to jump start it.

A knock on the window startled her. She glanced out to see Luke standing there. His brown hair appeared wet, like he'd just gotten out of the shower. She swallowed. She didn't need to carry that image with her to school.

She cranked the window down.

"Problems?"

What an understatement. She took a deep breath. "Yeah, it won't start."

"Open the hood."

She popped the hood and he lifted it up. She could see his big hands touching, moving wires. He reached for a rag on a shelf in the garage and checked the oil. He adjusted the battery cables. "Try again."

She turned the key and heard the same clicking noise.

"What time is your first class?" he asked, not taking his head out from beneath the hood.

"In about ten minutes," she replied anxiously, fearing she'd be late. Today she had her first test in the class and she'd spent the night studying.

"I'll take you and then come back and look at your car. I think it's just the battery, but I'll let you know."

Luke was being so nice to her. Taking her to school, looking at the car and helping her decide if she needed a mechanic. What she really needed was to jack this car up and slide a new one under it.

"You don't have to do that. I have an auto club membership. I could have them tow it to a mechanic."

He grinned at her. "What time are you out of school?"

"Two this afternoon."

"By the time you're out, I'll know whether or not you need to use the auto club," he said, wiping his hands on a rag. "Do you mind if we go on the bike?"

She glanced at the motorcycle parked in the garage. Fear gripped her insides like Teflon clinging to a pan. "No, but I have to warn you, I've never ridden on one."

"Just don't freak out on me. Hang on and don't move unexpectedly."

Oh she'd be sitting so still, praying that the ride was over. Yet clinging to Luke had its advantages.

"Okay," she said, nervously licking her lips.

"Here, put this helmet on. What building is your class in?"

"Sedgway building."

"Okay." He straddled the bike and walked it out of the garage before starting it up. The engine gave a healthy growl, unlike her car. He pulled his helmet over his head and motioned for her to do the same. She slipped her backpack over her shoulder, then pulled the helmet onto her head and tugged the chinstrap through the buckle.

Luke reached over and checked her helmet, his hands brushing her neck, sending a tingle of awareness racing down her spine. He made sure the straps were tight. Suddenly she was aware that she would be hanging onto this man, clinging to him, her breasts crushed against his back.

He pointed to the pegs and she lowered them. She glanced at him, took a deep breath and then swung her leg over the seat, her heart racing.

She wanted to try new things, to be daring and experience life. Though many would consider this nothing, it was a huge step for her. Putting her life in his hands was a tremendous leap for someone who had forgotten how to trust. Especially how to trust men.

Marianne wrapped her arms around his waist lightly. He touched her hands and then leaned back to shout at her over the engine, "Hold on tight. Whatever way my body leans, you lean yours the same direction. Are you ready?"

"Yes," she said, her voice sounding shaky. The rhythm of her heartbeat echoed in her ears.

"Here we go."

She tightened her arms around his waist and she could feel his muscles, strong and muscular. Suddenly, the motorcycle moved and they were zipping down the street.

A charge of exhilaration filled her as he picked up speed. Cold air rushed by her. Luke blocked most of the wind from her body, his strong back warm and sturdy.

"Are you okay?" he yelled over the roar of the engine and the wind.

"Yes," she said with a little laugh. "This is fun."

She felt him chuckle. They were traveling at a fast enough speed that she knew soon they would reach the school, but she didn't want to arrive. Couldn't they just keep driving, letting her experience this new sensation?

She didn't want the ride to end. She didn't want to let go of Luke. He felt warm and strong and she liked holding onto him. She liked riding on the back of his bike.

The bike came to a halt in front of her building and with trembling legs, she climbed off. Luke took off his helmet, but remained sitting on the cycle, gazing at her.

"So what do you think of your first bike ride?"

"That was fun," she said, taking the helmet off and shaking her hair. "I see why people enjoy it so much."

He smiled and she handed him the helmet. He quickly fastened it to a peg on the bike and then glanced at her. "What time should I pick you up?"

"Two o'clock," she said. "You know you didn't have to do this?"

He smiled at her. "I know. But I've been wanting to get you on my bike and this seemed like the perfect opportunity."

He wanted to get her on his bike? Whoa…alarm bells started ringing and yet other areas of her body were aroused, from both the ride and clinging to the professor.

She didn't know what to say, so she ignored his comment.

"Thanks for your help this morning. I left the keys in the ignition. If you need the auto club information it's in the glove box."

"You're welcome. I'll pick you up at two."

"Yeah…I'll see you then."

Marianne turned and hurried toward the safety of the building. What had she done? Luke wanted to get her on his bike and she'd enjoyed riding with him this morning.

She'd loved the way his body felt against hers, yet there was no room in her life for a man.

No, her priorities were school, her daughter, and learning to live large. Nothing was going to stop her from graduating this time, especially a man. But, dang, she had forgotten how good it felt to wrap her arms around a warm, muscular man and breathe in his special aroma.

~

Katie and Crystal gazed around the room at the party and then glanced at each other and smiled.

"This is so cool. Our first college party," Crystal said. "Oh, I see the cute guy in my Spanish class. I'm going to go say hello. I'll be right back."

She walked away, leaving Katie to stand awkwardly gazing around at the mass of students.

"Hey, you," a big guy with muscle bound arms said, pointing at her. "Freshman! Get over here."

Katie frowned at the guy, but strolled over. "Yeah, what?"

"Do you want a beer?" he asked, his voice lower.

"Sure," she said, taking a bottle from his hand.

The boy was gorgeous as sin and was flirting with her. She liked what she saw.

She grinned at him and took a swig from the bottle. "I'm Jake."

"Hi, Jake," she said, liking the way his shirt clung to his abs.

"So, do you have a name?"

"Maybe. How did you know I was a freshman?"

"I could see the lonely, frightened expression on your face. First party at college and you stood there looking a little lost."

She raised her brows and smiled. Damn. She didn't want to look frightened. In fact, she'd been doing her best to hide the emotion and obviously hadn't done a very good job. "What are you, a psychology major?"

"No, but I recognized the look. I felt that way two years ago." He gave her a once over. "So, did your parents forget to name you? Or do I have to guess?"

She grinned. She was going to make him work for her name. If he could make fun of her, she could do the same to him. "Guess."

"And if I guess right what's in it for me? After all, you already owe me for the beer."

"Owe you?"

"Not money," he wiggled his eyebrows. Oh, he was crazy if he thought she was going to put out for a beer. Not happening.

"Put it on my tab."

"You don't have a tab."

"Then start one."

"Okay, but if I guess your name correctly, your tab is going to be quite large."

"And after three tries, if you don't guess my name, my tab is clear."

Her name was just unusual enough that she had no fear he would guess and even if he did, she wasn't giving him what he wanted. Oh no, he was going to have to work a lot harder than just giving her a beer and guessing her name.

He nodded. "Okay, but I think I can guess."

He walked around her, staring at her, checking her out completely. "Let's see. Jennifer is a popular name."

"No."

"Sarah?"

"Last chance," she said, smiling, knowing she had this one in the bag and wishing she'd upped her prize, so that she could have maybe gotten a little more from this handsome player.

He frowned and stared at her. "Ashley."

She smiled. "Clear my tab, Jake."

"Damn, I like it when girls owe me. It works to my advantage."

"Not this time."

"So what's your name and what dorm are you in?"

"Katie," she said, keeping her dorm name to herself. She wasn't ready to give him that information.

"I never would have guessed that name. Did they name you after your grandmother or something?"

"Nope, it's short for Kathryn, spelled with a K."

"Katie," he said letting the name roll off his tongue. "With a K."

"Jake," A skinny blonde girl walked up and tugged on his shirt. "What are you doing?"

"Oh hi, Jennifer," he said, as she wrapped her arm possessively around his waist.

His brows rose in a reflective manner, and Katie couldn't help the surge of disappointment that she firmly suppressed. She'd been enjoying their conversation before this girl had claimed him.

"Jennifer, meet Katie with a K. She's a freshman."

"Hi," Jennifer said, not friendly.

"Hi," Katie said, picking up on the 'he's mine' vibes that radiated from Jennifer's eyes.

"Come on, Honey. Some of us are going to start a new game. I told them you would be my partner."

Jake grinned at her. "Sorry, Katie, I have to go play with Jennifer now."

She nodded. "Nice to meet you."

"I'm sure I'll see you around."

Oh yeah, she'd see him around, but if there was a girl hanging on his arm, she'd be looking the other direction. She didn't need the aggravation of stealing someone's boyfriend.

"Nice to meet you, too, Jennifer," Katie said pointedly,

though the girl ignored her.

"Oh yeah. See ya."

Katie sipped on her beer and watched the two of them walk away. He was definitely nice-looking and had muscles that rocked. But he was clearly taken.

Katie sighed just as Crystal walked up. "Where did you get the beer?"

Katie smiled. "If I told you, I'd have to kill you."

"Hey, I'm your roomie. Share!"

"Try the cooler under the table."

"Who was that you were talking to? He was a gorgeous hunk."

"Yeah, he was. His name was Jake."

And somehow she knew he was probably a nice kind of trouble walking away. She sighed and glanced around the room. There were probably other available men here and she was going to check out the scenery.

A tall handsome black boy with dark eyes walked up to them. "Hey Ladies, how are you doing tonight? Can I hook you up with anything or anyone?"

"Thanks, but no," Crystal replied.

"Well, my name is Frank and I am here to make sure that all the girls have a great time tonight." Frank winked. "This is the kick-off party of the school year, after all."

"Thanks," Katie said.

"Which one of you is Katie?" Frank asked.

"Me," Katie said, looking at him inquiringly, wondering how he would know her name.

"Jake, one of my good buddies, said to give you this," he pulled out a card and gave it to Katie.

She turned it over in her hand. The card said, '*You're receiving this card because I think you're hot. Call me.*'

His phone number was printed on the card, and he'd signed it Jake Ballard.

Katie looked at Frank a little stunned. "So how many of

these does he pass out at each party?"

Frank held up his hands, his beer bottle glinting in the light. "I don't know. I'm just the messenger and this is the only one I've handed out tonight."

Katie glanced over at the other side of the room where Jake sat playing video games, his girlfriend draped across him like a body extension. So was he breaking up with her or was he wanting to date more than one girl at a time?

"Does she know about this?"

Frank shook his head. "I don't know. Like I said, I'm just the messenger."

"That's pretty cocky."

Suddenly she felt icky, like just because she was the newbie on campus this guy thought he come on to her when he had a girlfriend.

She held the card in her hand and turned it over. She could make a scene or she could accept his card.

She looked at Crystal. "Do you have a pen on you?"

"Yeah." Her friend dug in her purse until she found the instrument and handed it to Katie.

Katie quickly wrote on the card. *When you're no longer hooked up, call me.* She wrote her number on the card.

Then she handed the card back to Frank. "Return this to Jake."

He read the note and glanced at his friend. "You know he's a player."

"Obviously," Katie said, still interested. There was something about him that made her insides get all soft and wet, and she wanted to date him. But not his girlfriend and him.

"I'm certain there are any number of guys in this room that would love to test your skills at the game," he told Katie.

"The game?" she asked.

He smiled. "The hide the weenie game."

"I don't like weenies. I prefer bratwurst with a dollop of mustard and covered in onions. It's a man's weenie. I'm sure that's not available tonight."

Frank laughed at Katie. "I'll keep that in mind."

He turned and headed toward Jake, who still held a controller in his hand blasting away aliens. She watched as he slid the card into Jake's hand and then moved on.

She heard Jake ask Jennifer to get him another beer and when she walked away, he read the card. Slowly, he turned and glanced at Katie, then touched his fingers to his forehead in a mock salute.

God, he was handsome enough to melt the clothes right off her body. Every girl in here knew exactly what to expect from him. He was a player and he was after her.

Maybe she should let him catch her.

<u>**Chapter Six**</u>

Several days later, Marianne drove her car with its brand new battery into the Burger Grill parking lot, where Katie told her they could meet. The drive to Boulder had taken longer than expected, and a quick glance at her watch showed she was fifteen minutes late.

Boulder, a beautiful mid-sized college town nestled at the bottom of the mountains, boasted a fair amount of upwardly mobile professionals, a hopping nightlife, and plenty of restaurants and shopping. Music spilled out into the street from an open-air patio into the cool night.

She got out of the car and hurried toward the entrance of the Burger Grill glancing around for her daughter.

For some odd reason, Katie had wanted to meet her at the restaurant and promised a surprise. Probably she wanted her mother to meet her friends.

Marianne opened the door and glanced at the tables filled with college students. She searched the faces, looking for Katie among the people waiting to get a table in the vestibule.

"Excuse me, can you tell me if Katie Larson has been seated?" she asked the hostess.

"Mom, there you are," her daughter said, rushing towards her, appearing even more beautiful than when she'd seen her two weeks ago. College seemed to be agreeing with her, though there was a tenseness Marianne could see in her daughters eyes.

"I was worried."

They spoke often on the phone, but Marianne hadn't seen Katie since the day she had helped Marianne move. She hugged her daughter to her.

"Sorry, it took me longer to get here than I expected," Marianne said, watching her daughter closely as she nervously twisted her hands.

"Come on, we already have a table in the back," Katie said as she led the way through the dining area of the restaurant.

Marianne wanted to ask who "we" was, but Katie led the way, hurrying through the tables toward the back. Marianne followed her daughter, curious about the tautness radiating from Katie.

When they reached the table, Marianne went cold with anger, her body going rigid. Sitting next to a blonde Marianne had never met, was Daniel. Katie glanced at her apologetically.

"Dad came to visit me this weekend."

Suddenly everything came crystal clear as Marianne looked at Daniel who swallowed, his Adam's apple bobbing. He seemed ill at ease.

Their daughter stood watching her anxiously.

"Hello Daniel," she said. It was the first time she'd seen him since the divorce. Though occasionally he still called and begged her to come home. "How are you? I haven't heard from you in a while."

"Marianne," he replied, as he twisted his hands. "Let me introduce you to Cheryl."

"Hello," his latest blonde said, offering Marianne her hand.

Marianne politely shook the woman's hand. A wave of pity swept through her for this naïve woman. "Nice to meet you."

An awkward silence filled the air. Marianne didn't want to sit across from her ex-husband all evening, not even for her daughter.

She glanced at Katie who had taken her seat, but watched her mother expectantly. Now she understood her daughter's unease. Now the lines of anger were clearly visible to her on Katie's face. Daniel must have brought his girlfriend without his daughter's knowledge, ruining her planned reunion dinner.

They were both a victim of Katie's manipulation and she was suddenly sick of her daughter not accepting the reality of the situation.

"Excuse me. Could I see you outside, Katie?" Marianne asked.

Her daughter's face grew anxious as Marianne spun around and walked back through the restaurant towards the parking lot. This was a conversation that needed a private place.

As she opened the door, the cool evening breeze did little to settle the tumultuous anger gripping her insides like a lion with its prey. It wasn't the fact that Daniel sat with another woman that bothered her. Katie had known of Daniel's visit and had set her mother up.

Marianne marched across the parking lot, unlocked her car door and commanded her daughter, "Get in."

Katie reluctantly opened the door and sat on the cracked leather seat. "Mom, I didn't know he was bringing her."

"But you knew he was coming."

"Well, yes."

"And you thought I would want to see your father?"

"After all this time, is it so crazy that I thought you might want to see him again? The three of us having dinner like old times, and maybe you might…"

"Get back together," she said, finishing the sentence for her daughter.

Silence filled the car, until Marianne repeated the question.

"Is that what you thought, Katie?"

"Yes," her daughter said quietly.

Marianne's body shook with barely suppressed rage. She knew she had to impress upon her daughter not to ever put her in this awkward situation again, though Daniel's surprise girlfriend must have ruined her daughter's plans.

"I have tried to be patient with you, hoping you would realize I am never going back to your father. No more," Marianne said with finality.

Katie's head jerked and she met her mother's gaze, her eyes large and wide. "I didn't know he was going to bring her."

"She doesn't matter,"" Marianne said, her voice trembling with barely suppressed fury. "Kill the fantasy that we'll ever get back together. Our marriage is over."

Silence filled the car until Katie broke it.

"I—I just thought that maybe with time, you would realize your mistake."

Over the summer, she had hoped her daughter would realize the reasons behind the divorce, but obviously not.

"My mistake?" Marianne said, her voice thundering in the small confines of the car. "The marriage should have ended years ago. Do you understand?"

A sniffle filled the car. "Yes."

"So answer me, do you still think your father and me will ever get back together?"

Katie murmured, "No."

"Good. Now, I'm going home."

There was no way that Marianne would go back into that restaurant and stare across the table at the two of them while she ate dinner. It just wasn't going to happen.

Katie wiped her eyes and glanced at her mother. "You're not going with me into the restaurant?"

"No."

"But...but Dad is expecting you and me."

Marianne sighed and tried to control the rage that still flowed through her veins like a flash flood. "I hope the three of you have a lovely dinner, but I'm not staying."

Katie stared at her mother in disbelief. In the past, Marianne would have endured the meal, but now, not even for Katie would she spend a miserable hour with Daniel.

"What am I supposed to tell Dad?"

"I don't give a damn what you tell him. I'm not the one who planned this reunion dinner."

Katie's bottom lip trembled, but Marianne held tough, knowing it was yet another form of her daughter's manipulation. Not even tears could persuade her to stay.

"Come on. Mom, I don't want to sit in there with *her* and dad. Stay for me."

"No."

There was a lengthy moment of silence as the two of them stared at one another, testing their wills. Finally, Katie wiped her eyes and opened the car door.

"Fine! Go home to your dumpy apartment. I'll tell Dad and his Barbie that you got into a snit and went home."

Frankly, she didn't care what her daughter told her father or his new play thing. She was not staying. It wouldn't be healthy for herself or her daughter.

Katie got out of the car.

"I don't care what you tell your father. It doesn't matter how dramatic you act, I'm not sitting through another tense dinner with your father."

Katie slammed the car door. Marianne rolled down the window and started the car.

"Goodnight," she called to her daughter who stomped across the parking lot, ignoring her.

Marianne watched Katie disappear inside, unable to leave until she knew her daughter had made it safely indoors. She hated that it had come to this, but it was past time for Katie to give up on ever getting her parents back together.

Marianne pulled out of the parking lot and, with an odd sense of relief, headed back to her life in Fort Collins. She couldn't wait to get home to her little apartment.

Pity filled her for this Cheryl woman. And

Daniel…well, how did she stay married to that man for so long?

She sighed and a calm sense of contentment came over her. Seeing Daniel helped her realize she liked her new life. Even if Katie didn't understand, Marianne was happy in her homey little apartment.

For the first time in years, she felt a sense of rightness and satisfaction. No, everything wasn't perfect, but she liked her life. And it was time her daughter accepted the divorce was final and Marianne had moved on.

~

The radio blared in the big RV, filling the welcome silence. On Monday, Brenda had wished the newlyweds good luck and then stopped by the hospital to say goodbye to James. He was doing fine and his daughter had arrived to take him home. Brenda wished him a speedy recovery and headed the gypsy RV west.

After seeing James's daughter, the need to see Marianne had her hopping on the I-10 driving across country toward the mountains where she now lived.

She longed to see her daughter. They had barely spoken in the three months she'd been on the road and she missed both her granddaughter and daughter. They were her only family left, except for a couple of distant cousins who couldn't care less if she lived or died.

Maybe the time apart had helped them all appreciate one another. Maybe they both had needed a fresh start. Maybe it had taken Brenda's road trip to realize she needed a new beginning.

She turned up the radio and sang along to a song on the radio. "Love hurts! Love scars…" She hadn't heard the tune in years and she laughed, enjoying being alone.

Last night, she'd stayed in Pensacola and tonight she'd park somewhere close to Baton Rouge, Louisiana. She might even stop and donate some money to the Casinos tomorrow. But right now, she'd driven a long way and needed to rest.

Brenda watched the last rays of the sun sink behind the endless road. She'd driven further than she intended and darkness had descended. Being alone, she wanted a park where lots of people camped. Tired, she realized that today she'd traveled almost three hundred miles.

An hour later, she finally saw a place that said RV Park and, with relief, she turned the big rig in. After she paid her money for the night, she drove to her assigned spot. Only a few campers were parked in the park and no one near her. A river of unease traveled along her spine. It would be okay. She had George's pistol and she knew how to pull the trigger. Tomorrow, she'd stop before it became dark.

She'd keep the doors locked, sleep lightly, and keep the pistol handy. She backed the camper in, and since it was after nine o'clock, decided she didn't need to set up the lights outside. If she decided to stay a second night, she could always set up camp tomorrow, but her plan was to be on the road again first thing in the morning.

Exhausted, she made herself a light supper and crawled into bed to watch TV. With the satellite dish, she could pick up channels anywhere and she soon fell asleep watching a movie.

Hours later, a consistent clinking noise dragged her from a deep sleep. She lay in bed, listening, trying to decipher what the noise could be, until she heard voices.

After an hour, the TV had automatically shut itself off. A light glowed over the kitchen sink, but the rest of the camper was dark.

The clank of metal came again and she got out of bed, sliding the pistol from the nightstand drawer. She walked slowly to the front of the RV, her hands shaking.

Curtains blocked the view from the front window of the

RV. Slowly, she pulled the material back and peaked out into the darkness. She could hear voices and realized they seem to be coming from beneath the RV.

"Did you find it?" a voice asked.

"Yeah, but the bolts are screwed on tight. I'm working on it. I think I heard someone walking."

Her first instinct was to go outside and give them a blast of the pistol. Instead, she stepped very carefully to the back of the RV, picked up her cell phone and dialed 911.

A voice came on the line, "What's your emergency?"

"I'm in the Springs RV Park on highway 91 and someone is underneath my RV," Brenda said, her heart racing inside her chest like a hot rod at a competition.

"Can you see the individuals?"

Good grief, what part of being underneath her RV did the woman not understand? Didn't she realize that meant she couldn't see them?

"They're underneath my RV," Brenda repeated, her words terse.

"Okay, ma'am, a patrol car is on the way."

"How long will it take them to get here?" she whispered, knowing she couldn't wait much longer without them doing damage to her vehicle or even getting away. And these bastards were not going to slip into the night after causing damage.

"Ten minutes, at least."

"By that time, they'll be done."

"Just hang on ma'am, the police are on their way."

Brenda hit the end of call button and tiptoed back to the front of the RV. The thieves' tools clinked in the still night air.

"I think I hear her moving around," a man said in a low voice.

"You're paranoid. The old broad is dead asleep."

The old broad was not dead asleep and that last remark

was enough. To hell with the police.

She sat down in the driver's seat and turned the key, starting the engine. Like the sound of a race car engine, the RV's motor roared in the night.

She pushed the curtains out of the way and hit the headlights, lighting the area around the camper.

A crash, followed by loud cursing came from beneath the camper.

"Damn! She's going to run over me," she heard the man scream.

She couldn't help but laugh. Served the bastards right. She left the car in park, but she revved the engine, the motor roaring in the darkness.

In the glow of the headlights two men scrambled from beneath the RV, trying to get away, just as two patrol cars pulled up, lights flashing, blocking the RV in. The cops jumped from their vehicles.

"Drop to the ground, now!" she heard an officer yell.

"You, in the RV, come out!" the other man demanded.

She turned off the engine, left her pistol behind, and walked to the door. She flipped the lock and stepped outside, her heart beating hard in her chest. She'd thought she had excitement with Sandy traveling with her.

The patrol officer glanced at her, his gun drawn, his face serious. "Did you call in the emergency?"

"Yes, I did." She swallowed and wondered how the officer would feel about the gun in her RV.

Two young men lay on the ground. They were cuffed and lying on their stomachs with their wrists behind them.

"Hey, he checked me in here," she said, pointing to one of the young men on the ground, shocked.

The other officer returned from the patrol car. "These two are wanted for questioning in a series of thefts of catalytic converters. It seems they like to hit the campgrounds."

"Officer, she tried to kill me. She started the engine, while I was beneath it. I want to press charges."

"Shut up, Bobbie," the other guy said.

"Well, she did."

"If I wanted to run over you, you'd be a flat spot on the road right now," Brenda said, disgusted as she gazed at the two boys on the ground. "Book 'em, Officer…" she gazed at his uniform, "Bailey."

The patrol officer grinned at her, while the other policeman hauled the thieves up and led them to the squad car.

The flashing lights of the patrol cars had drawn a crowd around her campsite, but she didn't care.

"Can we go in your RV and talk for a few minutes?" Officer Bailey asked.

"Sure, come on in," she said and opened the door. He followed her in. "My gun is laying on the table, so don't be alarmed. It's loaded and ready to use in case I needed it."

He picked up the weapon, put the safety on, and handed the gun to her.

"I'm going to pretend that I didn't see it and I'm not going to ask if you have a concealed handgun license."

She shrugged. "My husband made me get one. Would you like some coffee?" she asked.

"No thanks, ma'am. My shift is over in an hour and I'd like to get some sleep."

"You and me both," she said.

"Tell me what happened," the officer asked.

Brenda proceeded to tell him how she'd awakened to the clinking noise and what had transpired after she called the police.

When she finished, the officer looked at her. "Can I ask you a personal question?"

"Sure," she said.

"What are you doing out here all alone?"

"I'm a widow. I can either choose to die or I can continue to live my life," she said.

She sat there stunned at the words that had just popped out of her mouth. It was true. She had come to the conclusion that she hadn't died with George and somehow she had to find the way to live without him. And no, it hadn't been easy. She still loved him and missed him every single day. And people lied when they said it got easier with time.

"I'm sorry to hear about your husband, ma'am. I just don't know if it's safe for you to be traveling on the road by yourself."

She nodded her understanding. "Well, if it makes you feel any better, I had another woman traveling with me until two days ago. But she found herself a man and decided to get married.

"Look, I've proven two things to myself on this trip. I can drive this camper across the country and I can chase off bad guys. If I go down, it won't be without a fight."

He stood. "Well, ma'am, I hope that you find someone else to travel the road of life with."

She thought for a moment. "That would be nice, but I don't know if I will ever find anyone as good as my George."

The officer stepped out of the camper. "Be safe, ma'am."

Brenda watched the young man leave and laughed. She hadn't had that much fun the entire trip. Outwitting those crooks had felt good, damn good.

Deep in her heart, she'd known she was a survivor, but it had taken two thieves to remind her she had courage.

<u>**Chapter Seven**</u>

"I can't believe you signed me up for speed dating," Marianne said to Paige as they hurried into the restaurant. "I had to skip my biology class."

The woman just wouldn't quit. She'd signed her up for online dating which was a bust, a spa day that had mixed results, and now speed dating. Good grief, when would Paige realize she wasn't interested in finding a man?

"So you miss one class. It's not going to kill you. Besides, we both need some new excitement in our lives."

"What happened to John?"

Paige shrugged. "He keeps calling, but I'm just bored with the whole experience. There's no thrill anymore."

So far in the last four months she'd gone through five guys, none lasting more than five to ten days.

"So you're dumping him?"

"You are so conventional. If not for the thrill, why be involved? Really, I thought you'd left the old Marianne in Texas."

The effect of her words had Marianne sizzling like fried bacon and questioning her decision to come today. "I can only be myself."

Before Paige could respond, they stepped inside the restaurant. A sign directed them to a banquet room where an attendant handed them a sheet of rules and regulations, gave them a name badge, and told them to take a seat.

Fifteen men and, with their arrival, fifteen women, filled the banquet room, all eager to make that lifetime connection.

Or at least fourteen of them were. Marianne wasn't certain Paige wanted to connect with just one person and spend the rest of her life with that man. But then again, she wasn't ready to reattach the ball and chain of marriage to herself anytime soon.

So what in the hell was she doing here? She needed to learn how to say no.

She took the first vacant seat, relieved that Paige sat at the other end of the room. They were divided up into small little tables where the conversation could be intimate between them.

The leader of the group tapped a fork on a glass to get attention.

"Hello everyone. Thank you for coming. If you're new, I'll explain how this works. For five minutes, you'll talk to the person across the table from you. If you think there's a connection with this person, then either during the five minutes or at the end, you can share contact information with each other. Remember, we do not screen our members. You do not have to give your last name, and in fact, we recommend that the first few dates be in a public place until you know more about this person."

Great, just great. She could be meeting a serial killer, a rapist, or a child molester. Just what she needed, more drama in her life.

"At the end of the five minutes, the men will move to the next table. Afterwards, we invite everyone to hang around for the lunch buffet. I'm setting the timer now. Let's all have fun today."

Marianne gazed across the table at the geeky guy whose wrinkled shirt was only missing a pocket protector. She felt nothing, no interest whatsoever, and wondered again if she'd made a huge mistake in coming. Biology was her best subject, but still, she shouldn't have skipped class.

"Hi," he said nervously. "What do you do?"

"For a living?" she asked, wanting to confirm the question.

"Yes," he responded, licking his lips. "I'm a systems analyst."

"Great," she replied, thinking this could be the longest

five minutes of her life. "I'm a full-time college student."

He nodded. "Aren't you a little old to still be in school?"

She forced a smile while she envisioned penciling in horns and a mustache on his face. Why had she come? "Yes, it's my second time around."

"Oh," he said, his voice toneless, no enthusiasm as monotone as a robot. "What's your major?"

It was a fair question and one she had yet to determine. What did she want to spend the rest of her life doing? Definitely not speed dating.

"Marketing," she said, just to answer him, knowing that was the furthest from what she wanted to do.

"One minute," the coordinator yelled.

Thank God. She glanced down the line of men. She had fourteen more of these to go? Dear Lord, how would she do it?

He leaned into her. "Do you like oral sex?" he asked, in a hushed voice.

"What?" she asked, uncertain she'd heard his question correctly.

"It's a question I ask all the girls I date. I don't date anyone who doesn't like oral sex."

She gawked at him in astonishment, his question like a slap to the face. She drew her body up like a prizefighter prepared to fight, anger her shield.

"That is none of your business. I don't date anyone who asks me that question before they ask me my name."

"Oh, I did forget to ask, didn't I? It's just oral sex is so important to me. You worship my penis."

She was just about to tell him to get the hell away from her. Never in her life had she had anyone say such a stupid thing to her.

"*Time.*"

"So, can I call you?"

"Absolutely not," Marianne said and watched as he moved to the next chair. Thank goodness, he was gone. If that was the type of people she was going to meet, then this would be over long before she made it through the men who were here today.

A tall, dark-haired man took his seat. He smiled and she took a deep breath and tried to return his smile. Her hands were clenched and she slowly unwound them. The nerve of the creep. She had to fight the urge to leave.

"Hi, my name is Brett."

"Hi, Brett, I'm Marianne."

"I've never seen you at these before. Is this your first time?"

"Yes," she said, thinking at least that this guy appeared articulate.

He leaned in closer. "Let me give you the lowdown." He took a deep breath. "Todd, the guy you just spoke to, is into sex games, or so the girls tell me. John, at the end of the table, is a player. He wines, dines, promises forever, and then moves on to the next. David is going through his third divorce and he bemoans how the world is treating him. Phil, the slick older guy, just likes to date, and Bob is rumored to be bi."

The man bombarded Marianne with information overload, overwhelming and leaving her with a strange distaste. Talk about TMI. "What about you, Brett? What's your deal?"

He grinned. "Me, I'm just a hard-working Joe. When I meet a woman I'm interested in, I go for what I want. And you're one pretty piece of flesh."

In zero-to-sixty, she went from mildly interested to freezer burned. Something about being described as a 'pretty piece of flesh' let her know she'd just be a bauble on his arm and that wasn't what she was looking for.

"One minute," the timekeeper called.

He pulled out a business card and laid it in her palm. "Here is my information. I expect a phone call from you. We'll go to Sambini's and spend the weekend discovering one another."

She smiled, knowing the card would be in the city dump on the next trash pick-up day. She'd already discovered everything she wanted to know about Brett. He was a loser.

She glanced at Paige, who smiled at her and held up two cards. Why in the world did she let her friend talk her into these stupid adult games that didn't interest her? This was a total waste of her time.

The next three guys were even less interesting, though one insisted that she take his card, and the other two mumbled, asking for hers. She became very blunt, telling them she wasn't going to waste their time.

The next candidate moved into the hot seat. With relief, she realized he was the last one. He took her hand in his and introduced himself. "Hi my name is Stuart Wymer and I'm a real estate agent." He released her hand. "I've been married once for twelve years and have two children that are in high school. I don't get out much, because most of my time is spent with my boys."

A flicker of interest had her sitting up straighter in her chair. He actually seemed normal. "Hi my name is Marianne. I was married for nineteen years and my only daughter is in college."

"You have a daughter in college?" he asked, his eyes wide with apparent surprise. "Did you have her when you were ten?"

She laughed. "Hardly." She stopped and asked a daring question. "Why did your marriage end?"

He took a deep breath. "It was my fault. I let my business get in the way and I didn't spend enough time with my wife and kids. My wife had an affair and now she's married to the guy."

"I'm sorry," she said and volunteered the reason her marriage ended.

"Wow," he said. "I guess I'm thankful Pam didn't get into games."

The timekeeper called time.

Stuart gazed at her, his big brown eyes earnest. "So, would you like to have dinner some night?"

"Yes, I would," she offered, surprised by her response.

He gave her his card. "Call me. I'd really like to see you again."

"Me, too," she said, and for the first time she meant it. She liked Stuart and wanted to see if her second impression was as good as her first. Maybe today hadn't been a total waste of her time.

~

Katie sat in her dorm room alone, working on her English Thesis. Friday night, date night, and she sat home alone. Her roommate, Crystal, was gone on a date, while Katie did her schoolwork, not really into it, but what else was there to do?

A knock on the door drew her attention from the paper she was writing. "Who is it?"

"Open up, its Jake."

Jake was here now? Crap! She sprinted into the bathroom and checked her hair and makeup, brushed lip-gloss over her lips and hurried to the door, throwing it open.

His right arm was braced against the doorframe, his blonde hair was tousled, his blue eyes twinkled with amusement, and he looked like he'd stepped out of a million dollar jean ad.

"Hi," she said, her heart beating excitedly.

"Hi," he responded, assessing her. "So why are you

alone tonight?"

"Who says I'm alone?"

He peered into the room. "I don't see anyone in there. Should I check under the bed?"

She laughed. "Hardly."

"So, you're alone?"

"Yeah, I was working on my English Thesis."

He frowned. "Boring."

"Yeah, but it is why I'm here."

While she wasn't a straight A student, she worked hard to pass her classes and knew that she was preparing for life ahead. A life that hopefully would bless her with a decent job.

"True, but when is the paper due?"

"Next Friday."

"God, you have a week, why are you spending the night inside this room, when you could come play with me?"

Katie folded her arms against her chest. So why was he here? And could she restrain the urge to jump up and down like a five year old?

"What about Jennifer?"

"What about her?"

She craned her neck to look behind him and down at his leg. "I don't see her attached any longer."

"That's because I set her free."

"So, you're unattached? No girlfriends?"

Her pulse beat a little faster. The boy was a player, but with her, she was certain he would be faithful. She'd keep him happy and he wouldn't have any reason to be looking at other girls.

"I'm always free. I just don't happen to have a lady right now. Some brunette taunted me to call her when I was free."

"And here you are."

Excitement catapulted through her at the fact that he'd

come to see her. Her English paper could wait. She wanted to go play with Jake.

"Yes, and I wondered if you'd eaten yet. Maybe we could grab a burger somewhere."

He was asking her out on a spur of the moment date and she couldn't be more pleased. She smiled and tilted her head playfully.

"We could," she said slowly. "Do I have to worry about other girls attacking me for being out with you?"

"I'll protect you," he said, leaning into her, his voice deep and husky. "I'll let them know that you're the one."

Katie shook her head at him. "For the moment."

He grinned. "Life is but a series of moments. I try to make sure they are all moments of pleasure."

"I just bet you do," she said.

"So are you in or not?" he asked and she knew he meant more than just hamburgers.

"Let me get my jacket."

~

Three hours later, Katie and Jake strolled slowly down the street toward her dorm room. They'd gone to eat and spent time at a local game room where they'd played video games. Katie had showed off her prowess and managed to at least make it to the fourth level before being annihilated.

Jake seemed impressed and told her she should play with him in the college tournament. She didn't know if she was that good, but she enjoyed the compliment.

Halfway home, he'd taken her hand and tucked it inside his pocket, pulling her close. His body was warm and solid against her and sent delicious shivers through her body, straight to her middle. The boy could arouse a woman without even really trying.

The aroma of Jake surrounded her and she had to concentrate on what he was saying, her mind wandering to what else they could soon be doing. Visions of the two of them intertwined ran through her mind in a naked slideshow.

"So anyway, my Mom says that my grades have to come up or she's no longer paying my tuition."

Thank goodness her parents had warned her in advance that she would receive four years of paid college, but after that it was all up to her. She had a set amount of money and once it was gone, the party was over.

"We could study together," she volunteered.

"Could you help me with my history term paper?"

"Sure. What are you writing about?"

"The constitution and how it relates to us today."

She nodded her head. "We could write it together."

He nodded his head. "Thanks. That would be a big help."

"So what's your major?"

He shrugged. "Something that will make a lot of money. I keep thinking I should become a doctor, but I love video games."

"That's a given. I don't think any of us want to live in poverty, but how do you plan on making all this money?" she asked, remembering her mother's words of advice and thinking Jake had no plan, only a wish.

"If I knew that, I'd have my major be something other than computer programming, which I find boring."

"So, what else interests you?" she asked.

"Besides video games, partying, and girls?" he asked.

"Yes, nerd swipe."

"Ohh...she's got a mean streak."

"You just named off typical boy stuff. What do you like to do when it's just you and no one else is around?"

"That's kind of personal," he said with a snicker.

Well he was certainly all boy. Junior high jokes and no plan on how to succeed.

"Would you be serious," she admonished. "Do you like to read? Build stuff? Work with your hands? Computers? What do you like to do?"

He stopped and pulled her until they were face to face. Close enough she could see his breath in the cool night air. Close enough she could feel his heart beating against her chest and see his eyes darken.

He leaned his head toward her and she didn't even hesitate to meet him halfway. His lips covered hers, desire blossoming inside, shaking her to her very core. She'd been kissed before, but never experienced a sizzle all the way to her toes.

His kiss was thorough, sensual, and left her wanting to rip her clothes off right there in the street. She had to get a hold of herself.

She placed a hand between them, needing a moment to collect her thoughts. She opened her eyes and stared into his, awed at the desire shimmering in his gaze. He wanted her and that knowledge made her feel powerful and desired. God, she relished in the feelings.

"My apartment is a couple of blocks from here. We could start on that term paper," he said, kissing her neck, his tongue lingering in her ear.

She leaned her neck back, giving him more access. Enjoying the moment for just a minute longer. She let him continue kissing her ear, a shiver rippling through her and settling like a tidal wave in her center.

She wanted her first time to be special, memorable.

"Come on, baby. My apartment is only a few blocks away."

"When is your term paper due?"

"Screw the paper. I want you," he openly declared.

Katie placed her hand between them. "And I want you, more than you know. But not tonight and not like this."

He tried to kiss her again. "Come on. It'll be good. I

promise." Gently, he bit her neck, sending hot flames of lust cascading through her.

She stepped out of his arms, knowing she had to get control over her emotions or wake up in his bed. "I have no doubt it will be good. Just not tonight."

Jake drew himself up, sighed, and took her hand. They continued walking toward her dorm room. "I really do want your help with my term paper."

She stopped in front of the outside door. Kids came and went by them, laughing and talking.

"I'll help you. Meet me at the library tomorrow."

He grinned at her. "Why can't we work at my apartment?"

"Do you have a copy of the constitution? Do you have the reference books we're going to need?"

Wrapping his arms around her, he held her, and they swayed together. "Probably not, but we could start our research there and end it at the library."

"You're doing things backwards. Research first."

"It's just so hard to do personal research at the library."

"There are ways," she said and leaned forward to kiss him goodnight.

He took her face in his hands and held her mouth to his while he explored her mouth, ravaging her until she felt like she would melt into a puddle at his feet.

"Hey, get a room," someone yelled and he abruptly released her.

Katie stood there stunned, regretting her decision not to go with him to his apartment. She wanted to jump his bones, but her conscience told her to move her feet inside.

"Good night, Katie," he said, smiling at her, knowing he'd left her wanting him.

"Good night," she said, trying to gather her wits about her. Her feet were weighted down with regret as she made her way inside.

She reached the door and turned to see him walking cockily down the street, his hands in his pockets.

Oh yeah, she was definitely giving her virginity to him.

~

Brenda stood on the fishing dock and watched the sun go down over Lake Proctor near Comanche, Texas. On her way to Colorado, she'd stopped to spend a few days doing laundry, resting and relaxing. And now here she stood, her fishing line disappearing into the depths of the lake, trying to catch some Crappie for supper.

Her bobber went under and she yanked, reeling her line in to land the fish. She had him to the top of the water, when with a shake of his head, he fell off the line, and splashed back into the lake.

"Damn!" she said, reeling her empty hook in.

"You pulled too hard," a male voice called.

She watched as a man in a small boat with a tiny troll motor wove in and out of the brush alongside the bank.

"Thank you," she said sarcastically. "I hadn't noticed."

Just what she needed, a man to critique her fishing capabilities.

He laughed. "Spoken just like a woman. Never open for any criticism."

"Excuse me," she said, raising her voice, irritated that her peaceful evening was disturbed by a jerk on the wrong end of the fishing line.

"What kind of bait are you using?" he asked, ignoring her sarcasm.

"I'm sure it's the wrong kind."

"It probably is, especially if you bought it from that crook at the convenience store."

She didn't say anything. She had bought her minnows and her worms from the convenience store close to camp. It was convenient.

"You're not responding," he said.

"Huh?" she asked. "Did you say something? Your noise is scaring the fish."

He laughed and shook his head. "Try buying your bait further down the highway at the Minnow Shack. They're honest, their bait is better quality, and you come away with at least 15-20 minnows instead of twelve."

"Thanks," she said reluctantly, running the hook through the minnow's back and then tossing her line in the water.

"How many have you caught?" he asked.

Brenda didn't know why, but she grabbed her fish basket and raised it proudly showing off her three twelve-inch crappie and two small Brine. Not bad for a couple of hours work.

"You do know how to fish."

Smartass, she thought to herself.

"What about yourself?" she asked, hoping his basket was empty.

He lifted his fish basket. It was half full.

"Damn," she said, wishing she'd beat him. "I'm glad I'm not cleaning all those fish."

He grinned. "We're having a fish fry tomorrow night over at the big camp area. You should come."

"And have to share my fish?" she shook her head. "I don't think so."

"Nah, I've been catching fish for several days and I'm due to go home on Sunday. We've got plenty of fish. We're asking people to bring either a salad or a dessert."

She thought about it a moment, intrigued by this man. "Who is we, kemosabe? I don't hang out with bikers or old geezers."

"How about geezer don't-wannabes?"

She laughed. "Now, that's a group I could possibly consider joining. As long as no one talks about their cholesterol meds or their blood pressure medicine."

He was an older gentleman, but he had a keen sense of humor and he seemed nice. Not that she was going to find out for sure.

"No guarantees, but the last time we all got together, one guy in camp was peddling natural herbs that promised to keep you young forever."

"Hmph. There is no such drug."

"Yeah, that's what I told him and he took a hike."

"What time do the grateful undead gather?"

It wouldn't hurt to check out the local senior group in the RV park. She'd soon be moving on to Colorado.

He smiled and shook his head. "Don't call them that or they will run you out of the park."

"I'll wait and see whether or not I like these people before I call them the grateful undead."

"Good idea."

Brenda felt a nibble on her line and turned her attention back to the fish at hand. When her bobber went under, she reeled the fish in and pulled him up onto the dock.

"Hey, that's a nice one."

"Thanks. I guess I didn't pull too hard on this one."

"Nope, you did a great job of setting the hook."

She gripped the fish in her hand and took the hook out of its mouth and then slid it into the basket. She wiped her slimy hands on a nearby rag.

He watched her and laughed. "My wife used to always wipe her hands, too."

His wife used to! He must be a widow. It seemed to be an epidemic among her age group.

"I love to fish, but I don't like that slimy icky feel or smell on my hands." She baited her hook and threw it back out in the water.

"My name is Paul McConnell, by the way."

"Nice to meet you Paul, I'm Brenda Jones."

They continued to fish, but with the introduction of names, it felt awkward. The spontaneity seemed to have disappeared along with the setting sun.

"It's getting dark," Paul said. "I guess I better head to the bank, so I can start cleaning fish. You could come help me."

There was no way she was going to follow this man back to his campsite and help him clean all those fish. It would take her just about five minutes and then her fish would be frying in a hot skillet. His would take hours.

"Yeah, and people in hell want ice water. It's time for me to head back to my camper," Brenda said.

"If you don't mind the cold, the fish usually bite here early in the morning or late in the evening, especially under that light."

She'd noticed the light on the other side of the dock, but chose to fish on this side of the pole.

"Thanks, I'll remember that."

He yanked the pull start on the trolling motor, until it finally sputtered to a start. The battery operated engine quieted to a purr.

"Maybe I'll run into you again."

"Yeah. See you around," she said.

He waved and she watched as he headed the little boat around the dock, keeping close to the shoreline. Soon, he disappeared into the darkness and she couldn't help but smile. The old man had been kind of fun.

<u>**Chapter Eight**</u>

A week later, Katie walked into her dorm room and shut the door. She sighed.

Crystal glanced up from her laptop. "Good date?"

"The best," she said kicking her boots off. "I think I could marry this boy."

"Whoa, wait a minute. We're in our first year of college. Who in the world gets married now?"

Katie plopped down on her bed and leaned back against the wall. After all the upheaval in her life, she'd like some stability. Something she could count on forever. Someone who wouldn't leave her.

"My mother did."

"And didn't you tell me she regretted getting pregnant and marrying your father?"

Since the time she was a little girl, her mother had told her 'you're going to college and you're going to finish'. At the time that had seemed like a great plan, but not now. Now, she didn't know what she wanted. She just felt lost.

"Yes, but don't you want to get married?" Katie asked.

"Sure, eventually. But for now I'm more focused on passing this semester – and flirting and partying, and just having fun. I don't want any kind of commitment beyond finals."

Sitting there, Katie thought about what she was saying. That was the person she'd been up until four months ago. She had just wanted to party, have a good time, and get into college. She had her life all planned out with her parents beaming at her when she walked across the stage to receive her college diploma. But now, nothing was the same. She wasn't even certain there was a good reason to finish college.

Crystal shook her head at her. "Besides, I'm still trying to figure out what to do with my life," Crystal said with a laugh. "I've seen my older sister with her husband and two kids. I'm not ready for dirty diapers, sick kids, and a husband who's more interested in watching sports than helping. Hopefully in four years, I'll be able to get my own place and have some fun before I commit to happily ever after with someone."

All of that had been Katie's plan, but now she felt empty. She wanted someone to make her feel alive again, and Jake made her laugh. For the first time in months, she'd smiled and had a good time. She needed that right now. She needed someone to think of her happiness.

Crystal frowned at her. "I thought you were just playing with him, like he likes to play with other girls. You knew the night you met him that he likes to string women along. Are you certain you want to commit to someone like that?"

She was right. But with her Jake was different. He was caring and sweet and made her forget her problems. She was the only girl in his life and she would do what it took to keep him from straying.

Shrugging, she said, "It's only been three dates. But I'm the only girl he's with right now. I like him a lot. Let's just say, if I was going to get married, he'd be at the top of my choices."

"Well, I hope he doesn't break your heart. And I hope at the end of this semester you focus more on school and less on guys and marriage."

In her heart, Katie knew she was right. She should be working harder at school, but right now she didn't feel like she could, not when she felt like she had nothing, no home, no family, no one, and it was the worst feeling in the world. The aloneness was frightening. She needed someone, and Jake was that someone, she was sure of it, because he needed her too.

~

Marianne glanced at Stuart, sitting in the car next to her. This was their third date. The 'obligatory' sex date. According to Paige, every man expected sex no later than the third date. And earlier in the evening, Stuart had informed her his kids were not at his house tonight.

"Look, it's starting to snow," she said excitedly. It was such a rare sight in Texas that she couldn't help but feel delighted. By the end of her first winter, everyone told her she would hate the white stuff, but right now the flakes spiraling to the ground were beautiful.

"You're worse than one of my kids," Stuart said, glancing at her and then patting her on the leg, where his hand remained.

Oh yeah, he was expecting a little something tonight.

"Can't help it," she said. "I can count the number of times I've witnessed snow in Texas. I love the sight."

"It will look even better by firelight," he said, smiling at her.

The sizzle in his gaze had her doing math problems in her head, trying to control her fear. "Do you want to stop and get a movie?" she asked, anything to distract him.

It sounded lame, even to her ears, but her nerves were playing Wimbledon and she was losing forty love. Stuart was kind. He'd sent her flowers after their first date, he'd called her almost every day, he understood when she had a test and couldn't go out with him. There were just so many nice things about him and yet she wasn't certain of her feelings.

He seemed almost too good to be true.

She wanted to really, really like him, and she did, but she wasn't convinced she liked him enough to have sex with him. She'd only had sex with one man and she couldn't remember how she was supposed to feel.

Stuart glanced over at her. "I have streaming video at home. We can choose a movie to watch."

"What kind of movies do you like?" she asked, trying to calm her nerves.

"Action adventure and some romantic comedies, but not all of them."

She smiled. "You'd sit through a chick flick with me?"

"Sure. I'm good for a chick flick as long as you are willing to sit through a James Bond movie for me."

"I can do that."

He smiled and reached for her hand. "Have I told you how much I enjoy being with you?"

Heat spread across her face. How long had it been since a man had said this to her? He treated her so special and yet she didn't know what to think of him. "You have, but I enjoy hearing it again."

He pulled into the driveway and her heart gave a little extra beat. Maybe she should just tell him to take her home. Maybe she should feign a stomachache. What the hell was she doing?

"Come on, let's go inside," he said.

"Okay," she replied her knees knocking. He got out of the car and came around to her side. Like an awkward ninny, she sat waiting for him to open her door.

He took her elbow and led her into the house. He swung open the door and flipped on a light illuminating a large room with a fireplace. She stood in the entryway, her nerves still slugging out the tennis match.

Stuart helped her out of her coat and laid it on the back of the sofa in the middle of the room. "Have a seat. I'm going to open another bottle of wine and light the fireplace. The restroom is right down the hall, if you want to freshen up."

"Thanks," she muttered.

If she went into the bathroom, she might lock herself in and never come out.

She strolled around the room, concentrating on her

breathing, glancing at the pictures of his kids. They were obviously very important in his life, and he displayed their pictures proudly. He returned, carrying a bottle and two glasses.

"That's Jason and Mark," he said.

She picked up a plaque. "Soccer Coach of the year?" He grinned. "For a while, I was the little league coach for Jason's soccer team. Until I got tired of out of control parents."

She strolled to his bookcase and looked at the titles. Most were college textbooks and real estate books, with a few fiction titles.

The lights dimmed and she turned to see him gazing at her, like she was cherry pie with whipped cream on top. Yet his gaze left her warm inside. Part of her was interested, part of her was uncertain, and part of her was terrified.

"As you see, I don't read much. I just don't have the time and when I do, I usually read industry manuals that I need to learn something from."

"That's the one thing I don't like about college. All my reading time is spent on textbooks," she responded.

"But it will pay off one day."

"Let's hope so."

With the flick of a switch, the gas logs in the fireplace blazed. He opened the bottle of wine and poured a glass for her. Her hands shook as she took the glass from him.

He lifted his glass and clicked it against hers. "To another great evening together and hopefully the beginning of something meaningful for both of us."

She smiled, warmth spreading through her. He said the nicest things. "Thanks."

"Have a seat," he said, and motioned to the pit group that was arranged around the fireplace.

She sank onto the sofa and sipped from her glass,

needing the liquid courage.

He took a seat beside her. "You know these last few days I've dreamed of you being in this room with me, with us sitting here talking. It's nice to see you here."

"I enjoy your company," she said sincerely. She had fun when she was with him. She liked him. So why the nerves? Why not just be with him and see if the physical side of their relationship was as good?

His mouth nuzzled her neck and she swallowed, feeling like a boulder was stuck in her neck. He took her glass from her hand and set it on the table. She gazed into his eyes and the passion burning there left her breathless.

His lips covered hers, his mouth magically clearing her mind of everything but Stuart. He leaned her back against the couch, while his lips continued their magic, his fingers beginning to unbutton her blouse.

"You're beautiful," he said, as cool air brushed her now bare nipples and she wondered when he'd unhooked her bra.

How long had it been since a man had wanted her, had said words of pleasure to her as he slowly undressed her?

"I've wanted you since the first day I met you," he said, his words so perfect they eased the doubts that had plagued her on the drive over. In her marriage, sex had become overrated. Great sex had been extinct since the honeymoon.

What was she waiting for? Why not take a test drive to see if her engine even remembered how to purr?

She reached out, wanting to be an active participant, and began to unbutton his shirt. Her hands made quick work to reach his chest, needing to feel his naked skin, needing Stuart to replace old memories with new ones.

~

Katie glanced around the dorm room. Candlelight flickered, casting a warm glow in the room. Crystal, her roommate, had gone to visit her parents for the weekend and everyone else had been warned she had plans this evening.

And she did. Seduction plans.

Music played in the background. She couldn't go for that soft elevator stuff her mother listened to, but banging guitars hadn't fit the mood, so she'd bought a John Mayer CD, which set the tone nicely.

Earlier in the day, she'd bought spaghetti and ravioli at a local restaurant and all she had to do was warm it up in the microwave.

She'd showered, put on her prettiest underwear, and sprinkled herself generously with perfume. She was ready for the big night – the night she gave Jake her virginity.

Katie glanced at the clock. He was twenty minutes late. What if he didn't show?

She took a deep breath. He'd be here. After all, this was their fourth date.

A knock on the door interrupted her panic attack and she hurried to answer it, her heart in her throat.

Katie flung open the door and Jake stood there in low hanging jeans and a t-shirt, a bulky ski coat over his body, his hair still damp from the shower. She grinned at him. Wasn't he in for a shock tonight?

"Hello," she said.

"What are we doing tonight?" he asked. "Some of the guys invited us to play Xbox."

"Come in," she said, grabbing his arm and pulling him into the room.

He gazed at the set-up, a slow smile spread across his face. "Candles? Music? Are you trying to seduce me?"

She swallowed and didn't answer his question. "I bought us spaghetti and ravioli from that restaurant on the corner of Main and Pacific."

"Later, babe. Right now I'm hungry for you." He pulled

her into his arms and kicked the door closed with his foot.

His mouth closed over hers and he drank from her lips like a man with an unquenchable thirst. She melted against his body, the feel of his chest strong and solid against her breasts.

She broke away, gasping for breath. "Don't you think we should eat first?"

"You're the only nourishment I need," he said, his lips against her neck, nibbling and teasing her, sending delicious shivers spiraling down her spine. His words thrilled her. She had the power to excite him and he definitely was making her desire him.

His hand slid beneath her shirt and she loved the way his warm palm felt against her skin. Hesitantly, she laid her own hand against his head, moving it down his neck. She didn't know how to make it pleasurable for him. And she couldn't help but worry about the fact that this was her first time. Would she be good enough for him?

His fingers touched her breast and she arched her back, giving him more access. They were standing in the middle of her dorm room with his hand on her breast, kissing until she couldn't breathe.

She stepped out of his arms, needing to gather her wits about her. He yanked off his coat, lifted his shirt over his head, and quickly shucked his jeans. He didn't have any underwear on and she stared at his gorgeous body, his penis jutting out proudly.

He was hot.

"Quit staring and take off your clothes," he said, his voice low and husky.

This wasn't exactly going the way she had imagined it. Somehow she thought they would have dinner, he would slowly seduce her and take off her clothes. But she wasn't willing to back out now.

She pulled her sweater over her head and unhooked her

bra, tossing it aside. He let out a low moan.

"Your tits are gorgeous," he said.

Before she could stop to think about what she was doing, she quickly shed her jeans and her panties.

He pulled a condom out of his jeans and rolled it on, then took her by the hand and led her to her bed. His lips covered hers again, while his fingers explored her nipple, tweaking it while a shudder ran through her. She skimmed her hand down the sleek muscles of his back, exploring awkwardly. She wanted to return the pleasure he was giving her, yet she didn't know what to do.

His mouth left hers and she wanted to cry out at the loss, until he suckled her breast and she moaned deep in the back of her throat. She arched her back and an urgent need to grind her hips against his gripped her.

As if he understood her need, his hand skimmed her mound and his finger delved into the moist center of her. She cried out with the unexpected thrill of his touch, moaning his name.

"Wow, you're so tight," he groaned.

Pleasure wound tighter and tighter within her and she clung to him, her arms wrapped around him.

He moved between her legs and before she knew his intent, plunged deep inside her. Pain ripped through her with a startling shock. She cried out, her body tensing as he thrust again.

"Oh my God, you're a freaking virgin," he said gazing at her in shock. "Why didn't you tell me?"

He rested deep inside her, her insides aching from his brutal entry. "I didn't think you needed to know."

"Baby, I would have been a little easier on you. We still would have done it, but this is your first time. It's going to hurt. Are you okay?"

The pain began to subside and she shifted a little to accommodate him better. "I'm okay."

He kissed her. "We've got all night to show you how much fun this can be."

"All night?"

He grinned, "Yeah, all night."

His fingers found the center of her again and the pleasure she'd felt earlier began to spiral through her again. He smiled as he watched her. "I'm going to make your first time great."

"Hmm…," she moaned, "it gets better than this?"

"Oh yeah," he said and kissed her deeply.

~

Sunlight peaked into the room, just beginning its ascent in the sky. Marianne eased from the bed, trying not to wake Stuart. He lay curled on his side, sleeping. She just wanted to go home. They'd done the nasty several times during the night, and while the sex had been good, the sunlight had awakened her overactive brain. She needed some time to think.

She picked her clothes up and carried them into the living room with her, where she quickly dressed and called a taxi.

Ten minutes later, her cell phone rang, letting her know the taxi waited outside. She opened the door, and Stuart appeared in the hallway, a sheet wrapped around him.

"Hey, where are you going?"

She stopped, the situation awkward. "I need to get home. I have a paper due next week and chapters to read."

He wrapped his arms around her and kissed her lips softly. "I had a great time last night."

"Uh, me too," she said, not really sure how she felt about last night. She liked Stuart. He was a nice guy and the sex had been good, but this morning her brain had overridden her heart and something wasn't right.

The physical side seemed forced, not natural and easy.

Something felt wrong.

"I'll call you later," he promised.

"Okay. I've got to go," she said. He released her and she hurried out the door. Once she reached outside, she turned to wave at him as he watched her leave.

She opened the taxi door and climbed in the back. She gave the driver her address and leaned against the seat. Tears pricked the back of her eyelids.

Stuart was a great guy. He cared about his kids. He wanted a relationship with her, yet her heart wasn't involved. Even after sex, she felt no emotional connection with him and that hurt. She wanted to love him. And yet there were no feelings, no stirring of passion, no can't-live-without-him feelings. Only emptiness.

There had been no emotion. Only two bodies connecting and now she knew she couldn't have sex just for the physical act itself. She craved the emotion, the bonding, and the intimacy of sharing her deepest emotions with another human being.

Sadness welled inside her and she realized she was going to break Stuart's heart.

She wasn't Paige and she knew she could never act like her friend. She decided right then that she would not have sex with another man until she was certain there was mutual emotion.

Body rubbing against body wasn't enough. She needed more. With a sigh, she leaned back, knowing last night she'd learned something about herself that she could never lose sight of again.

She needed emotional intimacy with the physical act. She needed love, and even though she wanted to feel different, her heart wasn't involved with Stuart.

The taxi stopped in front of Marianne's house. Her car was sitting in the driveway, with the hood up. She frowned, paid the driver, and stepped out of the taxi.

She looked like hell. No make-up, the same clothes she had on yesterday, her hair a mess, and she had yet to brush her teeth. She hated morning breath.

She shut the door of the taxi and watched him drive off.

Luke poked his head around from the front of the car. "Good morning, sunshine. Looks like you had a rough night."

"Not open for discussion," she replied automatically, her heart still bruised.

His brows drew together in a frown. "I took the liberty of checking out your car. I checked the anti-freeze levels, the brake fluid, your oil level, and your hoses. That little bit of snow we had last night is just the first taste of a winter-storm that will be arriving in the next few days."

"Was everything okay?"

She did not want to discuss this right now, she only wanted to escape into her apartment and lick her wounds. She'd made a mistake, a huge mistake, and she just wanted to forget last night.

"How fond are you of this car?"

"I hate it. Why?"

He laughed. "Then I guess you won't mind trading it in. It's not going to last much longer. And with the type of winters we have, it could die anytime."

"Crap!" she said. She really appreciated him taking a look at her car, but this was bad news at the worst possible moment. If she didn't get into the apartment, she was going to break down and cry right here in front of him.

"I thought you didn't like it."

"I don't, but it's paid for and for a full-time student that's great."

"Just get you another junker to last until you graduate."

"That would be good if I had any kind of idea as to when, or if, I will ever graduate."

He frowned. "Trouble in school?"

"Yeah, it's called 'what do I want to do with the rest of my life'."

He wiped his hands on a rag. "Sometimes, that's the hardest decision."

"I'm sorry," she said. "I appreciate everything you're doing. You didn't have to check out my car. I'm letting my experience from last night ruin today. Thanks for all your help."

"You're welcome. I like to tinker with cars and I was doing my own and thought I'd take a look at yours."

She smiled. Luke was a kind man, but right now she just wanted to hang her head in shame. "Should I trade it in now or wait for it to die?"

Right this moment she was not in a good emotional place to make decisions about anything and especially about buying a car.

"Just make sure you always have a cell phone with you and some extra blankets. Being broke down in Colorado is different from Texas."

"Okay."

"You look tired," he said. "Why don't you go in and get some rest."

"I have two papers to write, both due Monday."

"They may be easier to write after a little rest."

"Thanks. I also have to figure out how to break a man's heart." Stuart was a nice man and she wasn't looking forward to giving him the news that they weren't going any further.

Luke's head jerked from beneath the hood of the car and he banged it on the metal."

"Damn!" he said.

She laughed. "Sorry, I guess I shouldn't have said that while you were under the hood of the car."

"It was a little surprising."

"It's been twenty years, or longer, since I broke a man's

heart and it doesn't feel good."

"Dragging it out won't make it any easier for you or for him," he said softly.

She sighed. "No, it won't. And he's a nice man. That's what sucks."

Luke smiled. "Even nice men get their hearts broken. Sometimes more than the pricks."

"I think I will go take a hot shower and have a nap and see if that improves my thinking."

Luke started to say something and then bent beneath the hood. "See you later."

"Later," she said, wishing that he hadn't seen her come home in a taxi. He had to know she'd spent the night with another man. Then again, it was none of his business what she did with her life.

She liked Luke, he was easy to talk to and had a nice smile. All the more reason to avoid him and concentrate on school.

<h1 style="text-align:center"><u>Chapter Nine</u></h1>

Brenda strolled into the camping pavilion, the smell of frying fish drawing her into the gathering. She knew she looked hot tonight compared to the other retired women in the room. She'd worn her best jeans and her slinky top that hid her muffin roll, a new dye job on her hair hid the gray, and for a sixty-year old woman, as the kids would say, she had it going on.

And considering that most of the people in the pavilion were older couples, she'd wasted her time. It was pretty bad when you went to a campground to hook up with a man.

"Come on in," an elderly man motioned with his arm. "We got a fresh batch of catfish just coming out of the grease."

"Did you remove the cholesterol from that grease?" Brenda asked, a serious expression on her face.

"What's cholesterol? A cute young thing like you doesn't have to worry about HDL/LDL."

She smiled at him. "Right. Only strokes and heart attacks."

And she'd witnessed more of those than she cared to ever see again. First George and then James. She didn't want to witness another heart attack.

"Shh…" he said. "Those words are unmentionables at our age."

She laughed. "Where are the desserts? I brought banana pudding."

He smacked his lips. "You don't happen to put whipped cream in it do you?"

"Always," she said, thinking this man was a character. At least he seemed to enjoy life and that was what she wanted. Someone to share the fun times and even the sad times in life.

"God, what is your name? When my wife dies, I want you to be her replacement."

A woman stepped around from behind him. "You old coot. I'm going to outlive you, just so there can be no replacements and spend every dime of your money with the pool boy."

He winked at Brenda. "I knew she was behind me."

Brenda laughed. "I've never considered myself a replacement part and never intend to. I'm Brenda Jones."

"Nice to meet you Brenda, I'm Larry and this is my wife, Donna."

They seemed like nice people and Brenda was suddenly glad she'd come to the fish fry.

"Put your banana pudding on that table next to the wall," Donna told her. "Let me introduce you to some of the other campers."

Donna took her around and introduced her to everyone, and just when she decided he wasn't there, Paul came out of the kitchen wearing a ruffled apron tied around his waist in a big bow at the back.

"Hey," he called out. "You came to try my fish."

"Cute apron," Brenda said, giving him the once over.

"Is that a sexist comment?" he asked.

"When you wear an apron like that, it is."

"I want you to know it takes a real man to wear something like this. I'm secure in my masculinity."

She raised her brows and shook her head. The man certainly was handsome for someone his age. "I see."

Donna strolled by. "Shish. That was the only apron available."

Brenda smiled.

"Donna, remind me to tell that husband of yours to lock you in the camper the next time we have a fish fry."

"He knows better," she said, and continued on.

"Did you get any fish?" Paul asked.

"I was just going to grab a plate."

He took off the apron. "Mind if I join you?"

"That would be nice." And she meant it. Sitting with Paul would be fun and he was someone she knew.

They filled their plates and found two empty chairs at one of the tables. "How many fish did you catch yesterday?" he asked.

"I think it was five. I don't like to catch more than I can eat at one time."

"That's wise. Usually, I catch a lot and bring them here for the group to fry. Of course this will be our last fish fry until spring. A lot of these folks will be heading to South Texas. Snow birds."

She glanced around the room. She'd heard of people going down to the warmer climate in the winter and then going further north in the summer. Maybe she'd do that later this year.

"That's an idea," she said. "I've never gone to Brownsville before. Do you go?" Brenda asked, curious.

"I used to, but now I don't get more than a couple of hours away from Dallas. I need to be close to home."

"Do you have family close?" she asked.

"Yeah, a couple of grown children and three grand-kids. How about yourself?"

For the first time she noticed his sandy brown eyes twinkled with kindness, and there was a sprinkle of freckles on his cheeks.

"One daughter and one grand-daughter. Both of them are going to college now," she responded, a pang of longing cutting through her at the thought of them. She missed them.

"Are they close by?"

"No, they're in Colorado."

He gazed at her, his forehead creasing in a frown. "You're a long ways from Colorado."

"I used to live in Dallas, but about three months ago, I decided I wasn't going to wait a minute longer. I sold the house, bought the RV, and here I am traveling the open highway."

"Alone?" he asked in surprise.

She smiled, remembering her trek across the country with Sandy. God, she didn't miss her. "No, at first I had another woman traveling with me, but she found a man in Florida and married him. Me, I'm too mean to get married again."

He grinned. "That's pretty gutsy, traveling alone."

Thinking of the attempted robbery she nodded her head. Sure she got lonely, frightened, and even bored sometimes, but she was at least living.

"Well, I can't say I haven't had a big adventure and I think that's what I needed. I was dying in that big old house all by myself," she quietly admitted.

Paul reached out and patted her arm in a comforting gesture. "I never thought I'd be alone at this time in my life. I thought I'd be a lot older before that happened."

"How old are you?" she asked.

"I'm twenty-two. Can't you tell?" he said, teasing, abruptly making the mood lighter. "You don't believe me?"

"Yeah and I weigh 120 pounds."

He laughed.

Brenda tilted her head. "You do see that, right?"

"Oh yeah," he admitted.

Even though she looked like a hot mama at sixty, she still carried a few extra pounds. "Sorry, but at forty I think a woman's body shifts into matronly mode and the curves become chunks."

"Well your chunks are mighty fine," he said, winking at her.

"Thank you. I would have hit you if you'd lied and said

I was skinny.”

“At our age, I think I’m just happy to be in relatively good shape with most of my parts still in good working order,” he said, moving the food around on his plate.

She couldn’t help but agree with him, after witnessing so many friends and family fall ill and just seem to waste away. She hoped when it was her time, she’d just go to sleep and never wake up. She’d be happy if it were that easy.

“So you never confessed how old you really are.”

“I’m twenty-two.”

She shook her head at him. “Keep on telling yourself that and let me know if anyone else believes you.”

“Okay, so it’s times three,” he said, finishing his meal and pushing the plate away.

“Sixty-six. Hey, you’re still standing and that’s more than I can say for some people I know.” The others in the room began to clean up.

“What did you bring to eat tonight?” he asked.

“Banana Pudding.”

“Can you cook better than you can fish?”

Brenda drew her brows together and gave him a mean look. “What’s wrong with my fishing? If you recall, I think I caught more in that spot than you did.”

“Pshaw! You were fishing in the nursery. The fish I caught were twice the size of yours.”

She leaned close to him with twinkling eyes. “Listen closely. There’s a lesson you should have learned before now. Size does not matter.”

Reaching out, he wrapped his arm around her shoulder. “Honey, obviously you’re fishing in the wrong pond because size definitely matters with everything.”

She stopped and looked at him. “Paul McConnell, I think you’re flirting with me.”

“Is that what I’m doing?” he asked, stunned. “It’s been

so long, I've forgotten how. How am I doing?"

She laughed. "Keep it up and you might get lucky. I'll let you walk me to my camper, if you promise to be good."

"Oh, I'm good."

"That's a subject not open for discussion."

He grinned. "Not yet anyway."

A blush spread across Brenda's cheeks, like a sixteen-year-old virgin on her first date. "Where are you catching these monster fish?"

"That's top secret information. I'd have to kill you if I told you."

Brenda yawned. "Get in line. I think two guys are sitting in jail right now, wishing they could get a hold of me."

"What are you talking about?"

She told him about her catalytic converter thieves and how the police had caught them.

He laughed when she finished. "You get into all kinds of trouble, don't you?"

She shook her head, feeling proud of the way she had lived her life the past four months. The fear and loneliness had lessened to at least livable levels. "Life should be lived and I'm determined to make mine interesting. I didn't die with George, though at times it seemed that way."

He nodded his head as if he understood. "Grief can make you wish you were dead."

The room was almost empty. While they'd talked, most people had finished eating and begun to leave.

Larry walked up to their table. He placed the empty bowl of banana pudding down beside her. He took his finger and ran it along the inside and licked his finger. "I'd pick this bowl up and lick it, but my wife would give me hell, so I'm bringing it back to you to let you know that the next time we have a fish fry, you have to bring banana pudding. I haven't had good pudding with whip cream since my Mom use to make it."

Brenda hadn't felt so appreciated since before George died. Being here with these people today, she'd felt accepted. Like she'd finally found the right group where she belonged.

"Thanks, Larry. Maybe I'll make more and bring it over to you."

"Like hell," Paul said. "I didn't even get a chance to taste it. Larry ate it all."

"Wasn't my fault that you didn't get over there in time to get a taste. It was mighty good too."

"While I cooked, you ate it all."

"You were done cooking when she brought in this pudding," Larry admonished him.

"But I hadn't eaten yet. I was waiting for us to go get dessert," Paul said, staring at his friend.

"Too late!" Larry taunted.

"Boys, I'll make some more," Brenda said, laughing.

"Can I have my own bowl?" Larry teased.

"After I get my bowl," Paul insisted.

A surge of happiness swelled inside Brenda. For the first time in a long time, she'd had fun. No pressure, just good fun. And she liked Paul.

"After Paul takes me to his secret fishing hole, I'll come back and make more pudding."

"Take her first thing in the morning, Paul. You really need to try this pudding."

"Thanks for thinking of me, Larry," Paul scoffed.

"What are true friends for," Larry replied. "Gotta run, here comes the wife and she's going to give me hell for eating all this pudding."

"I guess we should go, since they've cleared the building," Paul said reluctantly.

"Yes, I guess we should," Brenda said, standing, not really wanting the evening to end just yet.

Paul stood and they meandered slowly to the door of the pavilion. "I tell you what, why don't you meet me at the dock in the morning at six o'clock and we'll just see who can catch the most fish."

"Can't we catch the nooner fish?" she asked.

"Nope, early in the morning is the best time."

"Okay, but I make no guarantees on my mood and coffee is a requirement."

He grinned and turned to leave. "See ya, shortcakes."

"See ya," she said, and began to walk back to her camper, the sound of a bullfrog on the lake calling out for a mate echoing in the night air.

Tonight, she'd had more fun than she could remember having in a long time. She couldn't wait to see Paul again. At least this group of people had seemed normal and not just into hooking up. Maybe she'd finally found a place she belonged and a companion to have fun with.

~

Marianne watched in awe as the medical personnel bustled around in the emergency room. Her college advisor had assigned her to the hospital as a volunteer to see if she would enjoy working in the medical field. Her first night as a volunteer, and she felt like a first-grader in college. They had assigned another volunteer, an older woman with graying hair, to show Marianne her duties.

"I'm glad it's quiet tonight," Trina said. "Sometimes it can get really busy."

"Tell me what you do?" Marianne asked, curious as to how she could help these trained professionals. It seemed her best bet was to stay out of their way.

"Come on and I'll show you where everything is."

Marianne followed Trina to a closet where a cart sat, a thick curtain covering it. She slid back the curtain and revealed sheets, pillowcases, and towels.

"This is the fresh bedding. When the rooms are empty, I stock them with fresh linens, latex gloves, and some medical supplies."

A nurse interrupted them. "Trina, can you run this to the lab for me?"

"Sure."

Marianne watched as Trina pulled latex gloves from her pocket and slipped them on. She took the plastic bag from the nurse. Inside was a sealed cup of urine and the patient's name was on the outside of the vial and the baggy.

"Always wear latex gloves whenever you handle any kind of lab work. I take urine, blood samples, everything to the lab for the nurses and I always wear gloves."

They hurried to the lab center. "Hey chica, how are you?" the lab technician asked.

"I'm fine."

"What have you got for me?"

"A urine sample that's a rush," Trina said.

"They're all a rush. Just sign it in."

"Bill, this is Marianne. She's a new volunteer."

"Welcome," he said.

Marianne watched as Trina signed a sheet on the desk. She wrote the name, the nurse, and the time.

They returned to the emergency room just as an ambulance backed in. The paramedics wheeled in a stretcher with an elderly woman lying prone. The nurses directed the EMTs into a room and stood by as they unloaded the patient onto the bed.

Marianne heard the paramedic say a possible stroke victim and she watched as the nurses began to take her vital signs and try to talk to her. The emergency room doctor arrived and asked the patient some questions. The elderly woman didn't appear to know where she was.

The doors swished open and a young couple ran in, carrying a baby. "She's not breathing," the young mother cried, her face distraught with fear.

The nurse behind the central desk hurried them into a room. "When did this start?"

"She's been running a low-grade fever, but tonight it shot up to 102. We were driving here when she stopped breathing."

A second nurse entered the room next door. "Excuse me, doctor, we need you next door. A baby isn't breathing."

He yanked his gloves off and hit the trashcan as he left the room. Marianne tried to watch from a distance to see what he was doing to the baby, but too many bodies blocked her view. Soon the baby screamed and she sighed in relief. Could she watch sick children come in and be treated, possibly even die, day after day?

She assessed her emotions and realized she didn't feel ill, only concerned. To lose a child must be the worst thing that could ever happen to a parent, and to witness something so tragic would be heartbreaking.

The volunteer took her by the arm, "Come on, let's get back to stocking the rooms. This is how it goes around here. One moment everything is calm and suddenly it gets busy. Or some nights it stays busy."

"Does this ever bother you?" Marianne asked.

The woman thought for a moment. "No. The doctors and the nurses are so good at their jobs and I know I'm helping them. I'm doing menial tasks that they don't have time for. As for the patients, I've seen some really bad accident victims, a burn victim, a lot of sick kids, several heart attacks and strokes, but they all received help when they arrived here and that makes me feel good."

"So what else do you do?"

She led Marianne into a vacated room. A rumpled sheet lay tossed aside on the bed and a nearby tray held several empty vials.

"We're going to clean this room." Trina said as she pulled out fresh gloves and slipped them on her hands. "Again always wear your gloves. Never touch the hazardous waste box. The cleaning crew handles all medical waste."

She yanked the sheets from the bed and showed Marianne the dirty linens box. Next, she took a bottle of disinfectant and sprayed the plastic mattress cover. "This disinfectant should kill the germs. Wipe anyplace someone might have touched."

She moved to the countertops and sprayed them down. Then, pulled out a fresh sheet and pillowcases from the cabinet. Marianne helped her make the bed.

As they finished the room, the sound of a siren announced the arrival of another ambulance.

"Looks like it's going to be a busy night," Trina said. "But that's good. I'll be able to show you everything."

The rest of the night, Marianne and Trina ran specimens to the lab, took a pregnant woman to the maternity ward, cleaned rooms, and generally helped the nurses any way they could.

At ten o'clock, when her time was up, Marianne went home tired but with a sense of satisfaction. Tonight had been interesting, but did she want to do this for a living?

Chapter Ten

Katie held the cell phone to her ear, unsure her mother would answer. Marianne had phoned her once after their confrontation at the restaurant, but Katie had told her she was too busy to talk. She wanted to speak to her mother, but she wanted to hurt her as well.

Marianne had killed Katie's dreams of her parents ever reconciling. It was the biggest fight they'd ever had and Katie's dreams had evaporated like vapor into the cold Colorado night sky.

She wanted to tell Marianne about Jake. She was just a little concerned about some of the changes that came with having Jake as her boyfriend – her grades were getting worse with every assignment, and she couldn't seem to stop it. Not that it should matter. Katie was planning a new life, one that didn't depend on her grades. There was so much she wanted to talk to her mother about but couldn't.

Their relationship had never recovered since the night she sat Katie down and told her that her parents were splitting. No matter how hard Katie wanted things to be the same between her mother and herself, she didn't know how to repair the damage. Angry, she wanted her mother to hurt like Katie ached for the life she'd lost.

The phone rang and her mother answered. A knot formed in Katie's chest.

"Hi, it's me," Katie said, keeping her voice even.

"Hi, how's school?" her mother asked excited.

Katie paused, then said, "Fine."

"Do you have tests coming up before the break?" Marianne asked.

"Yeah," Katie wanted the walls around her heart to collapse, but they were too strong and she couldn't will them away.

"I have two twenty-page papers that have to be

completed before the holidays," her mother rambled on, her voice chatty.

"You've still got a couple of weeks."

"I know, but they're weighing on my mind. How have you been?"

"Great," Katie said, sarcastically.

"You're doing okay in school?"

"Yes."

"Dating anyone special?"

"Not really." She wanted to tell her about Jake, but she couldn't. Not yet. Her dreams of starting a life with Jake, getting married and having his babies would not be approved of by her mother.

Silence filled the airways.

"How long are you going to be mad at me?" Marianne asked bluntly.

"I'm not mad," Katie lied. She just didn't know how to cope with this new world of her parents. She loved them both and didn't want to betray either of them.

"Then why haven't you called?"

"I've been busy," Katie responded hurriedly. She wanted to get off the phone and see Jake. She didn't want to get into a big emotional discussion. It was easier this way.

"Why did you call?"

"Dad bought me an airline ticket. I'm going home for Thanksgiving."

"Oh," Marianne said. "I thought since you spent the summer with him, you would spend the holidays with me."

"No, I'm going home."

A cricket could have been heard during the strained silence.

"Okay, why don't we plan on seeing each other the weekend before Thanksgiving?" Marianne said.

"Can't, I'm busy."

"Then I expect you the first weekend in December."

"That's too far off. I don't know what my plans will be," Katie said, not wanting to commit.

"Good, you can pencil me in on your busy calendar for the first weekend in December. I'll see you then."

Katie started to protest, but she didn't want to waste the energy in an argument and Jake was due any moment. She would find an excuse before then.

"All right, I'll see you then. I've got to run, I'm going out tonight."

"Have a good time." Her mother paused for a moment. "I love you, Katie."

"Bye Mom," Katie hurriedly said, wanting to hang up before the tears fell.

She disconnected and sank into the chair. Though she hated to admit it, she missed her mom. Katie had a right to be angry. She had a right to be upset, didn't she? But why did she feel like, in some ways, she'd been wrong? She certainly didn't know how to apologize if she *had* been wrong – which she wasn't entirely sure she was.

Part of her said, get over it. Her family wasn't any different from all the other families who had gone through a divorce. She wasn't the only kid who'd had to deal with dual families.

She had wanted her parents to be together one more time. Instead, Dad had brought his new girlfriend, and her mother had gotten mad. Everyone seemed to have moved on, except her. At this point, she'd just settle for the tension being gone between all of them.

Her parents were divorced. They would never get back together again, but she didn't know how to handle these new arrangements without feeling disloyal to one of them. It was a new world and she was still trying to cope with how to deal with the two of them separately. And so far she was doing a lousy job.

She realized now she'd screwed up majorly with her mother. After the holidays, she'd find some way to make it right. She just didn't know how.

~

Brenda arrived at the boat dock at five minutes to six. She'd spent a restless night waiting for the alarm clock to buzz, excitement making her too eager to sleep. She was too old to react this way. Sixty-year old women didn't anticipate a date like a teenager, but that's exactly how she felt. She liked Paul.

It was cold, the sun had yet to come up, yet here she sat, bundled, waiting. The sputter of an engine and the splashing of a boat making its way through the early morning fog had her peering into the darkness.

A glimmer of light could be seen poking its way over the horizon, chasing away the night shadows.

"Ahoy," he called. "I'm looking for a good-looking babe to take fishing."

Oh the man was quite the charmer. She was going to have to watch him or find herself in his arms.

"Sorry, you're stuck with me," she said, picking up her tackle box and fishing poles. "We won't be sitting out in middle of the lake in this fog, will we?"

"Nope, as long as I miss the stumps we'll be sitting in a cove."

He held out his hand and helped her step on board the boat.

"Stumps? Oh joy, nothing like a little adventure on a cold morning with the possibility of a swim."

"I just told you that so you'd cuddle up next to me when you get scared."

She laughed, shaking her head at him, wondering if he knew how much she enjoyed being with him. "There are better ways to get me to cuddle."

"I'm all ears."

"Later. The fish are getting away."

He stood and peered over the windshield of the boat to see through the fog. He put the boat in reverse and backed away from the dock. Swiftly, he turned the wheel and directed the boat across the smooth water.

In the predawn mist, they were the only souls on the lake. A sense of peace settled over Brenda as the boat skimmed the still water.

He drove slowly. "The fog makes it quiet."

"Isn't it great?" she said. "Kind of eerie and spooky, but kind of soothing."

He glanced at her and smiled. "I thought I was the only one who enjoyed the different seasons."

"Oh no, I like it when Mother Nature gives us a little surprise. All except tornados. That's where I draw the line. She can keep those."

"My wife always loved this time of year, because the leaves were changing, the temperatures were cooler, and it was right before the holidays."

He'd never told her much about his wife. Just mentioned her in passing and yet Brenda recognized the sound of sadness in his voice when he talked about her.

"Yeah, George always wanted to go fishing in the fall. He said all the water skiers were gone and the lake was quiet."

Paul turned the boat into a cove. "Okay, you are sworn to secrecy about this place. This is my baited fishing hole."

She chuckled and gazed at him like he was crazy. The sun was just starting to rise and she knew that soon the quiet peace would be interrupted by other fishermen. "And who would I tell?"

"I don't know, but you should feel honored. You're the first woman I've brought to my fishing spot."

"When do I receive the promise ring?"

Startled, he glanced at her his eyes wide. Then he realized she was kidding. "God, woman, don't scare me like that. I thought you were serious."

Brenda laughed. "I noticed that. Kind of skittish, are you, on the topic of promise rings?"

"I'm a little old for such nonsense." He killed the engine and threw an anchor overboard. The splash rippled the water and sent a bird fluttering on the shoreline. "The only thing I can promise you is to catch a lot of fish."

"At this time in my life, that's all I need."

He smiled. "But you still can't tell anyone where my fishing hole is."

"Shut up and hand me the minnow bucket. I've got to get my hook in the water and catch the first fish before you."

He handed the bucket of minnows to her. "When we reach twenty, we go home."

She dropped her line over the side of the boat and sat back, quietly contemplating the joy of the moment. "You know, George and I used to always bet with one another. Whoever caught the most didn't have to clean them and whoever caught the biggest had to…"

She laughed at the memory and glanced over at Paul. It was so easy to talk to him about George and she knew they would have been friends.

"You didn't finish that."

"And I'm not going to."

"Sounds very interesting."

"No, it was fun. We always had a good time together."

"That's the way it was with my Marjorie. Don't you feel lucky to have had a good marriage and have so many happy memories?"

She glanced over at Paul who had finished baiting his line and was gazing at her, a smile on his face.

"Yes, I was very lucky, and I guess that's why I'd like

to get married again, but I'm afraid. I don't know if I could be so lucky the second time."

So many people were unhappy or in bad relationships and she just didn't know if she would be so fortunate a second time around.

He dropped his line in the water. "Yeah, I know. With the divorce rate as high as it is, how could you be so blessed to have two good marriages?"

"Exactly," she said. "Sometimes, George and I would have a disagreement and occasionally we'd have a knock down fight. Nothing physical, but oh how we made up afterwards."

"Marjorie could freeze me out when I pissed her off," Paul said, smiling at the memory. "But Lord all that woman had to do was ask for something she needed and I would give her the moon. We had a great life together and I miss her."

Brenda felt a stirring in her chest, it wasn't often a man expressed strong emotions about a woman, especially his wife. It was obvious he'd loved her very much.

A tapping on her line had her focused on fishing again. She waited. The fish took the hook and she turned the reel. Excited she began to pull the fish in. "I've got one."

She reeled and reeled until she pulled the fish up and into the boat.

"Humph! Not bad, but not big either."

"Hey, it's the first one. I'm just warming up."

For the next two hours, they laughed, told stories, and caught fish. Brenda couldn't remember having such a good time. Soon they had caught twenty fish, ending their morning together.

Paul started rolling in his line. "That's twenty, it's time to go."

"Oh, are you sure we've caught twenty?" Brenda said, dismayed. "I know it is, but this was so much fun."

"We'll come again," he assured her.

She began to reel her line in, not ready to end her morning with Paul. She was having fun. She enjoyed being with him.

"It's only nine o'clock. Why don't we go back to my place and I'll make breakfast?"

She trusted Paul enough to invite him to her camper. And she was looking forward to feeding him. She liked to cook and had no one to share her meals with.

He finished pulling in the anchor and put it in a plastic box. He glanced over at her.

"I'm starved. What do you have in mind?"

"I make a mean southwestern style omelet."

"The meaner they are, the more I like 'em," he said, gazing at her, his eyes wide in mock anticipation.

"You're in store for a treat," she promised him.

He laid her fishing poles in the boat. The sun had risen and burned off the early morning fog, clearing the lake. He started the engine, and when the motor caught, he put it in gear. They bounced across the lake, the cool wind whipping at her hair.

Soon they pulled alongside the dock and he tied the boat. He stepped onto the dock and reached back to help her.

Their hands touched and he pulled her up onto the dock. When her feet were firmly planted, she turned, and they were shoulder to shoulder, face to face, and eye to eye. They seem to fit together perfectly.

Her breath caught in her throat as she gazed in his brown eyes and could see the passion stirring there. She met his lips part way. It wasn't a fervent tongue-down-your-throat kiss, just a simple tasting and testing of one another. His lips grazed hers and her arms reached to wrap around him, pressing her breasts into his chest.

He felt strong and he tasted like a sweet spice. Desire,

frozen so long within her, suddenly jump-started back to life. Happiness filled the empty void inside her. She hadn't known if she would ever experience that emotion again.

The sound of a boat caused him to step out of her arms. She smiled. So he wasn't into public displays of affection, so what?

"That was the best catch of the morning," she said.

He grinned at her. "I'm going to drive the boat around to my camping spot. I'll be at your place in just a few minutes."

Brenda all but danced back to her camper. Humming happily, she began to cook breakfast. Soon the eggs were done and there was still no sight of Paul. She looked out the door, anxiously waiting. Time moved slowly and she began to worry about him. What if something had happened?

Thirty minutes later, she turned off the warmer and strode out the door. When she walked over to his camper, she found him busily packing everything up. He was almost ready to pull out.

"Hey, I thought you were coming over for breakfast," she said, trying to keep the irritation from her voice.

"Sorry, something's come up. I've got to return to Dallas."

"Did that kiss frighten you so bad, you decided to run?" she asked, unable to keep the sarcasm out of her voice.

He stopped his hurried motions and stared at her. "No, nothing like that. My son called and told me I needed to get home. I'm sorry, Brenda. I've got to go."

He threw the last things into the boat and walked around to the front of the camper.

She stood uncertain, disappointment choking her.

"I'll be back in a day or two. Don't go anywhere. Wait for me."

"Maybe," she said, unable to commit.

"No, maybe. I'll be back soon." He paused at the door. He brushed his lips against hers and climbed into the cab of the camper. "I have no choice, I've got to go."

He started the engine and she watched as he pulled out of the spot.

"Damn! That's a first," she said. "Kiss a man and he runs."

~

Marianne sat in a chair by the window overlooking the big back yard. The sun shone brightly, not a cloud in the sky. It was an absolutely gorgeous fall day, the kind that made her long to be outside. The weatherman had said today the high would climb to near sixty-five degrees before another cold spell came through tomorrow. She ached to go to the park, to go for a walk, to take a drive into the mountains, to share this day with someone. Instead, she read her English textbook and tried to convince herself she was being a good student.

A knock at the door startled her. She jumped up and hurried to the portal. Luke stood there in his motorcycle leathers.

"Hi," he said, looking like a Greek god, his muscles firm, his arm leaning against the frame.

"Hi," she responded, her pulse accelerating at the sight of this fine specimen of a man. She got a little breathless each time she saw him.

"I'm taking the bike for a ride into the Mountains. I thought maybe you'd like to go along."

Most of her school work was done and what wasn't, could wait. She deserved an outing. Especially a ride through the mountains on the back of his motorcycle.

Marianne glanced at the textbook in her hand. "When are you leaving?"

"As soon as you're ready."

She paused for just a moment, knowing she should stay, but needing a break.

"Yes, I can't sit inside here a moment longer and read this textbook."

He laughed. "It's too pretty a day to pass up. We'll be back in plenty of time for you to read later."

"How do I need to dress?"

Luke gazed at her jeans and sweatshirt. "You're fine. You'll need a jacket. It will be cooler on the bike. When we're up in the mountains, it will be a lot cooler."

She laid the textbook on her desk and grabbed her coat. She put her keys, some money and a lipstick in her coat pocket.

"I'm ready," she said, standing before him.

He laughed. "That's the quickest I've ever seen a woman get ready."

"I'm a little burned-out sitting inside and studying. I'm ready to escape for a while." They went out the door and she locked it behind her.

"I haven't seen you coming in late lately. In fact, your car has been home a lot."

"Yeah, well, I've put my classes ahead of my social life up until today. I'm not even hanging with my friend, Paige, much anymore."

After Stuart, she'd decided it was time to make her studies her priority and put her social life on the back burner. In fact, she didn't ever intend to live the life that Paige lived and she was giving up even trying.

Luke straddled the bike and backed it out of the garage. Then he handed her a helmet. "That's probably for the best."

"This is my only break until Thanksgiving."

"Then we better make this a good one. Climb on."

He checked her helmet straps to make sure they were tight and then climbed on the bike. He started it up and pulled out of the drive onto the street.

Marianne wrapped her arms snuggly around his waist and hung on as they turned a corner. A cool breeze blew against her and she was glad for the coat.

Luke was a watchful driver as he drove them onto the highway and turned onto the road that led up into the mountains. The two-lane road began a slow ascent, the smell of pine trees and spruce had her breathing in the clean, crisp air, clearing her brain.

The natural beauty soothed her in ways nothing else could. Though the mountain breeze was cold, Luke took the brunt of the wind, shielding her with his body. She leaned into his strong back, the masculine scent of him causing a flutter in her stomach.

The last snow had rid most of the trees of their leaves, but a few aspens still had gold leaves clinging. A doe and her fawn watched from a safe distance on the side of the road as they rumbled past.

After an hour, they reached the town of Estes Park. Luke pulled over at a restaurant and turned off the bike.

He took off his helmet. "I thought maybe we'd have some lunch while we're here."

"Good, I'm starved."

He helped her with her helmet and locked them on a peg. He took her elbow and led her into the restaurant that had an outside patio eating area. Soon they were seated and she picked up a menu. She stared at her hands, they felt like they still trembled from the bike.

"My hands are vibrating. I feel like I'm still on the cycle."

He took her hand in his and held it for a moment. "Nope. They're a little cold."

His hand was warm and the texture of his skin rough against her own. He didn't release her, but continued to hold her hand.

"What's good here?" she asked, enjoying the feel of his touch, but nervous about the possible meaning.

"My favorite is the buffalo burger."

"Buffalo?" Marianne asked, startled.

"Yeah, it's different."

"I see they have a turkey burger," she said.

"That's good, too."

"Do you like weird food?" she asked.

"I like to try new things. Life is about adventure and I want to experience as much as I can while I'm here," he said thoughtfully.

This was the attitude she wanted to adopt. To experience, life at its fullest and yet in a sensible way. All the partying hadn't fit her and it was okay to be focused on her dreams.

She smiled at him. "That's the kind of attitude I am looking to adopt. I want to try new things. I'll take a buffalo burger."

"You'll be surprised that the meat is not that different in flavor," he said, gazing at her.

"We'll see."

When the waitress approached them, they both ordered coffee and a buffalo burger with sweet potato fries. It was the first time they had sat across from another. For a moment, Marianne felt awkward.

"Tell me about your classes at the college," she asked him. "What do you teach?"

"I teach Philosophy to juniors and Politics to seniors."

She couldn't imagine standing in front of young people and discussing politics with them in a way that hopefully they would listen to with an open mind. So many times their families and even television had already set their political values.

"Impressive."

"Thank you. I enjoy teaching and I especially delight in

the type of lifestyle it affords me."

"Tell me what you love about teaching?"

He thought for a moment. "I like to show young men and women that there are different ways to look at things in life. I try to open their minds to different philosophers and teach them the different perspectives."

"Sounds complicated."

"It is and I enjoy it."

"You teach politics?"

He smiled. "It's my favorite subject. And my students are required to help a political campaign. They need to get involved and they must be a registered voter to be in my class."

He was an interesting man and she liked that he seemed calm and rational and not trying to sell people on his life values.

She laughed. "Do you take them to the polls?"

"Nope. How they vote is their business, but I encourage debate in my classes and participation in the political process," he said enthusiastically.

"Sounds like you like your job very much."

"I do," he said. "Tell me how you came to be at Fort Collins University at this time in your life."

He was asking her about her life and that made her feel good. How many men had she met who wanted to know about her? Most of the time it seemed they just wanted to get into her pants. And she didn't have time any longer to deal with jerks like that. She was done.

"You mean you want to know why an old lady is going back to college?"

"I didn't say that. People return to school at all ages. I had a sixty-seven year old in my class last semester and she was one of my best students."

"Well, I'm not sixty-seven yet. In my previous life I was a homemaker. When I separated from my husband, I realized I had no marketable skills. And I didn't think working at a big box store would support me in the lifestyle I wanted."

"How long were you married?"

"Eighteen years."

"That's a long time."

"Yes, especially when the marriage died about ten years in."

"Ouch."

It was true. Now as she looked back on her life with Daniel, the marriage had flat-lined about ten years in, when he'd gotten his big promotion. Maybe at that time she hadn't been enough for him or maybe he'd just gotten bored, but whatever happened had killed their marriage.

"Yes, but I had a daughter to raise and I kept believing things would change. And they did. I changed."

He laughed. "You don't miss being married."

She thought about that time. There were some things she missed, but she enjoyed her life now. She'd been alone in the marriage, the same as now. "No, I really don't. Life is a lot simpler now."

"A lot of divorced women go out and find someone and remarry right away."

"My priority is to finish school. I have dated some and I probably will continue to date occasionally, but I'm not looking for husband number two," she said with confidence. She had settled into her life and she liked it. "What about you? How long have you been divorced?"

"Almost three years. She said I was boring and left. She wanted us to belong to the country club and get involved in the social scene. Not for me."

Marianne almost giggled out loud. "And why haven't you remarried?"

"Haven't found anyone I wanted to spend that much time with. I'm not exactly the most social guy and I like unusual things. Going out partying is not what I consider a fun evening."

"I'm quickly learning it's not that much fun. In fact, I've given it up."

"My idea of a nice evening is a fire in the fireplace, reading a good book, or watching a documentary."

"Sounds perfectly boring and wonderful," she said, with a laugh.

He smiled. "Yeah, most women think so, until the newness wears off."

Yet for her the newness had worn off of going to clubs and speed dating and online dating.

"My friend, Paige, has been upset with me because I stopped going out partying with her and am concentrating on my studies. She thinks I'm wasting time and that I just need to find a good lay."

He threw back his head and laughed. "She sounds like a party girl."

"She is. I dated Stuart for a while, but it wasn't easy and it felt awkward," she admitted. "I decided to concentrate on my classes and I've been happier."

"There's nothing wrong with getting laid, but if the relationship isn't ready, it can create more problems than it solves," he said, his gaze steady and assuring.

Tilting her head she stared at him, wondering if he was being honest with her.

"Are you telling me if a woman offered you a one-night stand, you'd turn her down?"

"Are you offering?" he said with a smile on his face.

Startled at his bluntness, she realized he was teasing. "Keep dreaming."

He lifted his coffee cup and sipped from it and then sat the cup down. "I don't do one-night stands anymore. Usually, you regret the decision the next morning."

"You're telling me, in the last three years since your

divorce, you have not had a one-night stand?"

"Like I said, I don't do them anymore. The first six months after my wife left, I made some horrible decisions. Once the fog began to clear, I realized that casual sex was dangerous and unfulfilling." He took a deep breath. "Don't take this the wrong way, I like sex just like any other man, but I'm choosy."

A smile spread across her face. "How did we get on this conversation?"

He grinned at her. "I don't know. We just did, and it's been enlightening."

She dipped her head and looked at him coyly, "At least it tells me we're going to be good friends. We can talk about anything."

He leaned over and brushed his lips against hers, startling her.

They were warm and she could tell from the way his green eyes twinkled with merriment that he'd deliberately taken her off guard.

"Oh, I think we're going to be more than just good friends."

<u>**Chapter Eleven**</u>

Marianne dialed her mother's number. She had not spoken to her in over a week, though they had both promised to stay in touch. Many times, her mother was simply too busy to talk or had very little to say. With the coming Thanksgiving Holiday, Marianne wanted to spend some time with her mother, but didn't know if she was still close to Dallas or had ventured down the road.

After several rings, her mother answered the phone.

"Hello."

"Hi, Mom."

"Who's this?" Brenda asked.

Oh God, it was going to be one of those kinds of calls.

"You know who it is, Mom."

"Marianne. I hardly recognized your voice," she said sarcasm dripping from her words like water from a leaky faucet. "It's been weeks since you called."

"Hey the phone lines go both ways. As does the highway," Marianne responded, thinking that normally she was the one who made the effort to stay in touch.

"Well, I wouldn't think of keeping you from your school work," Brenda replied.

"I always have time for you, Mother," Marianne said, trying very hard to keep the cynicism out of her own voice. If her mother wanted to have this type of call, then Marianne could counter her sarcasm with some of her own.

"You're still full of bull."

"I learned from the best. Where are you?" Marianne asked, changing the subject before they got into an argument.

"I'm still at Proctor Lake."

"Why don't you come to Fort Collins for Thanksgiving? The weather is supposed to be cold, but nice. No snow until the week after."

A long pause followed and Marianne knew she was considering coming.

"You haven't seen my place yet," she encouraged.

"I don't know. Give me a few days and I'll let you know," Brenda said.

"What's keeping you in Proctor?"

"Good fishing. You should try it sometime; it's therapeutic. Clears the head and sharpens the brain."

That wasn't what was keeping her at that lake and Marianne knew it, but until her mother decided to confide, she wasn't going to push her.

"Mom, I'd like to see you. It's been a long time," Marianne said, hoping she didn't sound whiny, but wanting to see her mother. They hadn't parted on good terms and she wanted to mend the rift between them.

"I don't know Marianne. I'll think about it. I am not ready to leave here, but I will consider coming. I can't give you an answer tonight, but I will next week."

"Okay, but I'd really like you to come spend Thanksgiving with me, and I insist you come for Christmas."

"We'll see."

"Are you still traveling alone?" Marianne asked.

"Yes, and I'm loving it. I don't have to listen to anyone chattering all the time, and I don't have a hussy picking up any and every man she meets."

Marianne laughed. Her mother never changed. While Marianne loved living here in Colorado, she missed seeing her and wished they were closer.

"What about you? Are you dating anyone?"

For a moment the image of Luke came to mind, and she quickly shoved his rock hard pectorals out of her mind. They were not dating. They had gone for a motorcycle ride, had lunch together, and he'd kissed her that did not make them a couple. But she'd enjoyed being with him.

"I'm concentrating on school. How about you?" she asked her mother. "Are you dating anyone?"

"Just me and the crappie."

"The what?" Marianne wasn't certain she'd understood.

"Fish."

"Oh. Any of them marriage material?"

"Not a one so far," Brenda responded. "Look, I gotta go. I'm meeting some of the ladies and we're playing Bridge tonight. I gotta run."

"Okay, but call me and let me know about Thanksgiving."

Marianne was wishing her mom would just come and spend some time with her. While she was married, they saw each other once a week, and now, nothing.

"I will."

"Be safe, Mom. I love you."

"I always am. I love you too," Brenda responded, ending the call.

Marianne hit the end button on her mobile phone. She sat there a moment, realizing her Mother wouldn't be visiting. Past experience revealed that whenever her mother hesitated, she didn't want to come. She quickly dialed her friend, Paige.

Paige answered the phone. "Hey girl, how are you?"

"I'm doing good."

"Still dating Stuart?" Paige asked.

"Nope, I ended it," Marianne said, knowing she'd been right to end that relationship. The man had been nice, but there just wasn't the emotional tug she needed.

"Why?"

"It just didn't feel right."

"Who the hell cares how it feels! If he was good in the sack, you should have made him your fuck buddy. You need a few of those you can call."

That was certainly not appealing. Sure she could

understand if some women wanted that type of relationship, but she wanted more.

"Paige, I don't want a buddy. I don't need one."

"Oh, honey, I've been dating that one guy I met at lunch and, oh my God, he is so great in bed."

"That's good," Marianne said, trying to be excited for her friend, but bored with the constant sex conversations. Didn't she have anything else in her life? All she focused on was sex, and that just didn't appeal to Marianne.

"I mean he knows positions I'd never dreamed of and can last forever. It's been a lot of fun."

"I'm happy for you. Do you like him?"

"Hell no, he's not at all my type, but he's so good in bed that I'm going to hang on to him for a while," she said with a giggle.

Marianne shook her head, suddenly feeling sorry for the man. "Paige, I admire you for your boldness."

"You could be having fun too."

"No, I've come to accept that's just not me." Sleeping with any and everyone wasn't fun, and Marianne didn't want to change that about herself. Paige had a right to live her life her way. That was her business.

"Honey, if you'd loosen up a little, you could enjoy the same pleasures."

"No, Paige, I've come to the conclusion that I cannot be anyone but myself. So I'm giving up the one-night stands. I'm not going out to meet men, I'm not out dancing and acting wild, trying to find someone. I'm concentrating on getting through college and finding my way in life alone. I think that's what I need to do right now."

And for the first time in years, Marianne felt a sense of happiness and purpose. She was doing what she needed and liked her life.

"You could be doing both and getting a little in the process. I mean, how can you do without sex?"

Marianne realized, without the right partner, she didn't want sex. She was taking a time-out on the physical side of life.

"Paige we've always been different, and I think I let myself get caught up in the idea that I need to be different because of my failed marriage. Again, I can only be the same old Marianne that I've always been. As for sex…I miss it, but it's not the end of the world."

She loved Paige, but Paige just didn't get it.

"Oh, honey, I know just the man to hook you up with. He will rock your world."

"No, Paige. I'm not interested."

A long awkward silence filled the line.

"Well, when you're bored, give me a call and I'll do what I can to spice up your life."

"I'll do that," she said, knowing she would pass. "What are your plans for Thanksgiving?"

"Scott is taking me skiing in Canada. He has more money than he knows what to do with, so we're going first class all the way. I can hardly wait. Why, what did you have in mind?"

"Nothing, I just wanted to make sure that you had some place to go at Thanksgiving."

"Are you spending time with your Mother and Katie?"

"Yeah, we're getting together." Marianne lied, unable to confess to her friend she would be alone on Thanksgiving, unless her Mother came to visit. "Have a great time in Canada. Don't break a leg on the ski slopes and come home safe and sound."

"I don't plan on getting on those ski slopes except to wear my little bunny outfit and show off my great ass in my tight ski pants."

Marianne laughed. Paige always had a way of making her feel good, and yet she was glad that it was Paige's life, not hers.

They ended the call and Marianne sank onto the couch. For the first time in her life, she would spend a holiday alone. She focused inward to see if it bothered her and felt nothing. In fact, she was actually looking forward to the break from college and some restful time alone.

~

Brenda threw her baited line into the water, the sun beating down on her as she sat on the dock. A week had passed since Paul left, and while part of her wanted to pack the camper and continue on her way to visit Marianne, another voice urged her to stay. That's what Paul had asked her to do. But she owed her allegiance to no man, no one, not even her daughter.

Instead of loading up the motor home and hitting the road, she came fishing. She played Bridge with the ladies in camp, took long walks, and enjoyed the changing fall leaves. In Texas, the leaves didn't reach their fall brilliance until right before Thanksgiving, and even then, they didn't fall until the absolute end of November.

She missed Paul, and that left her feeling vulnerable, which she hated. They hadn't known each other that long, but the connection with him had been more instant than a hot cup of coffee.

They both had come from good marriages and missed their spouses. They enjoyed the same type of life, and she had thought they had the beginning of something. Now she worried she'd dreamed the connection between the two of them.

Sure, he'd kissed her, but what did that mean?

"You still trying to catch fish out of the nursery?"

At the sound of his deep voice, she whipped her head around. He stood, dressed in blue jeans, a ball cap pulled low over his head, gazing at her. Her heart did a little extra curricular dance.

"No, I caught all the small fish and took them out to some old man's fishing hole and baited it for him. Now, all he should catch is small ones."

It was all she could do not to throw her arms around him. He was a welcome sight and gave her pulse a little extra excitement.

"Leave you alone for five days and you become vicious," he responded, walking to her.

"How's the emergency?" she asked.

"Resolved for now," he answered.

"Care to share why you had to leave?"

She watched his face and could see the dark circles under his eyes.

"Not on such a beautiful afternoon. I've had to deal with gloom and doom for a week, I'd like to spend some quality time with a good-looking babe hiking in the woods. Want to join me?"

Brenda was tempted to tell him to take a permanent hike, but part of her knew it really wasn't any of her business where he'd been. What if it was something bad? The dark circles beneath his eyes branded the stress on his face. Shouldn't she give him a break?"

She reeled her line in and they strolled to her camper and stored her fishing gear.

Paths meandered along the bank of the lake, weaving around it for over a mile. Brenda had walked the trails several times, but never with Paul.

When they were out of sight of the road, he took her hand. "Hey, I'm sorry I had to leave like I did."

"Yeah, me too."

"I wouldn't have been surprised if you were gone when I returned. I couldn't wait to get back here and see if you waited for me. I'm happy you stayed."

"Well, I only stayed because the weather has been warm and the fish have been biting and…

He pulled her to him and his lips covered hers, his mouth telling her what she already knew. Passion filled his kiss as his lips took possession of hers, and he pressed his strong and solid body against hers. She leaned into him, needing more contact. Her arms wound around his neck, and she melted into his embrace.

When they parted, he smiled. "Now that's a welcome home worth coming back for. Have I convinced you I really hoped you'd wait for me?"

"I just thought that was a gun in your pocket."

He laughed and hugged her. "That's what I enjoy about you. Your quick wit chases away the darkness."

"Yeah, I chase away the darkness, usually about six o'clock in the morning."

"Speaking of, are you up for fishing tomorrow morning?"

"Why not? I have to show you how I stocked your fishing spot with babies."

They continued walking along the path, his weathered palm holding her hand in his. "So are you disappearing for Thanksgiving?" she asked.

He sighed. "My son is having a family gathering and I'm expected to appear."

Brenda waited for his invitation, hoping that he would want her to meet his family.

"My daughter has asked me to come to Colorado."

He stopped. His fingers brushed her brow and pushed back a wayward strand of hair from her face. "Are you going to go?"

"I haven't seen her since the summer and I'm considering it. It's just that she is in far North Colorado and I hate driving all the way there in winter with the chance of snow and ice."

He didn't say anything and they resumed walking.

"I would be gone at least two weeks."

He stopped and pulled her into his arms and kissed her again. His lips moved over hers until she was breathless, her pulse racing like an overworked engine. When he stepped back, she stood there shocked and stunned and so not wanting him to stop. She'd forgotten how good kissing felt.

"I know you want to see your daughter, but that kiss was to remind you of what will be waiting for you here when you come home. Or if you don't go, I promise I will return just as quick as I can."

"What if we had Thanksgiving together?" Brenda asked, hating herself for bringing it up but wanting the option out on the table.

Standing beside her, she noticed the way his body tensed and he didn't say anything. Taking a deep breath, he moved away from her. "Brenda, my family has gone through lot in the last year, and while I enjoy the time we spend together, and eventually I want my family to meet you, I'm just not ready to take that step."

"Yet, you want me to spend Thanksgiving alone, waiting for you."

"I'll understand if you decide to go to Colorado. I'll be sad that you're gone, but I understand."

Brenda wanted to be angry with him, she wanted to tell him she was going to Colorado, but a part of her understood his need to take it slow. She hadn't even mentioned him to her daughter. Thanksgiving was just the beginning of the holiday season. Christmas would be spent with Marianne.

"Thanksgiving, I'll be in Proctor, cooking my own turkey, dressing, and giblet gravy. Homemade pumpkin pie made from real pumpkins, not that canned stuff. I'm going to invite some of the campers for lunch, watch some football, and spend the day being thankful for the people in my life. If you choose to share some of that day with me, then you know where to find me."

Paul stared at her. "I don't know who sent you to be in my life, but I'm thankful that you're here."

They strolled toward her camper just as the sun shimmered beneath the horizon, its rays spreading across the clouds, casting them in purple and gold streaks. "You're starting to sound sappy, old man."

"Humph. Meet me at the dock in the morning and I'll show you that there's a lot of sap left in this old man."

She knew that was true, just from the way he'd felt hard against her thigh when he'd held her.

"I beat you last time and I can do it again. In fact, if my record is correct, I've beaten you every time we've been fishing together."

"Then your reign must end."

"You can kiss my grits, too."

"Oh honey, I'd love to kiss your grits. I like 'em."

She giggled like a schoolgirl, her heart swelling with an emotion she wasn't ready to acknowledge. She didn't know where this was going, but she was glad she had waited. She was in no hurry and she wanted to see where this relationship was headed. She happened to like this old man.

Chapter Twelve

Katie waited impatiently by the door, her bags packed, for Jake to appear and take her to the airport. She could have ridden with Crystal, but no, she'd wanted Jake to take her. Her flight left from Denver and the airport was in the middle of nowhere, over two hours away. She was supposed to be there two hours before her flight and, apparently, Jake had disappeared off the face of the earth.

She'd called his cell phone repeatedly, and even called one of his gaming buddies trying to find him. If he didn't show up in ten minutes, she was going to drive herself to the airport and leave the car at the terminal. It would cost a freaking fortune, but that was better than missing her flight.

Katie checked the room one last time to make sure that she'd packed everything.

She was ready, but no Jake!

God, she was furious with him. The man had no respect for time, his or anyone else's. If he was in the middle of one of his games, he wouldn't leave until he was finished.

What if he was with a girl?

That pesky voice creeped into her conscience. They'd been together for over a month. She was the only girl he was with and they were progressing as a couple. They went everywhere together and hung out all the time. He'd filled the gap left by her family and she couldn't think of life without him.

Part of her was ready to commit to forever, but then he would do something like today.

To hell with him!

She grabbed her dorm key and her bag. Opening the door, she lugged the suitcase down the stairs, opened the back of her jeep, and threw it in. She ran back upstairs and grabbed the second bag from the room and her purse. Locking the door behind her, she scampered down the stairs. Her flight left in three hours exactly and she had no choice but to get on the road.

Katie pushed open the dormitory door with enough frustrated anger to send it slamming against the brick wall. And saw Jake strolling up the sidewalk with a grin on his face, looking like a million dollars, strolling along with his hands in his pockets like it was just another day.

Grrr!

"Hey babe, where you going?"

"To the airport. I've already packed the car."

"It's only three hours before your flight, what's the rush?"

The man had no sense of time, no sense of anything but his damn games.

"Traffic, possible snow, possible wrecks, possible boyfriend forgetting that I asked him to be here an hour ago."

"Babe, it's okay, I'm here now."

He wrapped his arms around her. "Come on, we'll load up my car and I'll drive you in."

"No!" she said, her temper flaring along her spine like a flash fire. "I'm driving myself."

She stopped, stunned, her eyes searching his neck. A bruise marked a spot just above his shoulder that reminded her of a hickey. "What's that on your neck?"
He pulled back his shirt. "What?"

"That bruise?"

"Babe, you're starting to sound suspicious." He tried to glance at the mark. "Oh that! Frank ran me into the wall at the student center. We were playing darts. I slammed into it pretty hard, I guess it bruised me."

She couldn't help but think it sounded fishy. Was she crazy for being involved with him? He hadn't answered his phone. Could he have been with someone else?

Was Crystal right that he would never be someone to

commit to?

"Did you get that paper done for me?"

She was late and he wanted to discuss his freaking English paper? God, he infuriated her. He should have been here on time if he wanted to discuss his English paper.

"I told you, I would help you with it, but I'm not writing it for you."

"You know, if I'm going to be in this gaming tournament, I have to practice."

"Yes, but it's not my responsibility to do your schoolwork for you."

"Can't you help me out?"

She stopped for a moment and carefully studied him. Was he using her for schoolwork and maybe sex?

"Let's see, I've written your last two papers. I think I've been helping you out." Before she could stop herself, she blurted out. "Is that all you want from me? Sex and your homework completed?"

He stiffened. "Believe me, I could get just about any girl on campus for sex, and as for the homework, I'll take care of it. I just thought you cared enough about our future to help me."

Great, now she felt bad for her suspicions. "I don't even know if we have a future," she said.

He wrapped his arms around her and nuzzled her neck. "Oh babe, don't you know that with you I want to be successful? It's for our future. When you get back, I think it's time you met my mother."

Katie couldn't suppress the flutter of excitement that filled her stomach. Meeting the parents was pretty close to an engagement. Did this mean what she hoped it did?

"I've got to go," she said. "I'll miss my flight if I don't leave now."

His lips covered hers and he kissed her deeply, his mouth moving over hers, sending tingles all the way to her toes.

Slowly, he released her lips and kissed her again softly. "That was to remind you of what will be waiting for you here. I love you, babe."

Katie's heart swelled with love, her heartbeat pulsating with emotion. He'd never said the L word before. "Oh, Jake, I love you, too."

"Call me when you get to Texas to let me know you arrived safe."

"Oh honey, I will. Have a wonderful holiday."

"You, too. Maybe we can spend Christmas together with one of our families."

She smiled and climbed into the car. "I'd love that. I've got to go, Jake."

He closed the door. "Drive safe."

"Bye," she said and started the engine.

He loved her. Oh God, that felt so wonderful, and just like that, she wasn't angry anymore.

~

Brenda sank onto a rock at the top of the ridge. She took a deep breath and let her aching feet rest for a moment as she caught her breath.

"Getting tired?"

She sliced him with a glare that let him know she was feeling the pain. "I thought we were taking an afternoon walk, not a hike to Dallas."

He laughed. "I brought you here to see the view of the lake before I have to leave."

She stared out at the sparkling lake below them. He was leaving again. She'd known it was coming, but didn't want him to go. The leaves on the trees had finally begun to change and colored the landscape with a golden hue.

"Now, don't you think the hike was worth coming up here?"

"It's breathtaking, but I think I'm going to need a helicopter to get me back to camp."

Paul sank down beside her and wrapped his arm around her waist. "I wanted to share this view with you," he said and leaned over, kissing her on the mouth gently.

Brenda liked his kisses and she enjoyed the feel of his body against hers. It made her long for a more intimate setting, and her thoughts turned, as they kept doing lately, to wondering what Paul would be like in bed. She couldn't help but imagine the two of them entwined together, his flesh on hers.

She glanced at the water and took a calming breath. "You know, Paul, we've talked about a lot of things about our spouses, but we've never talked about our sex lives."

He almost choked and began to cough. She slapped him on the back. "I didn't think it was that big a deal."

"God, woman, you could kill a man with your directness. Subtlety is not your style."

"If you wanted subtlety, you would not be hanging around me. Tact is for weak women."

He laughed. "I guess you're right. It just catches me off guard sometimes."

They sat quietly, both staring off at the water, relaxing together on the rock, knowing soon they would be forced to part.

"So, who's going first?" she asked.

"Is this something we really need to discuss? I mean it's kind of private and how does it pertain to us?"

"I'm not asking for intimate details. I just wanted to know if you had a good sex life together. Do you have to take Viagra? Have you slept with anyone other than your wife since she died? Are you into S&M?"

It had been a long time since she'd thought about sleeping with someone other than her George. It would be first for her and she wasn't doing it lightly.

He chuckled and she gave him a solemn look. "I'm serious. In this day and age, these are questions I need to know before I will ever consider sleeping with you."

Paul stopped laughing and stared at her, his eyes searching her face. "Are you saying you're ready to sleep with me?"

"No, but it's starting to percolate in the back of my mind. There may come a day when I'm ready."

Grinning, he picked up her hand. "Marjorie and I had a good sex life until her illness. We enjoyed each other. I never cheated on her, because I was happy. I don't have to take Viagra, changing positions is about as kinky as I get, and there has not been anyone else."

"So I'd be your first, if we slept together."

"Sweetie, you are my first in so many ways that you don't realize," he said softly.

"Oh, I like that idea," she said, smiling and wishing he wasn't about to disappear on her again. What kept dragging him back, besides his kids?

"So, what about you and George? Any kinkiness I should be aware of?"

"You wish," she said. "George is the only man I've ever been with. We had a good sex life and I miss it."

"Sex or George?" Paul asked.

"Both," Brenda said softly.

The wind rustled the leaves in the trees and a bird screeched its lonesome call as they sat there on the rock, looking over the lake, holding hands.

"You know, I can't replace George," Paul said softly. "And you can't replace Marjorie."

"Ya think?" Brenda said sarcastically. "Look, I'm not searching for a cloned George. I know that things would be different, but what I had with George is the only model I have of love, sex, and marriage. It's the only thing I can compare.

It's like buying a car. I know my Ford ran smoothly and gave me no trouble and the only Oldsmobile I ever bought left me stranded on the road. I want to make sure whatever model I get involved with is more like a Ford."

He laughed out loud at her. "Well, I like the idea of being compared to a Ford, only I've got about seventy-five thousand miles on me. I've never had to have an engine overhaul and my transmission can still shift gears."

"Hmmm…can you go into overdrive?"

"Zero to sixty in no time at all."

He kissed her mouth, his lips covering hers, his hands pulling her closer to him as he gave her a thorough tasting.

She pulled back, ending the kiss because this rock was not where she wanted to make love to Paul the first time. Maybe in her youth, under the stars or hiking up a mountain, would have appealed to her, but now the comfort of a bed was where she wanted to explore this relationship. Yet, she wasn't quite ready to take that final step.

"When are you leaving?" she asked.

"When we get back," he answered somberly. "But I'll be back tomorrow."

She thought about driving to Denver and quickly dismissed the idea. She wanted to stay here and invest time with Paul. She wanted to see where this relationship was headed, and that meant waiting for him. And she wanted to have sex with Paul.

"I'll be here," she said. "Maybe I'll be waiting naked with whip cream on my breasts."

He gazed up at the clear blue sky, shaking his head. "God, you know how to torture a man."

"Or maybe I'll be playing cards with all the other single men in camp."

Picking up her hand, he brought it to his mouth. "I'll miss you and will return as fast as humanly possible," Paul said. He fidgeted as if he were uncomfortable, his eyes darkening and the tone of his voice deepened. "When I return, we need to have a serious discussion."

"What about?"

"Our relationship."

She thought for a moment. "I'll save the whip cream for later then."

"Geez woman, I'm supposed to leave after you tell me this."

"Hopefully, the image of me waiting with whip cream on my breasts will make you hurry that much faster to get back to me." She hopped down from the rock. "Have a safe trip and a wonderful Thanksgiving with your children."

~

Marianne stepped outside. The sun was bright, the air crisp, and she couldn't imagine a more perfect Thanksgiving morning. This was her first holiday alone, and so far, she was enjoying her day. She'd cleaned her little place, baked a pie for later, and now she was going to watch a movie before the football game came on at three.

"Hey, you, why are you home?" Luke called out, standing on his back porch. "I thought you'd be with Katie and your mother."

"No. Katie's in Texas and so is Mom. I decided I was staying home for Thanksgiving."

Luke walked over to the stairs and strode up them, and her heart did a little dance. The sight of him set off her hormones in ways she'd never dreamed.

He wrapped his arms around her. "Good, you can come over and help me with my turkey."

His arms were strong and secure around her, yet part of her still hesitated. She liked living here, and a relationship with Luke could complicate things.

"Oh no, I've picked out a good movie, I've baked a pumpkin pie, and I bought a small turkey dinner for one."

He frowned at her. "Please, tell me it's not a TV dinner?"

"Well…okay, let's just say a packaged dinner."

Holding her in his arms, he leaned his mouth to her neck and kissed her softly. As he trailed kisses up the side of her neck, sending delicious shivers through her, he said, "I have a real bird cooking in my oven with all the trimmings. Some friends of mine are coming over at noon and I'd really like for you to come spend the day with me. I would have invited you before, but I assumed you would go home for Thanksgiving."

He picked up her hand and kissed the back of it. "You could help me with the dressing." His voice was cajoling and persuasive at the same time. "The two couples that are coming over are my best friends and I'd like for you to meet them."

At the thought of spending time with Luke and his friends, she felt her body warm with anticipation.

"I promise it will be fun," he said, swaying her within his arms.

The idea of relaxing with his friends was intriguing. She enjoyed being with people and an entire afternoon with Luke would be fun.

"Okay, as long as I can bring my pie for dessert."

"Oh, honey, they will love your pie. Mine are store bought and we'll just save them for later in the week."

"What time?"

"I could use your help, so anytime you want to come over is fine."

She smiled at him, noticing again the twinkle in his green eyes. She enjoyed being with him, he was easy and fun. But, oh, how he set off her pheromones, putting her insides on full alert.

"Okay, let me clean up and put some lipstick on and I'll be there."

He frowned and then his lips covered hers in a kiss that almost knocked her off her feet. Her body leapt to life. Why did she react so strongly to this man? He was dangerous and part of her enjoyed living perilously.

His mouth moved over hers, creating images of the two of them naked and entwined together. She could feel herself melting in his arms.

She put her hand between them and stepped away. She took a deep breath and tried to quell her traitorous body. She gazed into his emerald eyes and wanted to languish in the pool of green.

She wanted to tell him to stop, but instead all she could do was return his smile.

"I thought I'd kiss you before you put lipstick on."

"Oh and what about after I put lipstick on?"

"Don't tempt me or we won't get any cooking done."

She laughed. "You know this could become awkward," she said, trying to warn him off.

"I know. I thought about that. I've never kissed one of my tenants before. Of course, you're the first one that wasn't twenty years old. It'll be okay," he reassured her. "We'll deal with it. I have to get back to my turkey. See you in a few minutes?"

"I'll be there," Marianne promised, suddenly excited about spending the day with Luke and his friends.

She went inside and changed her clothes, freshened her make-up, put some lipstick on, and hurried down the stairs eager to see Luke again.

She knocked on his back door.

"It's open! Come on in."

She walked through a utility room that led directly into his kitchen. Her first time in his house and she took in the homey look and feel.

A fire roared in the fireplace, knocking the chill from the air. A big, flat screen television hung over the fireplace.

A stereo system and books filled shelves on either side of the fireplace, along with pictures and knick-knacks. A huge, soft pit sofa filled the room and separated the living area and the kitchen.

Luke stood in the kitchen, crumbling cornbread into a large bowl. Double ovens filled one corner of the wall. A tile and brick backsplash reminded Marianne of the home she once owned in Texas.

"You've never been inside my home before have you?"

"No," she responded, thinking she liked his taste. But then, she seemed to like so many things about her handsome landlord.

He smiled. "As you can see, it's an old house and I've lived here a long time."

"You're a great decorator. It has a nice, homey feel."

"Thanks."

"In fact, the kitchen reminds me of the home I use to own in Texas. It looks very similar," Marianne said, feeling nostalgic, missing the house, but not the life that went with it.

"When I was looking for ideas on how to upgrade the kitchen, I saw a magazine with a similar kitchen in it," Luke said, "I took the picture to the remodeler and said this is what I want."

She started to laugh. "Was it Better Homes and Gardens?"

He reflected for a moment. "Yes, I think it was. It's been years ago."

"I saw the same kitchen and had ours remodeled after it!"

"Seems like we share the same tastes."

"Yeah, it does."

"Speaking of taste, I have to make the dressing. Want to help me?" he invited.

"What do you need me to do?" she asked.

He grinned at her. "Sorry, my mind went in directions that are better left alone."

"Luke!"

"Hey, I'm a man," he said with a shrug. "I have all of the spices lined up. How about you start adding them in the dressing and I'll start pouring the broth?"

Marianne picked up the sage and poultry seasoning. She measured it out in her hand and sprinkled it in. Then she took the chopped onions and celery he had set aside and mixed it into the cornbread.

Luke came up behind her and wrapped his arms around her, trapping her next to the cabinets, the bowl of dressing in front of them. His body pressed against hers and she leaned into him. He slanted his head next to hers and poured the chicken broth into the cornbread mixture.

"I've never cooked like this before," Marianne said, her voice sounding breathless even to herself as her heartbeat raced.

"It makes the food taste even better, and the cooks, well, they have a great time too."

She took a big spoon and mixed the broth into the cornbread. Taking another spoon, she held it to his lips. He opened his mouth and tasted the mixture.

"More spice?"

"Always," he said, nuzzling her neck.

A shiver went through her as she tried to concentrate on adding more sage to the dressing.

She took a spoonful and held it to his lips. "How about now? Enough?"

"Delicious. Now, I need a taste of Marianne to go with it."

His mouth found hers and he kissed her playfully on the lips.

She giggled and turned in his arms. "I think we're ready for the pan to put the dressing in."

He kissed her cheeks, her nose, her lips, and his mouth trailed down her neck.

Marianne's breathing quickened, and the urge to open her blouse and give him more access as his mouth found her shoulder almost overcame her.

The sound of the doorbell had him lifting his lips from her and gazing into her eyes. "Damn. Don't they know we're busy cooking?"

"The kitchen is getting a little hot. It may be a good thing that they're here." She smiled at him and patted him on the cheek. "I think you better answer the door."

"Okay, but save the rest of that recipe for after the game."

~

Marianne glanced around the table at Luke's friends. Two married couples he'd known for years. When they opened the door, his friends had stood there, staring in surprise. She couldn't imagine what she looked like with her lips swollen from his kisses, her cheeks flushed with desire.

Yet they had welcomed her into their group and the morning had been spent happily preparing the meal. Now they gathered at the table to sample the feast.

Luke stood up and tapped his wine glass. "As you know, my family had a tradition of going around the table at Thanksgiving and everyone saying what they're thankful for. So I'll start by saying I'm thankful that each of you are here sharing this day with me and with my new friend, Marianne."

He turned to his friend Jim, who stood. "I'm thankful that the Bronco's aren't playing this afternoon." Everyone laughed. "And for everyone's good health."

He sat down and the next person, his wife, shook her head at her husband. "I'm thankful that we're still here in

Fort Collins and haven't been transferred."

Marianne had been given the place of honor at the end of the table, opposite from Luke. She stood nervous and yet wanting to make Luke glad he'd invited her. "I'm thankful that the journey of life has brought me here and I'm spending this Thanksgiving with all of you."

The next woman, Jill, stood. "I'm so grateful that Luke continues to cook every year and I don't have to."

The last man stood. A large man who reminded her of a big teddy bear. "I'm thankful the Pilgrims landed on Plymouth Rock and started this tradition of a day of gorging on turkey and pie. And I'm grateful for such good friends."

They all laughed and held up their wine glasses. "Happy Thanksgiving," Luke said, and everyone clinked their glasses together.

They passed the plates of food, everyone talking at once, happily sharing stories of previous Thanksgivings.

"How long have you known Luke?" Marianne asked Jill, the lady sitting next to her.

"We all went through grad school together, got married, moved away, and came back together. Through it all we've remained close."

How neat to have friends you'd known for years. People who no matter where you lived, they sought you out to spend quality time together.

"Wow. That's a long time."

"Yes, in college we were known as troublemakers," she laughed. "It's a wonder we didn't get kicked out. But somehow we've all survived."

"Luke was a troublemaker?"

"Hell, yes. The administration was reluctant to hire him, but then again, it was one way of keeping him under control."

She gazed with surprise at the mild-mannered man who

she couldn't imagine causing a problem of any kind. He radiated intelligence and strength of character. It was what attracted her to him.

"Back then we were going to change the world. Everything we did seemed so important, but now, looking back, it was nothing. I ran the school newspaper, Jim was a reporter, and Luke was the organizer of the Fort Collins Independent Political party, which no longer exists."

"Wow, I knew he was into politics, but I guess I didn't realize how much."

What she was learning not only surprised her, but kind of shocked her about this man. But it also let her know that when he believed in you, he stood behind you, and that trait she adored.

"Oh yeah, he once ran for city council and lost because he was the chairman of the Independent Party."

"Jill, quit telling her stories about me that aren't true."

"Luke, I don't have to make up stories about you. There are plenty to tell that are true."

Everyone was finished eating, but continued to sit at the table talking leisurely.

"Hey, the Cowboy game starts in thirty minutes," Jim stated. "Let's get the food put away, so we can watch them lose."

"Jim, can you go one Thanksgiving without watching the game?" his wife asked.

"No," all the men said in unison.

She shook her head. "Okay, I'm outvoted."

Marianne watched the couples, intrigued by their closeness and their ability to banter and tease one another.

"How long have you guys been dating?" Jill asked.

"Oh, I don't know if we're really dating," Marianne said. "We went motorcycle riding and he's helped me with my car."

The woman tilted her head down, her brows raised.

"Honey, if you went riding on Luke's bike, you're dating. He doesn't casually date. Even in college, he would pursue one woman, and until they broke up, there was no one else. He's a great guy, he's just been unlucky in love."

"Unlucky in love? What makes you say that?"

Jill leaned in close. "He's never found a woman who deserved him. We were all shocked to see you here today. He must be pretty serious to invite you to dinner."

"Oh no, I think he just felt bad that I had nowhere to go."

"Maybe, but from the way you two looked when you opened the door, that's the happiest I've seen him in a long time."

Marianne's cheeks bloomed with color, but she couldn't help but smile. She enjoyed being with Luke, and she liked his friends. Hopefully, they thought they were good together.

The group started cleaning up the table, and Marianne began stacking the dishes to carry to the kitchen.

Jim and Todd were in the living area getting the big screen TV all set for the game, while the women and Luke put everything away.

Luke came up behind Marianne and put his hand on her waist. "Don't let anything Jill tells you scare you away. She's a fiction writer and likes to create stories."

Jill popped him with the hand towel. "We've been talking girl talk and it's nothing you need to concern yourself about. Now, go play with the boys."

Luke wrapped his arm around Marianne. "Okay, but I'm taking Marianne with me."

They walked from the kitchen arm in arm and he leaned over and kissed her on the top of her head.

Marianne smiled up at him, surprised at how comfortable she felt around him and his friends.

Chapter Thirteen

Brenda gazed around the living area of her motor home at the empty table, the dirty dishes stacked by the sink. She'd invited three other campers over for lunch, and afterwards, they had sat and watched the Cowboy game together. Now, in the quiet camper, loneliness had set-in.

It was Thanksgiving. Earlier in the day, she had spoken to Marianne, Katie, and even Paul had called to wish her Happy Thanksgiving and tell her he'd been delayed until Sunday. He promised to tell her the reason when he returned.

He'd sounded stressed and distant. Whenever he came back from these trips with his family, he seemed detached. It took him a day or two to warm up and resume their friendship.

Something about his trips to Dallas made Paul different and she didn't know if it had something to do with his children or if going back still reminded him of his wife, reopening the pain of her death.

Brenda had no doubts that he'd loved his wife. And she was glad. It made her respect him as a man. Made her think he'd been a good husband. Made her think Paul would be a good companion.

Without a doubt, she was ready to take their friendship to the next level. But was Paul ready? He teased her, he flirted with her, he kissed her, but he wasn't physically pursuing her like most men.

She didn't doubt that he was attracted to her. She could see the desire in his eyes, but what kept him from trying to get her in the sack? Why was he holding back?

Did he have some religious stipulation that required him to wait until he was married before having sex again?

For the first time since she'd lost George, she was ready to experience love and even longed for sex with Paul.

But marriage? No, she wasn't ready to say I do, just yes to a little pleasure.

This time when he returned, he would find a sixty-year old sex kitten waiting to seduce him. Maybe kitten wasn't the appropriate word and cat didn't seem right, but a fire stilled burned in the oven and she intended to see if she could still stoke the flames of lust in a man once again.

She kind of felt sorry for Paul. He had no idea what was waiting for him when he returned. She intended to literally knock the socks off him when he walked in the door. She was going to have her way with him and could hardly wait for his return.

~

Needing to touch him, Katie leaned into Jake, and patiently knocked on her mother's door. Texas had been a huge mistake and she'd longed for Jake so bad, she'd finally told her Dad she had to get back to write a paper. She'd changed her flight to Friday and came home.

Now Saturday morning she stood with Jake in hand, waiting to introduce him to her mother. Since they both came from divorced families, it was the first of the meetings of the parents.

Marianne opened the door and she threw her arms around Katie. "I'm so glad you called and said you were coming today. It's been ages since I've seen you."

Katie hugged her Mom back. Her Mom's unconditional love was always there. Her dad loved her, but her mother showed her the depth of her commitment to her, in so many ways. Time spent with her Dad always proved her mother's devotion and helped Katie see the error of her ways. She owed her mother an apology and she hoped her visit today would lead them back to the mother-daughter link they once had.

"Mom, there's someone I want you to meet."

Her mother slowly released her and faced Jake. "Hello, I'm Marianne Larson."

"Jake Ballard," he said, ill at ease as he yanked his hand from his pocket.

"We've been hanging out together for a while now," Katie said happily as her mother studied Jake.

"How nice," her mother said. "Come on in you two. I fixed lunch and it should be ready in about an hour. In the meantime, we can get caught up."

Though Katie had told Jake her mother's apartment was really small, he seemed to fill the entire room. He wasn't an extremely large guy, but his presence overwhelmed the small room.

They sat down on the sofa and her mother took the chair.

"Jake, tell me about yourself. How long have you been in college?" her mother asked.

Katie smiled at him, so proud that she had managed to snag the best catch on campus. She hoped her mother would see that Jake had a great future ahead of him, especially with Katie urging him.

"This is my third year, but I've had to drop some classes, so I'm still a freshman."

"Oh," Marianne said, and Katie could see her mother's radar zoom in on Jake's lack of enthusiasm for college.

"He's studying to be a game programmer. You know, design video games," Katie said, laying her hand on his leg possessively. He was all hers and she couldn't wait for them to marry.

"That sounds exciting," Marianne said. "Are the classes difficult for your major?"

"Yes, you could say that, especially when I spend so much time trying to figure out how to make it to the next level on a really cool game. Plus I play in tournaments a lot."

"What kind of tournaments?" Marianne asked.

"Video game tournaments. I'm the auto champ on campus. I made it further than anyone in the tournament," Jake proudly proclaimed.

"How nice. By playing in these tournaments do you receive any credit towards your degree?"

Jake and Katie glanced at each other and burst out laughing. "No, mom, this isn't school sponsored."

"Oh, I see. So, how will this help you with your education?" Marianne said.

Katie could see her mother's body tensing. Her mother always focused on the end result, and sometimes it drove Katie nuts.

"It makes me very game-savvy and I'm hoping that someday I can create my own video games that I can sell," Jake responded.

"Aren't there classes that help with game design?"

"Yeah, but I'm not ready to take those yet."

Katie smiled over at Jake, while her insides cringed. So Jake wasn't a good prospect on paper, but with her help, he would be very successful. If only her mother could see what she saw in him, then she would accept Jake and hopefully, eventually, give her approval.

Marianne nodded and smiled politely at him. "What kind of classes do you have to take to get your degree?"

"Lots of computer programming. So far, though, I haven't made it far enough to take the classes I need."

Katie winced. That was not approval shining in her mother's gaze.

"Jake's the head of the Nintendo Nerds."

"Nintendo Nerds?"

"Yes, it's a group of us at school who are into games," Jake said, wrapping his arm around Katie.

Her mother cleared her throat and glanced at Katie, abruptly changing the topic. Another bad sign. Like she just wanted to forget that Jake was here.

"How was your trip to Texas? I didn't think you were coming home quite so soon."

That was a topic she really didn't want to discuss. The sight of her father and his girlfriend made her stomach crawl. They were just so ewwww.

Katie shook her head. "It was boring. Daddy's got a new girlfriend who's a female wrestler and all he wanted to do was talk about how wonderful she is." She shivered. "She can't cook and all they did was kiss all the time. It was gross. I left early."

Jake gazed at Katie, excitement on his face. "Babe, you didn't tell me she was a wrestler. I bet she was a hot chick! Maybe she's into mud wrestling."

Katie gave him a playful pat. "That's just gross. To think, my Dad is dating a woman with enough muscles to take him out."

"Bet she'd be fun to watch," Jake said with a leer, and Katie watched her mother stiffen visibly on the couch. This wasn't good.

"You aren't allowed to watch. You're off the market."

Katie glanced over at her mother to see if she'd caught the reference he was off the market.

"How long have you two been seeing each other?" her mother asked, right on cue.

She laid her head on Jake's shoulder and smiled up at him. "Since October."

"What? But you haven't said anything. Why?" Marianne asked.

"I didn't think the time was right," Katie lied. She'd been angry with her mother, but now after watching her father with the female wrestler, she was trying to make amends, without having to apologize.

"And now it is?" Marianne asked. Her face had an oddly stressful look.

"We want to spend the holidays together."

Jake brought her hand up to his mouth and kissed the back of it, sending delicious shivers through her. "I'm going to take her home to meet my parents."

Her mother took a deep breath and slowly released it. That was never a good sign as far as Katie was concerned. Usually, that meant she was about thirty seconds from a full meltdown. Katie held her breath, waiting for the explosions.

"Well, you're old enough to make your own decisions about where you want to spend the holidays. It's still several weeks away and you need to get through the end of the semester."

Shock filled Katie at her mother's lack of a reaction to Jake's announcement of meeting his parents and spending the holidays with him. She'd expected her to be upset.

"How are your grades?" Marianne asked.

Katie shrugged her shoulder. "Okay, I guess."

"You don't know?"

"They're fine, mother," Katie responded in a clipped tone, knowing they weren't the best, but she was doing homework for two, plus partying with Jake. "What about yours?"

"I can honestly admit I've been struggling all semester," Marianne said.

Jake laughed. "Welcome to my world. I've only had to drop one class this semester. I have a paper due on Monday that Katie's going to help me with."

She grinned at him. "I wrote it while I was in Texas."

"Atta girl."

"You wrote his paper," her mother said in disbelief.

Katie shrugged, wishing that Jake had kept that bit of information to himself. She knew exactly how her mother would feel about her doing his homework. "I'm trying to help him."

"Doing his homework is not going to help him. That's—that's plagiarism. It's cheating and could get you kicked out of school."

"Mom," Katie said indignantly, "he's got to improve his grades or his mother is not going to keep paying for his tuition."

Katie could see that her mother's opinion of Jake was quickly sliding right into the toilet. This wasn't going as well as she had hoped.

"I don't blame her. If you start failing, your father and I will have a serious discussion with you. But having someone else do your homework is wrong. Jake, you need to write your own papers."

He shrugged. "She wanted to help. I let her."

"Hey, Mom, tell me again where you and Dad were married?" she asked, needing to change the subject, curious as to the location of the chapel.

Her mother looked alarmed. Katie was certain that she'd managed to push her over the edge and Jake was going to experience one of her meltdowns.

"Why do you want to know?" she calmly asked.

It was too mild. Katie looked at Jake. "I'm just thinking about the future. It would be really cool to be married in the same chapel you and Dad were married in."

"There's plenty of time for that later. When you're ready for marriage. You still have three more years of college before you can consider marriage."

"Yes, you're right," Katie said, and winked at Jake when her mother wasn't looking.

"What is your class schedule looking like next semester?"

Katie shrugged. "Another sixteen hours of taking the same boring classes I had in high school. I may get to take one elective."

If her plans went the way she hoped, they would marry and attend college at the same time. She could help him and once he graduated he could start designing his own game while she finished college. They would be so happy living together.

"Have you signed up yet?"

"Not yet. I still have time."

"Katie, don't wait. There's three weeks left before the end of the semester. You should have signed up weeks ago," Marianne admonished.

"I've been busy," she said, glancing at Jake, an overwhelming sense of love filling her. She reached over and kissed his cheek.

Jake leaned into her and she smiled. Together they would be unstoppable and once again she would have a life filled with love and stability.

"I think lunch is about ready," her mother said. Her voice had that tense quality to it that she got when she was upset. "Why don't we eat?"

~

Marianne closed the door. From the window she watched as her daughter and Jake climbed into the car. God, he was getting Katie off focus. He was a good-looking, manipulating male who was using her daughter to complete his homework and he was taking advantage of the sex.

She wanted to march to the car, yank Jake out of the automobile, and beat the crap out of him, but it would only make matters worse. And she didn't want to be a feature story on the live at five news.

All these years, she'd thought she was teaching Katie to focus on her grades, but the first good-looking male comes along and everything she'd preached flew out the kid's brain. She should have saved her breath, because Katie was so wrapped up in this boy that she couldn't see the train wreck ahead.

She prayed her daughter was using protection and her life wouldn't follow the same path as Marianne's had.

Why did she feel history was about to repeat itself and her precious daughter was going to make the same mistakes she had made?

And what could she do to stop her? Nothing. Absolutely nothing. Whatever she said or did could run her daughter right into the arms of the bloodsucker.

She thought of her mother's reaction to the news of her pregnancy all those years ago and smiled. Brenda had shook her head and simply said, 'I hope like hell you know what you've gotten yourself into. Don't expect me to raise this child.'

Marianne hadn't known, and neither would Katie, the burden and all-consuming love of raising a child until she crossed that boundary. Oh how she hoped her daughter would wise up. She hoped that she'd preached enough about condoms and sexually transmitted diseases that somewhere in that child's brain it had stuck. And oh how she hoped Jake wouldn't hurt her daughter.

She leaned her head against the door and sighed. Some lessons in life you hoped your children never had to learn. Katie was about to take a fall and all Marianne could do was stand by and watch it happen.

All she could do was be there for her daughter when Jake broke her heart.

~

That night as she lay in Jake's arms in his apartment, he held her tightly and she felt like she'd found her place on this earth.

"I don't think your mother likes me," he said.

"She's just worried that I'm going to make the same

mistake she did."

He pulled her close. "What happened to her?"

"She got pregnant in college with me. She quit school and married my father. Now almost twenty years later, she's returned to school to finish her degree."

Katie loved the feel of his naked body next to hers. In his bed, she felt like she'd come home.

"I can understand why she's worried," he said. "You're her baby and she wants to protect you."

Katie laughed. "Maybe, but she should have thought of that before she left my dad."

"You need to get over that. My parents are divorced. My mother caught my old man cheating on her. She took him for every dime she could and I can't blame her."

A twinge of uneasiness rippled up Katie's spine. Her father would not have cheated on her mother. Jake would not cheat on her.

"When did your parents marry?"

"While they were in college."

He rolled over facing her. "I've been thinking." He lifted her hand and brought it to his mouth. "I think I do so much better in school when you're by my side, urging me on. Just this semester, since I've been with you, my grades have improved. I'm actually passing."

What could she say, his grades had improved because she was doing his homework.

He picked up her hand and brought it to his lips. "I think we should make this permanent."

Her heart slammed inside her chest, pumping with excitement. She loved Jake, she wanted to be his wife and spend her days by his side. He'd made her world stable again and she loved him just for that. He was a good man who needed to settle down and concentrate on his goals. And she wanted to help him become a success.

She put her hand over his mouth. "Stop. I'm not

moving in with you, if that's what you want. Sorry, but I'm just not. Now if you'd like to put a ring on my finger, I'd be thrilled. But you're not asking me here in bed. I want a proper proposal. So before you think about asking me to marry you, realize that I want a small wedding in the chapel where my parents married."

She removed her hand from over his mouth and he rolled over on top of her, grinning. "Freshman, I think you're coming out of your shell. You're starting to tell me what you want."

"Right now, I want you, inside me. Then I'd like a proper proposal."

"You got it, Miss Larson, soon to be Mrs. Ballard."

~

On Monday, Marianne tried to keep her mind off the previous weekend and on her duties as a volunteer at the hospital. She'd had a wonderful Thanksgiving, cooking with Luke, meeting his friends, and spending time with him.

Goosebumps popped up on her arms. In fact, it was scary the time spent with him had been so good. They seemed to mesh. They laughed, had fun, and he awoke parts of her she'd long forgotten. Her body clamored to connect with his the old fashioned way. She wanted to jump his bones and had even left before his friends, just because she knew once they were gone, she would be unable to say no.

Katie's visit on Saturday had all but sent her running to the phone to call her father. But what could she do? Katie was eighteen, old enough to make the same mistakes she'd made as a young woman.

It was obvious they were sleeping together. They couldn't keep their hands off each other the short time they'd visited. And how did she warn her daughter that the boy was using her without looking like the interfering mother?

A nurse stuck her head in the door. "We've got an ambulance coming in with two victims. Make sure we have a clean room."

"This one is almost ready," Marianne said, stuffing the dirty linen into the hamper. She rushed out to mark the room clean on the board.

The automatic doors opened and the paramedics pushed the stretcher in, their faces strained, the leader's voice commanding. "She needs blood stat!"

The nurses rushed into the room, following the stretcher. The paramedics lifted the board onto the bed and the nurses began taking her vitals. The emergency doctor hurried into the room and Marianne heard him giving orders.

The sound of a crying child took her attention as another paramedic carried in a little girl about two years old.

Marianne's heart broke at the sound of her cry. She hurried over to the young man. "Can I help you?"

One of the nurses rushed out of the room. "Take the child into trauma room 2. Marianne, you stay with the child. There are colors in the cabinet, try to keep her occupied until the doctor checks her out."

The little girl held out her arms to Marianne and the paramedic reluctantly handed the crying child to her.

"I'll get the colors. I know where they are."

Marianne started cooing. "It's okay, baby."

She said a quick prayer for the mother and held on to the baby girl trying to ease her fears.

"Mama" she said, and pointed to her mother.

"Yes, the doctor is helping your momma."

"The police contacted the father," the paramedic said, glancing in the room. "The child seems fine, but I can't say the same for her mother."

Marianne could see into the trauma room across the hall. Her breath left her at the sight of the young woman not moving, blood everywhere, the doctors and nurses huddled over her trying to stop the bleeding.

"They were hit by a drunk driver," the paramedic said, following her gaze.

Every parent's nightmare.

"Dear God," Marianne said, and hugged the child closer.

He handed the coloring book and crayons to Marianne who opened them. The little girl ignored the colors.

"The kid was strapped into a car seat in the rear of the car and that's the only reason she's still alive. The driver's side of the car is completely smashed. He had to be doing at least twenty miles over the speed limit."

"Please tell me he's in the morgue," Marianne said quietly, not wanting to wish anyone ill, but this child could have been killed and her mother was so desperately injured.

"Nope, he's sitting in the city jail. Four convictions on his record and now a fifth. These idiots don't ever learn," he said, not disguising his frustration. Anger radiated off of him as he glanced over at the child who had wrapped her arms around Marianne's neck and clung to her, the crayons completely forgotten.

The heart monitor alarm started beeping from the child's mother's bed, and the nurse handed the doctor the defibrillator paddles.

"Clear," she heard the doctor yell.

The child started crying again as if she sensed the tension radiating from the room.

Marianne blocked her view of the open door. She didn't want the child to see the frantic scene of the doctors and nurses working to save her mother's life. God, this child was so young.

The paramedic hurried across the hall to see if he could help.

"Momma?" the child said again.

"Look at the pretty crayons. Let's color this picture," Marianne said, trying to distract the child while the medical team worked to save her mother's life.

She sat down in a chair and held the child in her lap, her thoughts drifting back to her own daughter. Someday she would have grandchildren. This could be her daughter and granddaughter.

Somewhere, a young man rushed to the hospital, worried sick about his wife and daughter. Someone's daughter lay in that room, fighting for her life.

Marianne ran her hand across the child's head and picked glass out of her hair. "What's your name, sweetie?"

"Iris," she said, softly, her fingers wrapped around a red crayon, staring at it. "Momma?"

The swish of the automatic doors opened into the emergency room and Marianne peeked out the exam room. A young man rushed to the desk. "The police said they brought my wife and daughter here."

The nurse came around the desk. "Your wife's name?"

"Becky Rogers. Is she okay?"

"Your daughter is in exam room two, waiting to have the doctor check her out. A volunteer is with your daughter. She appears fine. The doctors are working on your wife."

Hearing the man's voice, the doctor came out of the room. Marianne noticed the nurses turning off the machines, a dejected look on their faces.

"I'm Dr. Patel. Please follow me."

"I'd like to see my wife," the young man said. "And my daughter."

Dr. Patel took him into a room and shut the door. In a few minutes, Marianne could hear the sounds of the young man's sobs through the room next door.

The paramedic came into the room. "How's she doing?"

"She's fine," Marianne said with the little girl still sitting on her lap. The child glanced at the paramedic and then went back to scribbling color on the page. "What about…"

He shook his head. "She didn't make it."

Marianne's heart shattered into little pieces. She hugged the now motherless child close to her. How did you explain to a two-year-old that her mother was gone?

The doors swished open again and an older couple rushed through the doors. "My daughter, Becky Rogers, they brought her here?"

The nurse took them to the room where the husband was.

"No…" the older woman wailed, instantly knowing at the sight of her son-in-law. She fell into the older man's arms sobbing.

They shut the door, closing the room so the family could grieve in private. Sympathy seemed to grip the hospital personnel. Though they continued doing their jobs, the tension radiated upon their faces. In the past few weeks, Marianne had witnessed many things in the ER, but nothing that affected the personnel like tonight.

Later, the woman came into the exam room where the child sat with Marianne, coloring.

When she saw the older woman, she cried out, "Nana," and held out her arms.

The older woman took the child in her arms, tears streaming down her cheeks. "Iris, sweetheart, you're okay."

"Momma?"

"Your daddy is here," she said.

But the little girl looked down the hall and pointed to where she'd last seen her mother. Marianne felt her own eyes tear up. "I'm so sorry," she said. "Your granddaughter is beautiful."

The woman hugged the child close to her breast. "Thank you for taking care of her."

Marianne stood and ran her hand through the child's hair. "Check her hair. I found glass in it."

The woman hugged the baby close to her, the tears spilling down her cheeks. "She's all I have left of my daughter."

Pain wrenched Marianne's gut as she couldn't help but think of her own little girl. "I'm so sorry."

She left the room to the grandmother and her granddaughter. Marianne glanced at the clock. Her shift had been over thirty minutes ago, but she'd been unable to leave.

As she went to the lockers, she passed the room where the father and grandfather sat beside the still body of the young mother.

Marianne grabbed her purse and hurried out the doors, the cool air a blast of much needed reality. She made it to her car, started the engine and somehow drove home, watching the traffic even more closely than normal. A drunk driver had run a red light in an intersection and killed the woman. He'd t-boned her small car.

Marianne drove home, numb. Her mind filled with the image of the young woman and her small child. The car seemed to find its way home without her guidance and she felt some relief when she realized she was sitting in the driveway, the motor running. It was then that the tears streamed unheeded down her cheeks.

Chapter Fourteen

Luke could have sworn he'd seen the lights of a car pulling into the drive, but he hadn't heard the slam of the car door. Still, he could hear the sound of a motor idling. He walked into the kitchen and glanced out the window at the driveway. Marianne's dilapidated car sat in the drive, the engine running.

In the darkness, he could see the outline of her body just sitting in the car, not moving. It appeared that her head was laying on the steering wheel. That was weird.

He opened the back door and glanced out into the night. She didn't move, but continued to just sit there. He hurried to her car and gently tapped on the window, not wanting to scare her, but worried. She raised her head and gazed at him, her eyes vacant and lost.

He yanked open the car door, reached in, and switched off the engine. "What's wrong? Are you okay?"

She didn't say anything, her gaze searching his face as if she were seeing him for the first time. She shuddered and a sob escaped. "It was a really bad night."

She'd been crying.

"You're home," he said. "Let's get you in the house." He placed his hand on her arm and guided her out of the car. She didn't resist, but moved slowly, and he could see that whatever had happened had knocked her completely off center.

"Come in and I'll fix you some hot tea," he said. She didn't protest or argue, but leaned against him as he led her into his house.

Once inside, he guided her to the couch and sat her down gently. He went into the kitchen and filled two cups with water, glancing back to check on her. She sat staring into space. The water seemed to take forever to heat. He gave her a fleeting look, wondering what had happened to drain the bubbly self-confidence completely from her.

Finally, the water boiled and he poured it over the tea bags and stirred in honey. Carefully, he carried the two cups of tea to a sofa table and sat them within reach.

He sank onto the couch beside her and pulled her into his arms, instinctively knowing she needed a hug. She didn't resist, she leaned into him, welcoming his embrace. He didn't ask what happened, but just held her for the longest time, knowing when she was ready to talk, she would.

After several minutes, she said, "I'm sorry. It's just, all I could think about tonight was this young woman looked like my daughter, Katie."

"But she wasn't Katie," he said, still unsure what had happened, but knowing something tragic had occurred.

"Only twenty-seven, this woman was killed by a drunk driver," she said. "A young mother with her whole life ahead of her. Her child miraculously survived."

He squeezed her tighter to him, understanding she must have witnessed a terrible ordeal tonight.

"I don't know if I can do this. I don't know if I can witness the horrible things that happen to people and not let it tear me apart," she said.

How health care personnel handled death and dying so well, he'd never understood, but he also realized they were special people who learned to cope. Could Marianne learn how to watch people die?

"I understand. It's something you need to consider," he said, supportive of her questioning the profession she'd chosen.

"The nurses and doctors tried to save her, but she'd lost so much blood. And while they worked on her, I held her small child as she cried for her mother."

She gazed at him, her blue eyes reflected a river of sadness. "How can I work in situations like that every day without it tearing me apart?"

"How did the medical professionals handle it?"

She paused and he could see her reflecting. "Everyone went about their jobs, but you could see on their faces, that they were affected."

"But they did everything they could to save her, right?" he asked, trying to remind her of the miracles the professionals performed. He had no idea how they dealt with patients dying, but somehow they had to see the good they did for people in need.

"Oh, yes, they spent over thirty minutes trying to stop her bleeding and when she crashed, they shocked her heart three times, trying to bring her back. They worked so hard, but it didn't do any good."

He rubbed his hand in soft circles on her back, comforting her the only way he knew how.

"Without them, she wouldn't have had a chance. They were there for her tonight, even though they couldn't save her."

"I know and I'm not questioning their dedication. I'm questioning whether I can deal with death and dying. Seeing accident victims, young and old. Seeing someone who reminds me of my daughter. See a family having to deal with the death of a loved one."

He didn't say anything, just continued to hold her, rubbing her back while she talked. She snuggled even closer to him, her breathing seeming to even out.

"Do you like working in the ER?" he asked.

"Yes," she said softly.

"Do you want to quit?"

There was silence as she contemplated his question. Finally she said against his neck, "No."

He continued to hold her, not saying anything, but just letting her slowly relax against him. If he continued to see her, he realized there would be times like this. Times when she would come home from the job beat down and depressed.

"Why are you being so good to me?" she asked.

He laughed softly. "Back to being suspicious."

"I can't help it. I have my reasons."

She'd told him about her ex-husband and all he knew was that he wanted her experience with him to be different. He cared for her and wanted to hold her and comfort her and let her know he would be there for anytime she needed him.

"You deserve to be treated special. I think you're a brave woman to go back to school and start her life over. I think sometimes in life we all need consoling. You needed to be held tonight. I care about you and want you to be happy."

"Thank you," she said, against his shirt. "I don't know how I made it home. I was on auto-pilot."

He ran his hand over her hair, stroking her. "You're here, safe and sound. Katie is safe at school, and you left the world of death and dying at the hospital."

She sighed, looked up and stared at him, her blue eyes glistening from her tears. "God, I don't deserve you, but I'm so glad you're here."

She lifted her mouth to his and he met her halfway. It was a kiss of desperation and longing, and it took Luke completely by surprise. Her mouth covered his, moving over his lips, seeking comfort in an age-old connection. And Luke was more than happy to return her kiss, eager, in fact, to soothe and remind her she was still alive.

He rolled her down onto the couch, the tea forgotten, feeling the crush of Marianne's breasts against him and the scent of gardenias enveloping him. His palms slid up her back. The touch of her warm, naked skin beneath his fingers was intoxicating.

She moaned, the sound encouraging him. Her hands

reached beneath his sweater and she let her fingernails gently rake his skin. Their lips broke apart and he raised up enough to yank his sweater over his head. Marianne undid the buttons on her shirt and removed her blouse, leaving only her bra.

He leaned over and kissed the tops of her breasts that spilled forth from her bra. His tongue trailed over her smooth skin and she leaned back, giving him access to her throat. Eagerly he took her cue and kissed his way across her chest and up her throat, lingering at her ear. He wanted to make her feel good. He wanted to comfort her and make the demons from the day disappear. He wanted to remove all thoughts and envelop her in sensual pleasure.

She disentangled her limbs from his and stood. Slowly, she slid down the zipper on her jeans and stepped out of her pants, leaving them on the floor. She stood before him, beautiful in her panties and bra.

"God, Marianne, you're stunning," he said, reaching for her.

She took his hand and pulled him until he was standing and then she unbuttoned his jeans and slid them down his legs.

At first, Luke was a little surprised by the way she took control. Marianne didn't seem like the type of person who wanted to be in the lead, but then he realized that tonight she needed to be in control of something in her life. Taking the lead in their lovemaking was the only thing she had.

He didn't mind. He'd wanted to get her in his bed since they took the motorcycle ride and had been impatiently waiting, knowing instinctively that this woman would somehow fill that empty part of him and hoping he did the same for her.

When she had him in his boxers, she pulled him towards the hallway. "I don't know where your bedroom is."

"In the back," he said, kissing the nape of her neck. She shuddered.

"If you don't stop, we're not going to make it to the bedroom," she whispered.

He twisted her up against the wall and pressed his body into hers, letting her feel his erection.

"God," she whispered, clinging to him. "I want you so badly."

Urgently his hands pushed her bra down and her breasts were free for his taking. His mouth wrapped around her nipple and he suckled until she moaned.

Her hands tugged him tightly against her and he was forced to release her breast. "Unless you want me to take you right here, I think we need to find a bed."

Her eyes had darkened with desire and her breathing was quick and heavy.

She took his hand and led him further down the hall, entering the last room. Two lamps on the nightstands cast a warm glow about the room.

Luke led her towards the bed in the center of the room. They both shed their remaining clothes quickly and he couldn't help but admire her body. No she wasn't a young girl, but rather a woman, with full hips and full breasts.

He lay beside her, his mouth hungrily seeking hers while he ran his hands over her body. He'd dreamed of this moment and now here she was.

She wrapped her fingers around his shaft and he moaned as she stroked him, the pleasure increasing. He didn't want her to stop, but tonight was all about giving her pleasure. He found her womanly center and caressed her as she gasped and writhed upon the bed. She needed this moment as much as he needed her.

His lips tasted her skin, he drank in her beauty, and soon he felt her body tense and shudder beneath his fingers.

"Luke," she cried, reaching her release and he smiled,

knowing he'd made her forget for the moment.

"Oh, my," she said, her breathing rapid and shallow. "Oh, my.

He grinned and kissed her on the lips before he released her and opened the nightstand drawer. Quickly, he found the foil packet and ripped it open. He stretched the condom over his penis.

Marianne wanted to ride him, so she rose to her knees and straddled Luke. This man had comforted her, he'd consoled her, he'd made her feel good, and she was not used to being taken care of.

Now she wanted to do the same for him. She wanted to return just a portion of the pleasure that he'd given her. Right now every emotion, every feeling, centered on Luke.

After everything she'd gone through tonight, coming home to Luke was a safe haven. A place where the world couldn't enter and destroy what they shared. She felt protected and cared for, and it had been years since she'd felt so safe.

She slid over him, his penis fitting snugly inside her. The rush of pleasure almost had her climaxing again. The intensity of her emotions and the pleasure he was giving her had her moving quickly, her body and heart swelling.

She wanted to take him to new heights of pleasure. She wanted him to give him her all. And so she did as she rode him, his hands on her breasts, her heart in her eyes.

"Marianne," he said out loud and she gazed into his desire-filled eyes, holding his gaze as the two of them flew away to the moon.

She could feel his muscles clenching, knew he was coming, and was determined to go with him. Staring into his gaze, she felt him explode inside her and then her own climax ripped through her as she called out his name.

With a mighty slam, he ground into her one last time. She collapsed on top of him, her body slumping as if made of Jello.

For several minutes they didn't move, and then he pulled out of her and rolled her to her side, spooning her. They lay there together, catching their breaths, their hearts slowly returning to earth.

"Marianne," he said, whispering her name against her ear. "That was fantastic."

She smiled. "You weren't too bad yourself."

~

The sound of a beeping noise coming from the living room awoke Marianne. She glanced over at Luke, who slept curled on his side, his breathing rhythmic. The night they shared had been wonderful. During the night, they had awoken and made love twice more, each time more fulfilling than the last.

She had to guard her heart from this man, because she could so easily fall in love with him. She had promised herself that this time, before she committed herself to love, she would finish school.

The beep came again from the living room and she realized it was her cell phone. She eased out of bed and found her discarded clothes. Quietly, she slipped them on.

She hurried down the hall to the living room and found her top and pants. Her purse lay on the couch and she opened it. Her message light was blinking.

She pushed the number and heard the message from her excited daughter. "Mom, call me just as soon as you get this message. I need to talk to you."

Katie didn't sound hurt, but elated about something. She had called late last night and Marianne quickly dialed her number. It was early Sunday morning, but she needed to be reassured everything was okay.

A sleepy Katie answered the phone. "Hello."

"Hey Katie-bug. What's going on?"

"Mom," she said excitedly.

The sound of a sleepy male voice in the background came through the phone, "It's only eight o'clock."

"Shh. Sorry Mom, my roommate is still trying to sleep."

Unless her roommate had a severe cold, that was a male voice. It sounded like Jake, the bastard who was taking advantage of her daughter.

"What's up? You called and left me a message," Marianne said, trying to ignore the fact that the boy was in bed with her daughter.

"Yeah, I tried to reach you and Dad both last night, but you both weren't answering your phone."

"It was my night to volunteer at the hospital."

"Oh,"

"So, what's the big news?"

"Jake asked me to marry him," she said, not quite as excited as her voice message had been, but still elated.

Marianne's supply of air was cut off as if someone had taken her off of oxygen support. She gasped. She'd known this boy was trouble, but she had tried to ignore the warning signs of an impending engagement. Her beautiful, intelligent daughter was about to make the biggest mistake of her life.

Marianne sat down abruptly.

How did she handle this without totally alienating Katie?

"Congratulations," Marianne said, trying to put some enthusiasm in her voice. He was an idiot, a total moron, and her daughter was buying his crap.

"You are planning on waiting until after you graduate, right?" Marianne said, hoping her daughter wasn't stupid enough to give up her education for this guy.

A moment of silence filled the line and Marianne feared the worst. How could her Katie have been pulled so completely off track by one stupid boy? How? After everything she'd said to her when she was growing up!

"We're thinking about a Christmas wedding."

"Christmas!" Marianne said, all pretense gone. "Are you pregnant?"

"Of course not," Katie said, her own voice rising.

"Then why so quickly? Give this some time, Katie. You've only known him since October."

"September, Mom," Katie had that petulant tone in her voice. "I'm going to quit school and support us while he continues working on his gaming abilities."

"You have got to be kidding me," Marianne said, the words coming out before she had a chance to stop them. "Don't do this, Katie. You will regret it the rest of your life," Marianne said softly. "I know."

"Mom, I love him and we want to be together."

"He's a loser, Katie, and he will never finish school," Marianne spoke without thinking, her thoughts spilling out like vomit.

"Mom, you are talking about the man I love! The man I intend to marry with or without your blessing," Katie insisted, a tearful note in her voice.

"How could I possibly give you my blessing? You're too young to get married! You're dropping out! You'll be working a minimum wage job, maybe two, while doing all his schoolwork and letting him skip out on half his classes! He's still a freaking freshman after three years of going to college, Katie! You are making the same mistake I did, only your father wasn't a complete loser."

Oh God, she'd lost control and let her emotions roar out like a lion on steroids. She'd been a horrible parent and done the worst thing she could do. She'd completely lost control.

The phone went click in her ear and she knew her daughter had hung up on her.

She took a deep breath and placed her phone back in her purse. When she glanced up, Luke was standing in the doorway with a towel wrapped around his waist, wet.

"Problems?"

"My daughter has decided to marry a gamer who doesn't go to class and has convinced Katie to do his schoolwork."

"Kids fall in and out of love all the time in college. Don't push it. They'll probably be broken up before Christmas."

"She's taking the exact same path I took, except I got pregnant. She swears she's not pregnant."

"Leave it be and let her learn on her own."

Marianne stood up, agitated. She had to get home and call Daniel. He had to help her stop their daughter.

"You've got that frightened-doe-in-the-headlights look again," Luke said calmly.

"I've got to go. Somehow I've got to stop this plan of hers to wreak her life."

He walked over to her and wrapped his arms around her. "Stay and have breakfast with me. We could go to a movie later this afternoon and then cook supper together."

It sounded like a nice peaceful afternoon, but she had a paper due on Monday and finals were coming up in the next two weeks.

She laid her head against his chest. "You are a temptation that is so hard to resist," she said. "I can't. I have schoolwork to do and I have to call Katie's father."

"You know, the more you interfere, the more determined she's going to become. Back off and let this thing play itself out. If he's as bad as you say he is, he'll screw up soon enough."

He was probably right. But this was her daughter, her beloved Katie, and she had to make her realize the mistake she was making. She didn't want her daughter to suffer like she had.

"I can't take that chance. He'll ruin her life."

"Just like you think you ruined yours," he said solemnly.

She gazed into his green eyes and saw the tension there. "Yes. She's my only daughter and I'm not going to let her make the same mistakes I did. I've got to stop her."

Luke didn't say anything else. He kissed the top of Marianne's head. "I guess I'll see you around."

So what did they do now? Were they a couple or had this just been a one-night stand? Suddenly it felt awkward and she didn't know how to handle this situation. She just wanted to get out of here and deal with her daughter. Later, she'd deal with Luke.

She picked up her purse. "Thanks for everything last night. I really mean it."

He shrugged, a wall clearly being erected between them, but Marianne didn't have time to fix the situation with Luke. She had to stop her daughter.

"No problem," he said, seeing her to the door. "See you around."

"Yeah, see you around," she said, and walked out of the house. For some reason, she felt like she'd done something wrong and she didn't know what.

He had to understand her first priority had to be school, and Katie was even trumping that right now.

She had to find a way to save her daughter from this testosterone-laden gamer.

~

A knock on the camper door had Brenda scrambling to answer it. She looked out and saw Paul standing there.

She opened the door and gave him the look she'd given Marianne whenever she was displeased about something. "You found your way back."

He stepped into the camper, kicked the door closed with his foot, and wrapped his arms around Brenda, his mouth coming down hard on hers. He kissed her with enough pent-up passion that she went from being angry to wanting to rip his clothes off in a few seconds flat. Finally she pushed back from him, breathing hard.

"Damn you, I wanted a good fight." She placed her mouth over his and kissed him again.

He pulled away, breathing hard as well, and he held her firmly against his chest. His hands had wound their way to her buttocks and he held her firm against him.

"Where's the whip cream?" he asked.

Startled, she remembered her promise. She'd been so angry, she'd forgotten.

"Don't tell me you forgot. The only thing that has kept me going all weekend is imaging your breasts with whip cream on top of them and me licking it off very slowly."

She gave a soft laugh. "Honey, if you want to lick my breasts, you don't need whip cream. They are yours for the licking."

"God, that's what I enjoy about you. You are direct."

"And I've been sitting here all weekend dreaming up ways to get you in my bed."

He was back. She wanted him and she didn't want to talk. She wanted to show him how she was falling in love with Paul and wanted more out of their friendship. She needed him in her bed.

"There's something we need to talk about before we go any further," Paul said, his tone turning serious.

Brenda was ready to explode with frustration. "Enough freaking yakking. We've been talking on cell phones for days. I've been waiting for you for days. I want you in my bed!" she said.

She stepped out of his arms and began to unbutton her blouse. She slipped the blouse from her arms and let it fall to the floor.

"Honey, believe me the only place I want to be is in your bed. But—"

"Talking is way overrated. I want you, now."

This was the first man she'd been interested in having sex with since George died. Sure they probably did need to talk, but not now. Not when she'd been waiting for what seemed liked forever for him. Whatever it was, they would deal with it later.

She unbuttoned her pants and let them slide to the floor. She stepped out of them, leaving them behind. She stood before him in her bra and underpants. Nerves made her breathing shallow and ragged. She was going out on a limb and she could feel the wood cracking. If he declined her now, she would never forgive him.

"I'll be in the bedroom," she said, turning to walk away, listening for his footsteps.

"Damn it, woman, you are the most frustrating, tempting, irrational human being I've ever met. How can I say no?" he called after her. "But how can I say yes?"

For a brief moment, Brenda wondered why he would question himself, but quickly shoved the thought from her mind.

She wanted Paul. She shed the rest of her clothes, and crawled under the covers, trying not to be nervous as a new bride.

He came into her bedroom and quickly shed his clothes. Brenda watched him and couldn't help but think that for sixty years old, he still had a firm body, nice legs, and a trim waist. When he took off his underwear, she all but sighed.

"Nice equipment," she commented.

He grinned at her and crawled under the covers. "You've got a nice ass," he said, reaching under the covers and grabbing her naked butt.

He kissed her lips, her eyes, her nose, her mouth. "I've wanted to be here for so long."

"And I've wanted you here with me. Now shut up and show me how that equipment of yours still works."

He laughed and ran his hand over her body, his touch caressing and tender. "With pleasure."

<u>**Chapter Fifteen**</u>

For the first time in over a year, Brenda rose early the next morning and cooked her man breakfast. As she fried eggs, Paul came and stood behind her, wrapping his arms around her, and kissing the side of her neck.

"Good morning," he said.

She turned in his arms. For the second time in her life, she was falling in love. After last night, she knew she wanted to give Paul her heart. No, he wasn't George, but he made her happy, he was good to her and she enjoyed spending time with him. And he rocked her world. "How did you sleep?"

"Very little. Some woman wouldn't let me rest. Then I worried the rest of the night," he said, rubbing his face with his hand.

"Why were you worried? Afraid your kids are going to be mad that you had sex?"

"No, but we have to talk."

"Okay, the eggs are just about ready and the bacon is cooked," she said. "Sit down at the table and it will be ready in a jiffy."

"I couldn't eat a bite right now," he said. "Not until after we talk."

She gazed at him, a sudden spurt of nerves making her shake as she poured his coffee. "Was the sex that bad?"

"God, no," he said. "The sex was great."

"Then, what is making you so serious this morning?" she asked.

She watched him, her heart in her throat. Could he be dying? Was that the reason he kept returning to Dallas and he just didn't want to tell her?

"Sit down," he said.

She took the spatula and piled the scrambled eggs on the platter and placed them on the table. She took a seat.

"What's wrong?" she asked.

He closed his eyes, took a deep breath, and gazed at her. "Brenda, I care about you. In fact, I'm falling in love with you."

Brenda's heart gave a little lurch of happiness.

"But you have to know something." He closed his eyes and clenched his fists. "Please hear me out and don't hate me."

"Okay, now you're starting to scare me," she said, a premonition filling her with fear. "If you tell me you're dying, I'll kill you myself."

He laughed. "No, not me." He took a deep breath. "There's no other way to say this. Brenda, I'm married."

She stared at him in shock. "What? I thought your wife died."

He ran his hand through his hair. "Margaret is in a nursing home. She has Alzheimer's."

Brenda couldn't breathe. Hot fury surged through her at the realization of his deception. She picked up the platter of eggs and hurled them at him.

"You son of a bitch. You're married? I thought you said you loved her, that your marriage was great, and yet you're cheating on her!"

Paul wiped the eggs from his face and picked them off his shirt. "I guess I deserved that. You have to understand, Margaret hasn't known me for the last two years. She doesn't know our children. She can't take care of herself. She's afraid of everything. I'm just some nice man who comes to visit. Every time, I have to reintroduce myself. It breaks my heart to see her like that."

"Don't you think she deserves your love to the end? Don't you think she deserves your faithfulness until she's gone?"

"Yes, and I didn't intend to get involved with you. This is why I've had to take off and be gone so long. I will never abandon her, because I do still love her, but she's already gone. All that's left is her body. My lovely wife is no longer with me."

Brenda shook her head in disbelief. She was the other woman, and she didn't like the position he'd put her in. Her soul was crushed. The man she'd fallen in love with was married. "You're cheating on her. You've made me the 'other woman'."

"I'm sorry. But I don't think of you that way. She's gone," he said, his voice breaking.

"'Til death do we part, you big jerk, or have you forgotten those vows?"

"No, I haven't forgotten them. I almost didn't come back here, because I've been so torn," he said, rubbing his head in his hands. "I tried to tell you last night, but, damn woman, you are such a temptation for me. You are the one bright spot in my life and I can't resist you."

Brenda stood. "Don't say anymore. I swore that I would never get involved with a married man. And you're still married. Even though your wife may not be here except in body, you are her husband. She deserves better."

Brenda turned away from him. "Get out, Paul. Get out and don't ever come around again. I am not a home-wrecker. I am not going to be the person who satisfies your loneliness."

Paul sighed heavily and she heard the scrape of the chair. "I never intended to hurt you, Brenda. I promise."

"Just get out!" she yelled. "Don't come around me!"

She kept her back to him, because she didn't want him to see the tears that tracked down her cheeks. She didn't want him to see how much he'd hurt her.

The door of the camper opened and closed quietly as he left.

Brenda wasn't a home-wrecker. She wasn't. And damn Paul, but she had fallen in love with him. She'd thought he was as good a guy as her George and couldn't believe her good fortune in finding a second good man.

She'd thought he was a good man, and he was a cheating, lying bastard.

Brenda sank down at the kitchen table. Tears spilled from her eyes as she sobbed, her heart breaking. She had to pack the camper and leave today or be tempted to see him again.

~

With the cancellation of her class, Katie wanted to surprise Jake on Monday evening. Engaged for nearly forty-eight hours, she wanted to spend time with her soon-to-be husband.

When she'd told her father, he'd responded by saying, "That's nice. Does your mother know yet?"

She didn't understand his remoteness these days.

Her mom had been furious, yet her father barely acknowledged her engagement. If she'd told him she passed her chemistry test, he would have been more responsive.

All in all, it had been an interesting day, with the reactions from their friends and family. Crystal, her roommate, told her she hoped she knew what she was doing, marrying a player like Jake, but Katie knew she was settling him down.

His grades had improved and he was favored in a game tournament starting on Friday. They had an exciting future ahead of them and she couldn't wait to see him.

Normally, he hung out at the student center where the college had a gaming center. She strolled into the building. Passing several students she knew, she waved hello and continued looking for Jake. He wasn't playing a game and he wasn't hanging out in the lounge.

Frank, one of his buddies walked over, "Hey girl, what

are you doing here?"

"Have you seen Jake?"

The boy shrugged. "I haven't seen him tonight."

He'd told her he was going to hang out here. How could she surprise him if she didn't know where he was?

"Thanks, see you later," she said, and hurried out the building. The only other place she could think he would be was his apartment, but Jake wasn't one to stay at home.

She walked the two blocks over to his off-campus apartment. He'd given her a key several weeks ago, so she could do his laundry. She hurried up the steps and stopped outside his door. Sometimes he hung out with his friends here, but the apartment was quiet.

She opened her purse and found her key. As soon as she turned the doorknob, uneasiness settled over her like a warning siren. The stereo played softly and the lights were dimmed.

Voices came from the bedroom. She walked slowly to the open door, knowing what she'd find, and had to fight the urge to puke.

Jake was fucking another girl in the bed they'd shared less than twenty-four hours earlier.

Katie gasped, her heart lurching into her chest, her stomach rolling with nausea. She hadn't changed him at all. How stupid could she be to believe that she had?

She threw her key at him, hitting him on the back. "Damn you!"

He whirled around, a surprised look on his face. She turned on her heel, needing to get away as quickly as possible.

"Katie," he yelled after her. "Stop."

She ran out the door, slamming it as she went. Tears sprang to her eyes and spilled down her cheeks.

She ran faster. She didn't want to see him, didn't want to talk to him. She just wanted to get as far away from the vision of him on top of another girl.

Near her dorm, she heard footsteps behind her.

"Katie, stop, I can explain."

What the hell could he say?

"Go away. I don't want to hear your excuses."

He grabbed her arm and yanked her to a stop.

She glared at him through her tears.

"Baby, I'm sorry. I had too many beers and she came on to me. You know you're the one I want."

She pulled away. "Don't touch me."

"We were both drunk,"

"You seem pretty sober now. Is this what our marriage would be like, both of us sleeping around?"

"No," Jake said.

"We're engaged not even two days and you're already cheating?"

"It was an accident, it will never happen again," he promised. "Forgive me."

She stared at him, her mind reeling with the pain of his betrayal. Where did they go from here?

"Babe, come home with me."

"And crawl in your bed after another woman has been there? I don't think so."

"No, come home and we'll talk."

"Fuck you. I don't want to talk right now. I'm so angry. Would you want to talk if you'd found me in bed with someone else?"

"Of course not." Jake ran his hand through his hair. "Are you calling off the engagement?"

Katie started to cry, sobs wracking her at the thought of breaking off her engagement to Jake. She loved him. She didn't want this to be the end of their relationship, but how could they go on?

Jake wrapped his arms around her. "I'm so sorry, babe. I promise you, it will never happen again. Give me another chance? You are the only woman for me."

She let him hold her in his arms as she cried, but she didn't say anything else. She didn't know what to say. She didn't know what she wanted and she just let him hold her.

After ten minutes of standing out in the cold, she pulled out of his arms. "I have to go in. I'll talk to you later."

He held her hand and gazed at her. "Are you okay? Are we okay?"

Fresh anger surged through her. "I'll be okay."

She pulled her hand away. "Bye Jake."

The cold wind swept right through her as she headed into the dorm. She'd been looking forward to seeing him and at this moment she hated him.

Maybe Crystal was right. Maybe Jake would always be a player that would never settle down with one woman. Maybe her mother was right and they weren't ready for marriage. What had she almost done?

~

By Tuesday evening, Brenda had driven the camper to another camping area on the other side of the lake, away from where Paul camped. She didn't know how long she'd be here, but right now she needed a day or two to let her wounds heal before she started the drive to Colorado.

She wasn't ready to face her daughter or her granddaughter and let them know a man had broken her heart. She was the tough old bird and right now she felt like she'd flown into the windshield of a Mack truck and was splattered all over the glass.

Now she could say she had loved again, but how did she explain she'd fallen in love with a married man?

Yes, his situation was unique, but by the laws of man and God, he was still married. He still had commitments to his previous wife and would until she passed away.

But Brenda kept seeing his pain-stricken face when

he'd told her the truth and he admitted to loving her.

Life was never easy. And love was often painful.

The phone rang and she looked down to see the caller ID. With relief, she recognized her granddaughter's number.

"Hi there," she said, happy to hear from Katie.

"Nana, I need your help," she said, her voice shaky.

"What's wrong, honey?" she asked.

"Daddy's in the hospital. They just called me and said he's had a heart attack. Mom's not answering her phone," Katie said, her voice panicky. "I took the first flight out of Denver, but they routed me to Kansas City and I'm laid over here. I'm trying to get to Dallas."

"How bad is he? Is it life-threatening?"

"They told me I needed to get there as quick as possible." Katie started to cry. "I don't know if I'm going to make it."

Oh dear. The jerk was dying, but all she could think about was her sweet granddaughter. How would she handle it? How could she help her?

"You just get on the next flight to Dallas and I'll find your Mom. Call me when you have your flight number and I'll be waiting for you at the airport in Dallas."

"Nana, I'm so afraid he's going to die."

"Honey, just say a prayer and get on the first airplane you can. I'm packing the camper right now. By the time you get to Dallas, I should be there."

"Thanks, Nana, you're the best. Tell Mom to call me."

"I will. You be careful. I love you," Brenda said, already in motion. Within a few minutes, she'd secured everything inside the camper and went outside to let down the air jacks. In less than thirty minutes, she was ready to hit the road.

She dialed Marianne's cell phone and only received her voice message.

"This is your mother. It's an emergency. Call me."

Brenda sat behind the wheel of the camper and glanced out into the night. Daniel had suffered a heart attack. Damn, if it didn't seem like poetic justice. She only hoped he didn't pass away before Katie learned the truth about her father. She deserved to hear Daniel admit to cheating on Marianne.

Brenda cranked up the engine and pulled the big RV out of the space, heading into the night.

Thirty minutes later, Marianne called.

"Where the hell have you been?" her mother asked. The woman could answer her phone occasionally. Especially when there was an emergency.

"I'm a volunteer at the hospital and I can't keep my phone with me. Katie has left me two frantic messages. What's going on? Is she okay? She's not answering her phone."

Brenda backed off, realizing her daughter was in a place where cell phones were prohibited and that she'd called as soon as she got the message.

"Katie's fine. She's stuck in an airport in Kansas City. Daniel had a heart attack and the hospital called her and told her to get to Dallas."

"Oh, dear God. My poor baby. Is she all right?"

"She's trying to get out of Kansas City and get to Dallas. I'm on my way to DFW Airport to pick her up."

"I'll be on the next flight to Dallas from Fort Collins or maybe even Denver. As soon as I know my flight number, I'll call you."

"I'll be waiting at the airport for both of you."

"God, Mother, is he going to live?"

"I don't know. Only the good die young, so probably."

"We've got to be there for Katie."

"Yes, we do."

"Be careful, Mom. I'll call you with my flight

information."

"You, too," she said, and disconnected.

She was going to see her daughter and granddaughter. Suddenly she was anxious to see both of them.

Chapter Sixteen

Marianne stepped off the plane from Fort Collins into the terminal at DFW. Numb with exhaustion and worry, she hurried through the terminal, bypassing the baggage claim, her carry-on bag in hand.

She didn't know how she felt exactly, but she knew she didn't want Daniel to die. He was Katie's father, and her daughter's life had barely begun. Marianne knew first-hand how it felt to lose your father. A young woman needed her dad.

Her mother was supposed to be waiting outside the gate in her RV. The electric door swished open for Marianne, and there her mother stood, arguing with a taxi driver.

"Damn it, I'll be gone from here in five minutes. It's after midnight and it's not like people are pouring out those doors right now."

"I'm calling security."

"Call them. I'll be gone by the time they arrive," Brenda yelled, hurrying towards Marianne.

She hugged her. "Hi, honey. It's good to see you."

"Yes, Mom, you too," Marianne said, glancing at the taxi driver who was on the telephone. "I think we better go."

They separated, and Brenda walked toward the RV. As she passed the taxi driver, she flipped him off and continued to the door.

Curses in a foreign language rent the air and Marianne quickly climbed into the RV and locked the door behind her.

"Colorful as always, Mom."

"I've been sitting here five minutes and that asshole acted like he owned that space of concrete."

Sometimes conflict followed Brenda like a jealous cat.

"It's called the taxi pick-up area."

"There was nowhere else to park that was close to the door. Five minutes is not going to hurt."

She pulled the big RV out of the parking spot and onto the service road. Marianne was amazed at how well her mother drove the lunking RV.

Marianne laughed. "So, where is Katie?"

"We have to pick her up at terminal two. She should be arriving about now."

"Have you heard anything else about Daniel?"

"No, I thought we would go to the hospital as soon as we pick up Katie."

Marianne remembered her last conversation with Katie and couldn't help but tense. "I'm surprised she called me. She hung up on me the last time we spoke."

"What now?" Brenda asked.

"She and Jake are engaged."

"Dear God, history repeats itself. Is she pregnant?" Brenda asked, glancing at Marianne.

"She said she wasn't. I just think this boy has conned her. She's doing his homework and he's talking wedding."

She hated that this was the last conversation she'd had with Katie, but she wanted the very best for her daughter.

Brenda shook her head. "This little prick is not going to ruin my granddaughter's life."

"The little prick is sleeping with her."

"And you're sure she's not pregnant?" Brenda asked.

"That's what she told me."

"Then why buy the bull when the sex is free?"

Marianne laughed. "Please don't say that to Katie."

"Someone needs to."

They rounded the corner of the terminal and there stood Katie, her suitcase at her feet, waiting. Marianne's heart leaped into her throat. She loved her daughter so much and wanted only the best for her. How was she going to react to Marianne?

Brenda pulled the RV to the curb and Marianne yanked open the door, anxious to reach her daughter. "Katie, I'm so sorry about your Dad."

"Mom, how did you beat me here?" Katie asked, shocked.

"I took a direct flight from Fort Collins. I think I caught the last flight of the day."

"God, I feel like I've been flying forever," Katie said, hugging her. "Any news on Dad?"

"Not that I know of," Marianne said.

"Nana," Katie said, releasing her mother and hugging her grandmother.

"I think you've gotten even more beautiful," her grandmother said, hugging her. "Let's get you in the RV and to the hospital."

Katie didn't know how she felt right now, besides numb. First the call from the hospital and now to see her mother here in town with her grandmother. She hadn't expected that.

"I'm so tired," Katie said, climbing into the RV while her grandmother grabbed her suitcase and placed it inside the vehicle. "I didn't think I would ever get out of Kansas City. Four hours sitting, waiting, and worrying."

Brenda climbed into the vehicle and pulled the RV back out into the non-existent airport traffic. At midnight, very few people were on the road besides the airport workers.

"What hospital is he in?" Brenda asked.

"Medical City in Dallas," Katie replied.

Brenda zoomed right through the tollbooth at the north end of the airport. It was silent in the RV as she took the freeway that would take them to the hospital.

"Your mom told me you're engaged," Brenda said.

Katie could feel herself bristle. This was not the time to admit that her mother was probably right about Jake. That he was a two-timing cheater. She felt hollow inside, no more room for any other pain.

"Yes, Jake asked me to marry him and I accepted. I'm going to meet his family at Christmas and we may get married then."

She hadn't made a permanent decision, but Crystal was telling her it was time to cut Jake loose, and the rational part of her agreed, while her heart slowly broke.

Silence prevailed in the RV.

"Are you pregnant?" Brenda asked out of the blue.

Her mom so was certain that history was going to repeat and she was going to get pregnant! She was too tired to deal with this now.

"No," Katie said, her voice rising. "Mom told you I was, didn't she?"

"I did not," Marianne interjected.

"No, but with your mother's history, it seemed likely. Your mom married your dad in the spring, quit school, and you came along seven months later. If you're not knocked up, what's the rush?"

"We're getting married because we want to be together," Katie said, defiantly staring out the window, her heart breaking inside. When had she become so enamored of getting married? It had seemed like the answer to everything. Something solid to build her life around. But would a man, especially Jake, bring security or more chaos?

"Yeah, well forever is a long time to be with the wrong one. Just look at your mother, she spent most of her life with the wrong man."

Oh goodness, her grandmother knew just the thing to say to piss her off.

"Mom, drop it," Marianne said

"No, she needs to realize the mistake she could be making. She needs to know how hard marriage is," Brenda said.

"He is the right one," Katie defended weakly, wishing with all her heart she could break down and tell them the truth. That she could confess she didn't know what she wanted anymore. "We love each other."

"Wait at least a year and if you still love each other, then get married," Brenda said.

"I don't want to wait," Katie replied, her voice cracking. "I want to wake up beside him each morning."

Or at least she had until she'd caught him in bed with someone else. God, this hurt.

"Well, aren't you doing that already?" Brenda asked.

An ugly silence filled the RV. Why were they assuming she was living with Jake? Sure she'd considered it, but it just hadn't felt right. Finally, she responded. "I live in the dorm and have a girl roommate."

"So, you're still a virgin?" Brenda asked.

She gasped. Good grief. Did being old give you the right to just pry into your grand-daughter's personal life?

"Mom, stop it," Marianne said. "You're not helping."

Now Katie understood. Her mother had convinced her Nana to try to convince her not to marry Jake. It was all beginning to make sense and it just pissed her off even more.

"I'm trying to keep your kid from making the same mistake you made," Brenda said, shooting Marianne an angry glance.

"Mom, you put her up to this, didn't you?" Katie accused. "You couldn't just come back to Dallas and be with Dad and me."

"Hey, I haven't said a word, except to tell your grandmother you were engaged before we picked you up. And I now see that was clearly a mistake."

If her mother wanted to fight unfairly, so could Katie. She could be just as mean.

"I know you don't love Daddy anymore, so why did you even come?" Katie said, her voice rising. "You destroyed our family. Are you here to finish Daddy off?"

"I came because I am worried about my daughter. I am concerned about Daniel and I wanted to be here for you if you needed me," Marianne responded, her own voice escalating.

"You should have just stayed in Denver with your lover. That's why I couldn't get in touch with you, isn't it? You were over at his house."

Brenda tried to say something and Marianne spoke over her.

"I was volunteering at the hospital, where I can't wear my cell phone," Marianne said.

Brenda tried again to say something and Katie spoke over her.

"You shouldn't have come if all you were going to do was stir up trouble. Dad doesn't need it, I don't need it, so why don't you just catch the next flight back to Denver where your boyfriend can pick you up?"

Suddenly, Brenda slammed on the brakes, the tires screeching in protest as the RV came to a halt in the middle of the freeway. Marianne braced herself for impact, but when they came to a halt she looked around in surprise.

Brenda put the RV in park, flipped on the hazard lights, turned in her seat, and faced both of them.

"Enough! Both of you!" she yelled, in the small confines. "You two bicker worse than any married couple I've ever met. It's got to stop. Marianne, it's time Katie learned the truth. You're not doing her any favors by keeping her in the dark."

"Mom, it's not your decision," Marianne said loudly. "We're sitting in the middle of the freeway. You need to move this RV."

"Not until we're all honest with each other."

"You're going to get us killed!" Marianne yelled.

"Then by God, we'll die exposing the secrets in this family."

"Mom, move this RV!"

"Marianne, she is about to make the same mistake you did. Tell her the truth!"

"What?" Katie said, her voice anxious suddenly feeling very nervous. What was her mother keeping secret from her?

Tears were streaming down her mother's face as she all but screamed, "What do you want me to say? That her father was fucking another woman?"

"Yes!"

This day couldn't get any worse. Why was her mother doing this? But when she looked at her face, her stomach clenched. Her expression was not one of a woman lying, but Katie couldn't be wrong. She'd treated her mother so horribly, if what she'd just said was true.

"You're lying," Katie said vehemently from the back.

"It wasn't the first time I caught him with someone else. It's the reason our marriage ended."

"Yes," Brenda said softer. "Be honest with her; tell her everything."

"I couldn't take it anymore, Katie. It had to end. Three times I caught your father. Three different times with different women."

Brenda reached out and patted Marianne on the shoulder. "Katie, your Mom tried to protect you. Your father cheated on her multiple times during their marriage. The last time was just too much for her to handle."

Why would they be telling her this, now, when he was lying in a hospital bed?

"Nana, how can you say this when he could literally be dying right now!" Katie said, staring at her grandmother in shock.

"Because you need to ask him the real reason why your mother left," Brenda said. "You need to know so that *YOU* don't make the same mistakes your mother did. You need to quit blaming your mother for your parents' divorce. Grow up, Katie."

Reeling, she felt like her Nana had just slapped her. Did she need to grow up? Was she making the same mistakes as her parents had by marrying Jake?

She could feel her heart pounding in her chest as she sat in the RV, trying to understand all that had happened. Was she at fault for the way her life was going?

The shouting had come to a halt and now silence deafened the inside of the RV, though cars honked as they moved around the parked vehicle.

Screeching tires had Marianne jumping. "Would you please start this damn thing and get us off this freeway before you kill us?"

Brenda took off the hazard lights and put the RV in drive. The rest of the drive was so quiet, even the turn signals sounded loud. Thankfully, they soon pulled into the hospital parking lot.

Numbly Katie followed her mother and her grandmother into the hospital. Exhausted, she wondered what else was life going to throw at her.

First Jake, then her father's heart attack, and now her mother's accusations that her father had committed adultery during their marriage. Ok so there were maybe a few signs that could possibly be pointing in that direction, but that didn't have to mean that he had been!

She felt tired, stunned, and she knew she had to speak to her father. She wanted to hear the truth from his lips.

The front desk told them he was still in ICU. They took the elevator to that floor in silence. Soon, they approached the nurse's desk.

"I'm Katie Larson. My father is Daniel Larson. Can

you tell me his condition and if I can see my dad?"

"He's stable for now. They're going to run tests on him in the morning to see if there is any blockage in his arteries or if the heart attack just came on due to the asphyxiation."

"Asphyxiation?" Katie asked, puzzled.

"…Yes, he got into some trouble and wasn't getting enough oxygen," the nurse said, not looking at Katie.

"What kind of trouble?" Katie asked, unable to comprehend what would cause him not to get enough oxygen.

"I'm sure he can explain it to you," she said. "I'll let you have ten minutes with him right now and then you can see him in the morning."

Katie looked at Marianne. "Can my mom go in with me?"

"Sure," the nurse said, and led them down the hall to his room. She opened the door. "Mr. Larson, your daughter is here to see you."

Fear spiraled down her spine at the sight of her father pale and lifeless in the bed. An IV dripped in her father's arm and a heart monitor beeped its steady rhythm. She took a hesitant step forward into the room.

"Daddy," she said, coming to his side. A red welt around his neck looked like a burn. Would a heart attack cause that redness around his neck?

"Katie-bug," he said, weakly. "You came."

"Yes, Daddy. How are you?"

"Better. Especially now that you're here."

She gripped his hand. Tears pricked her eyelids. "You scared me."

"Scared myself," he said.

"Mom came, too," Katie said.

He lifted his head weakly from the pillow and gazed at Marianne standing at the door.

She walked to the side of his bed. "Hi, Daniel."

"Marianne."

"Are you okay?" Marianne asked.

He shook his head. "Better now that my two favorite girls are here."

"Dad, maybe this isn't the time, but there is something I have to know and you are the only person who can answer this question."

Marianne shook her head, "Not now, Katie."

"No, Mom. If something happens during Dad's test tomorrow, this could be my only chance to know the truth. I won't believe it unless I hear what Daddy has to say."

"What, sweetheart?"

With her heart thumping loudly she swallowed and asked her father the question that frightened her the most. Because if he cheated on her mother, then she'd treated her horribly.

"Did you cheat on Mom while the two of you were married?"

Daniel looked away, cleared his throat, swallowed, and slowly returned his gaze to Katie, his eyes filled with trepidation as he stared at his daughter. A tear rolled down his cheek.

Katie knew the answer from the expression on his face.

"Katie, I haven't been the man I should have been for your Mom. I did cheat on her while we were married. I'm the reason our marriage failed, not your Mom. I should have told you months ago."

Katie whimpered. "Oh, Daddy, I've blamed Mom this entire time. And you let me."

"I know, honey. I was wrong to let you continue believing it was your mother's fault. She deserves better." He looked at Marianne. "I'm sorry, Marianne. We'd still be married if I hadn't screwed it up."

Stunned, Marianne stood there, staring at Daniel and wondering at the sudden turn of events. He looked so pitiful and sounded so beat down. She no longer hated Daniel. She didn't want him to die. She just felt sorry for him. But most of all, she felt bad for Katie. She was learning the truth about her father at the worst possible time.

"It's okay, Daniel. You need to concentrate on getting better."

He frowned, but before he could respond, the nurse stepped in the doorway. "Sorry, guys, time is up. He needs to rest."

Katie leaned over and kissed his cheek. "Bye Daddy. We'll be here in the morning."

He nodded. "Forgive me, Katie. I can't change how I acted, but I do love you."

"I know," she said, and walked out of the room.

Marianne glanced at her ex-husband and mouthed the words, "Thank you." Then quietly exited the room.

The night's emotions showed on their faces and she was so tired and numb. In the flash of an instant, her daughter had learned the truth regarding her father and while part of her was relieved, the other part was sad that she now knew what kind of man he truly was.

Standing in the hall, Katie appeared exhausted.

"Come on, let's go find your grandmother and go sleep in her camper."

"I don't know if I can," Katie said.

"There's nothing else we can do for your dad. We'll be right here if they need us and we'll be here before they take him up for the test in the morning."

"Mom," she said softly. Katie turned and fell into Marianne's arms, sobbing. "I'm so sorry for the way I've treated you. Everything makes sense now. Why you acted the way you did and everything. I treated you so badly."

"It's okay, Katie," Marianne said, feeling her heart shatter into a thousand pieces. This was her baby and she could never be angry with her for long. She loved her from the depths of her heart.

"No, Mom, over the last six months, I've come to realize that you were always there for me. Even when I was a kid, it was you, not Dad. But when you announced the divorce, I couldn't believe you'd leave him."

"Your father loves you."

"But Mom, you took the blame. You let me believe that you were the one who wanted the divorce."

She'd sacrificed herself for her daughter and while it had hurt, she realized that Katie was now more mature and understood things better than she had when she told her of the separation. If she had to, she would do it all over again. Her daughter was growing into a fine young woman.

"I couldn't let you think of your father in a bad way. I knew you loved him. Besides, if I had told you about your father cheating on me, you wouldn't have believed me. You needed to hear it from him."

Katie squeezed her mother hard. "You're right, I wouldn't have believed Daddy could do this."

"I always knew that eventually you would learn the truth, but I didn't want that to happen until you were ready," Marianne said, holding the daughter she loved with all her heart.

"I don't know if I was ready, but I'm glad that I know the truth now." She stepped out of her mother's arms and they both wiped their eyes. "Since we're clearing the air, I think there's something you should know."

Her mother gazed at her. "What?"

"I don't know if I'm going to marry Jake."

Marianne didn't say anything, just gazed at her steadily, giving thanks in her heart that somehow her daughter's eyes had been opened to the fact that this boy wasn't good enough for her.

"I caught him with another girl."

"Oh honey, I'm so sorry."

"You know, Mom, when Nana kept talking about history repeating itself, I couldn't help but think, 'oh God, I could have gotten pregnant'. And then when I learned that Dad cheated on you, I couldn't believe the coincidences. I know you had to get married, but did you really want me? I mean, I screwed up your entire life."

Marianne laughed. "Oh, honey, I thank God every day that you are in my life. Your arrival wasn't exactly planned, but I wanted you. I loved you almost the minute they confirmed that I was pregnant, though I kept thinking, 'not now!' I'm sorry about Jake. Did you break up?"

"He promised me it would never happen again. But Mom, if he can't be faithful now, what will he do when we're married?"

"I don't know," Marianne answered truthfully. "Katie, you are a bright, intelligent young woman. You are at that stage in life when whatever choices you make, you will have to live with them the rest of your life. But no matter what you choose, remember I will always love you, no matter what."

"So, are you saying that if I decide to marry Jake, you're okay with that?"

"I have faith in your decisions. If you marry Jake, then that is your choice in life and I will stand behind your choices."

Though secretly she was hoping that this boy had fried his goose and her daughter would walk away from him.

"Oh Mom," Katie said. "You've always been there for me."

"And I always will," Marianne said. "Let's go find your grandmother and see if we can get her to go to bed."

Katie laughed. "You know I'm just starting to realize how much of a character Nana can be. Could you believe her stopping that RV on the freeway?"

"I think I aged twenty years."

Katie laughed. "The women in this family are definitely a little screwy."

"But full of love for one another," her mother said and linked her arm with hers. "Come on Katie-bug, let's go find your grandmother."

~

Brenda went to the cafeteria looking for a cup of coffee. This was going to be a long sleepless night and the way things were going, tension would be served for breakfast. She was starting to realize that her daughter and granddaughter were chips off the old block. They were more like her than she'd ever realized.

High-strung and high-maintenance emotionally, but strong, tough women, and she was proud they were hers.

It was past time the kid knew about her father and she was tired of Marianne shouldering the blame. So she'd taken the matter into her own hands.

She hurried past the emergency room, and in shocked disbelief, saw Liz walking towards her.

"Liz," Brenda asked. "Is that you?"

"Oh my God, Brenda, what are you doing here?" she said, giving her a hug. "It's been so long."

Brenda took a step back, surprised at how happy her friend seemed to see her. This was the very woman who had all but run her out of water aerobics class.

"What are you doing here?" Brenda asked.

"It's Dean. He collapsed and the ambulance brought him in. They're checking him now."

"I'm sorry," Brenda, said.

"What about you? What are you doing here?"

"Daniel, Marianne's ex, had a heart attack and we came to support Katie."

"Oh my, I hope he's doing better."

"That son of a bitch deserves to die, but for Katie's sake, I hope he lives a little longer."

Now that most everything was out in the open regarding Daniel, she was willing to let him be here just a little longer for Katie's sake.

Liz laughed. "Oh Brenda, I can't tell you how much I've missed you. I'm sorry that things happened the way they did."

Brenda smiled, the apology easing some of the sting of betrayal from her oldest friend. "I'm okay. I've had quite the adventure since I left water aerobics in such a snit."

Well, she was in some respects. In others, her heart was still aching for a certain old man who was married.

"I'm so glad to hear that. Call me sometime when you're in town and we'll do lunch," she said.

"I'd like that."

"Ms. Webster?" A very serious doctor came out of the room and looked at her."

"That's me," Liz said.

"Your husband is critical. Have you called in the family?" he asked.

Brenda saw Liz sag from the news and she stepped up to her friend and wrapped her arm around her. When the doctor glanced at her, she gave him her sternest look. "I'm her friend."

"My children are on their way," Liz said.

"He's in and out of consciousness. We're trying to keep him comfortable, but he's slipping away. If you want to stay with him, I'll tell the nurses to watch for your children."

Liz stood frozen. "I'm not ready to lose my husband," she said.

"We never are," Brenda said, and hugged her friend. "Do you want me to stay with you?"

Liz gazed at her and Brenda could tell she was thinking

of all their years together and everything they'd gone through. Brenda knew the journey that Liz was about to begin and she couldn't help but want to comfort her friend.

"Do you mind?" Liz asked.

"Not at all. I'll stay with you until your children arrive," Brenda said. She'd traveled this road and it was not an easy journey. Maybe it was Liz's husband's time, but you never wanted to let go. Just like Paul didn't want to let go of his wife, even though it was only her shell laying in that bed.

Liz took her by the hand and together the two women walked into her husband's room, leaving the doctor behind.

Standing over the dying man, Brenda couldn't help but think that this was where this stage of her life had started. She had come full circle.

Chapter Seventeen

Marianne sat across from her mother in the hospital cafeteria. "Where were you last night? Katie and I searched everywhere for you. We finally gave up and returned to the camper."

She looked tired and Marianne worried about her. She wasn't as young and spry as she once was. They were all growing older.

"You remember Liz and her husband Dean? They were your father's and my best friends for many years, until your dad passed away."

"Yes, you guys used to go on cruises together."

"When the two of you went in to see Daniel, I went to find coffee and saw Liz in the emergency room. Dean had a stroke. I stayed with Liz until her children arrived. He passed away last night."

"Oh my," Marianne said. "I'm sorry to hear that."

Brenda glanced down at her coffee cup in her hand and sighed. "Marianne, I don't have many surreal moments in life, but being with her while her husband was dying, well it made me realize how much I've changed and grown in the eighteen months since your father died."

"I thought you hated her."

"I did until last night." Brenda stared into her coffee and then glanced at Marianne. "We had a fight at water aerobics class and that's when I realized how alone I really was. But then again, I hated everyone after your father died. I was angry that he'd left me. I was lonely. I missed him so much I could hardly function."

This was why she'd acted out so much when Marianne had told her about her divorce from Daniel and then the move.

"Oh, Mom, I knew you were grieving for Dad, but I guess, I was so wrapped up in hiding my own personal hell that I didn't notice until everything imploded. I'm sorry."

"It's okay, I don't know that I would have heard anything you had to say." Brenda laid her hand on Marianne's. "You know, if my friends hadn't abandoned me, I wouldn't have set out on this journey across the country and learned I could make a new life for myself."

"You look good Mom. The trip has somehow revitalized you."

"Yes, it has." Brenda took a deep breath and gazed at Marianne, her eyes teary. "It's not often that I say I'm sorry, but you must be very angry with me for telling Katie about Daniel. As your mother, I couldn't let her blame you any longer. I'm sorry I interfered, but I couldn't help myself."

Marianne sighed and smiled at her mother, shaking her head. The woman was a fierce defender of her daughter, and she'd become quite independent. Marianne was proud of her.

"You're not mad?" Brenda asked, surprised.

"No, in fact I should thank you. Because of you, my daughter and I had a very heart-warming talk for the first time in months. Daniel told Katie the truth."

"Good. I'm glad."

"Mom, why don't you come back to Denver with me? We could spend some time together."

"I'd like that, except right now, I can't," Brenda said. "Last night, seeing Liz watch her husband die helped me get my priorities straight."

"How?"

Brenda took a deep breath. "Marianne, I have a confession to make. I know how you feel about infidelity in a marriage." She glanced over at her daughter. "I met a man, a great guy. I fell in love with him and even slept with him."

"So why are saying confession and infidelity in the

same sentence?" Marianne asked, almost afraid to hear the answer. The thought of her mother sleeping with anyone other than her father was kind of weird.

Brenda held up her hand. "Paul would disappear for days at a time from the RV Park where we both were camped. I knew he went to Dallas, but didn't know why. Day before yesterday, he confessed he's married."

"Oh, Mom."

"We had great sex and then he dropped the bomb that he was married," Brenda said, her eyes filling with tears. "His wife has been in an Alzheimer's care unit for two years. She doesn't know who he is, but he's still married. I couldn't help but think of how Daniel treated you and how you would have felt."

Marianne felt alarm for her mother. Was the man a con artist and just using an older woman or was he a good man who she'd fallen in love with?

"Why didn't he tell you he was married when you first met?"

"He said he tried. Married is married. He even said he thought of not returning to the campsite, but couldn't stay away."

"Is he a good guy, other than not telling you about his wife?" Marianne asked.

"Yes, I think so," Brenda replied. "He still cares for his wife. But he talks about her as if she's dead."

"Does she even know he's there?"

"No, he says her mind is gone, but her body is still alive."

Marianne couldn't imagine how the man must feel taking care of a woman who doesn't even know you're there. And then comes her very vibrant mother who no one could ignore.

"Oh my God, think how hard that must be to witness someone you love wasting away. He must be lonely. He's growing old all alone," Marianne said suddenly.

Brenda sat and stared at her daughter. "I miss him so much, I can't stand it. Dean's death made me realize we may not have much time left together. Yes, he's married, but she's not really there."

If the man was as good as Brenda thought, then she'd be so happy that her mother had found someone to love again, but if he was taking advantage of her, then he'd have Marianne to answer to.

"Mom, take it slow. Tell him you won't hide from his friends and family and give him comfort when he's sad about his wife. He has to be grieving for her, just like you grieved for dad, only her body is still there, not her mind."

Brenda sat back and shook her head at her daughter. "I didn't intend to date someone who is not free to commit. I never dreamed I'd fall in love with a married man."

"It's okay, Mom. I want you to be happy."

"I was afraid that you would be reminded of Daniel's cheating," Brenda said, staring at her daughter.

"No, mother. It's not even close to being the same. Take it slow and if he's the right man for you, go for it."

Katie came running up to their table, her face red. "You are not going to believe what the doctor just told me," she said, breathing hard.

"What?" Marianne said, almost afraid of what her daughter had just learned.

"I was so embarrassed, I could have just died."

Marianne gazed at her dramatic daughter and gingerly asked, "What did he tell you?"

"Dad has no cardiac blockages, which is a good thing. But what triggered this heart attack was that his dominatrix almost killed him when her chokehold was too tight. He wasn't getting enough oxygen, which made his heart start racing which caused the heart attack. My father gets off by almost dying! That's just sick!"

Marianne watched her daughter shake her head. "Mom, if you are into kinky sex stuff, I really don't want to know."

Brenda started laughing. "He almost died because of his dominatrix! That's classic!"

Marianne couldn't suppress a giggle. Her daughter was going to learn so much about her father that she didn't know. Boy, was she going to be shocked.

"At first, I didn't believe the doctor, but then he explained that's why he has such a red ring around his neck." Katie rolled her eyes and tried not to laugh. "Please, this is my father who could have died that we're laughing at!"

Both women were laughing so hard, they had tears rolling down their cheeks.

"Your father is into kinky sex," Marianne said, trying to control her laughter.

"No, duh!" Katie said, shaking her head. "I'm starting to understand more by the minute why you guys divorced."

Brenda wiped her eyes. "Shall we tell her how you ended your marriage to Daniel?"

"Mom, please! I don't know if I'm ready for my daughter to know everything."

Katie looked between the two of them, obviously intrigued.

Brenda smiled. "Your mother knew he was at his dominatrix's place. She took his clothes, all packed up, over to the woman's apartment and rang the doorbell."

"Oh God, Mother," Katie said, gazing at her mother with new respect. "You go, girl. What a way to dump someone."

"It wasn't as funny as it sounds. It was actually traumatic and life changing. But I'm glad I did it."

The three women looked at each other and laughed.

Marianne gazed at the strong women in her family and her heart swelled with pride. "Promise me that nothing will ever come between us again. Not men, babies, or money. That we'll always talk when we have a problem."

Katie held up her hand and gave her mother a high five and then her grandmother. "Never again," she said.

"Never again," said Brenda.

"Never again," said Marianne.

They laughed and it was such a pleasant sound that Marianne couldn't believe they were here for a serious reason.

"Did the doctor say when they would release him?"

"Possibly tomorrow."

Marianne nodded. "I don't want to leave, but I have finals next week and I can't miss much more time at school."

"Yeah, I know. Me too," said Katie.

"Let's get together at Christmas," Brenda said.

Katie frowned. "Maybe."

"Oh, that's right. You're going to the fiancé's parents," Brenda said.

Katie frowned. "I don't know if he's still my fiancé. Let's just say boyfriend for now."

Brenda raised her eyebrows, but didn't say anything.

Marianne smiled. "We'll all try to meet either the week of Christmas or the week after, whenever it's convenient."

Brenda grinned. "Maybe I'll bring Paul."

Katie frowned. "Who's Paul?"

"Your grandmother has a serious boyfriend."

Marianne felt a sense of peace settle over her. Her relationship with the other women in her life was better than ever. Daniel was the past, and now she couldn't wait to get on that airplane and return to her life in Colorado. She had classes to attend, tests to take, and a man she couldn't wait to see.

~

Two days later, Katie glanced around the room at the party. She hadn't been attending these since dating Jake, but tonight she'd decided what the hay? She'd gotten back in town late last night. She'd caught up on her studies and now she needed to have some fun.

Jake was playing in a gaming tournament and couldn't go with her. So to hell with him. She and Crystal went out, and so far, she was having a good time.

"Hey, girl," Frank said, plopping down beside her on the couch. "Where's your other half?"

"He's playing in some tournament in Denver."

"And you're partying without him," he asked in astonishment.

She looked at her hand. "I don't see a ring on my finger, so I'm free to do what I want."

"I thought you were fiancé number three."

What was he talking about? There had been other women before her that Jake had been engaged to?"

"Fiancé number three?"

"You're like the third girl he's asked to marry him. Usually whenever Mamma's talking about cutting off the funds if his grades don't improve."

Katie moved closer to Frank and put her hand on his arm. "Tell me everything."

"Girl, he's a man-whore. He's done half the women on this campus and the others he has in his line-of-sight," Frank said, close to her ear so that she would hear him over the loud pounding of the music.

Anger filled her at the idea that Jake had slept with so many women on campus and used them to further himself. She'd been used by him. It wasn't one drunken mistake with one girl, it wasn't even a hundred drunken mistakes, it was – calculated! Everything about their relationship had been a lie.

"You don't think you're the only one he's banging right

now, do you?”

Oh God, yes, she thought they were a couple. She'd put her faith in him, had spent so much time dreaming about their future together.

“Who else?” Katie asked.

“While you were gone, he was doing Shanda Reynolds.”

“You’re kidding me.”

She was in a class with Shanda. They sat not far from one another.

“No,” he said. “Ask her. She’s here somewhere.”

“What about Jennifer, the girl he used to date?”

“No, she finally wised up. He was using her to do his biology homework.”

“So, I did his English and History, and she did his biology,” Katie said, with disbelief.

“Yes and Shanda was doing his sociology papers,” Frank said, his lips touching her ear lobe.

What the hell?

She drew back and gave him the once over. He wasn’t half bad looking. Why hadn’t she ever noticed him before?

Because she’d been blinded by Jake.

But that didn't mean she was ready to jump in with someone new. Right now, she needed to get herself together and a man would only complicate things. Not happening.

She drew back a little more and locked her gaze with his. “Do you know if he reads these papers we write for him before he turns them in?”

“Only if he has time,” he said.

Katie pulled Frank a little closer and leaned into his ear. “I think I have an idea of how to get even with him. Thank you for being honest with me.”

Standing, she glanced around the room. “Gotta run. I see someone I need to talk to.”

Katie crossed the room and tapped Shanda Reynolds on the back. "Hey, can I talk to you for a moment?"

~

Brenda hummed as she drove the RV into the state park. She pulled up to the gate.

"Hey, Ed," she said as she rolled down the window. "Can you tell me if Paul is still here?"

The attendant checked his records. "He's supposed to check out today."

"Like hell," she said. "Here. I'm paying his and my spaces for the next two days. I'm hanging out a Do Not Disturb sign, so keep everyone away, will you?"

"As long as the trailer's a-rocking, we won't come a knocking." The guy laughed.

She shook her head at him. "Can't you come up with anything better than that?"

"All I can say is we are so glad to see you. He's been in a hell of a mood since you left."

"Well, I'm going to sweeten him up for you."

"Thank God," he replied, and waved her through.

Brenda drove her RV into the space she'd been assigned, put the motor home in park, and turned off the key. She checked her makeup and put on some fresh lipstick, and then hurried out the door.

Time was a-wasting. She had to catch Paul before he pulled out.

She strolled over to the parking spot she'd been told he was in and saw him busy packing up.

"Hey," she called.

He turned and gazed at her, a shocked expression on his face.

Her heart seemed to race at the welcome sight of him. His brown hair and big brown eyes were shadowed with pain.

"I hear you've been kind of cranky since I've been gone."

He sauntered over to her, his face not revealing his emotions at seeing her. "I haven't been Miss Mary Sunshine, if that's what you've been told."

She took his hand. "I haven't been too happy myself. To me married is married. It took my daughter, whose husband actually cheated on her, to help me see that though you're still married, it's different with us. If your wife was mentally there, you wouldn't be here."

"Absolutely. I'd be at her side if this was only physical, but she's gone," Paul said. "I'm sorry, I know I should have told you before we slept together."

She could see the pain cross his face and his expression turned dark.

"You should have told me when we first met."

He nodded. "It's hard to talk about and there are days I try not to think of her in that place. It keeps me all torn up inside. You were a bright spot in my life that chased away the loneliness."

Brenda took his hand. "I enjoy your company; we have fun together. We just seem to fit together like two old shoes. But I'm not willing to hide our relationship. I would like to be here for you. I don't know what tomorrow will bring, but I'm willing to hang around and find out."

Paul drew her into his arms and held her tight against him. "God, I've missed you so much. I've been miserable. I can't eat. I can't sleep. I should have told you sooner."

"That would have been nice," Brenda said, wrapping her arms around him, knowing she'd found a companion to spend the rest of her days with. He was a good man, even if he was married.

"So, were you comparing me to tough old leather shoes?" Paul asked.

"Hey, you're catching on."

"You can call me an old boot anytime, as long as you're by my side."

"There is one thing I'd like," Brenda said.

"Anything," Paul said, still holding her.

"I'd like to meet your wife," she said. "I'd like to see the woman who first captured your heart."

"Next time I go see her, I'll take you with me. I'd like for you to meet her. She was a wonderful wife and mother and I'll always love her," he said, gazing at Brenda. "But you've shown me there's room in my heart for another love. A love that knows who I am."

Brenda squeezed him a little tighter and thought of how her life had moved on since George's death. She thought of her friend, Liz, who was just beginning the journey.

"I love you, Paul," she said, "And I'm happy to have you in my life."

"I love you, Brenda," he said. "Stay with me until the end."

"I'll be here as long as I can," she said and kissed him.

Chapter Eighteen

Katie stood anxiously waiting for Jake with Shanda and Jennifer alongside her. Crystal, her roommate, was hidden with a camera. They had his term papers ready for him to turn in.

Jake came around the corner, hurrying toward them until he saw all three girls standing there. He hesitated, his face tightening in a frown, but then strode forward in his cocky manner.

"Hey," he said, glancing at each of them. "What's up?"

"Jake, I ran into Shanda at a party the other night and found out we have a common interest. You. And then when we compared notes, I learned about Jennifer. Together, we all figured out that we're pretty much taking care of your schoolwork for you."

He looked from girl to girl, his gaze darting desperately between them. "Ladies, without you, I wouldn't be able to compete in tournaments."

"Or have time to sleep with each one of us," Shanda replied.

"Or tell us we're the only one," Jennifer said.

"Or ask us to marry you," Katie replied. "I learned from someone else that I'm the third fiancé in six months."

His face went white.

Her mother was right. He wasn't good enough for her and she deserved better. Her focus was now in the right place and she wasn't going to waste any more time after today on this loser.

"We thought about taking out an ad in the campus newsletter to warn other women about you, but you'd just say we were a couple of mean bitches who were out to get you," Shanda said.

Jennifer smiled at him. "Normally we'd just walk away, but we know that as soon as you walk away from us, you'll be finding someone else to use. We can't stop you, but maybe we can warn others."

Katie stared at the boy who'd been her first. "So Jake, smile into the camera. Ready Girls?"

He glanced around, looking to see who held the camera, and Crystal waved her hand as she zoomed in on his expression.

They each took out a cigarette lighter, held up the papers they had written, and set fire to them. The paper burned quickly, dropping the ashes onto the snow and extinguishing the flames.

Jake groaned. "I'm going to fail. My mother is going to refuse to pay for my tuition."

"Oh and by the way Jake," Katie said. "Your third engagement is over."

The girls joined arms, turned, and walked away, laughing. Katie couldn't help but think how much she'd grown in the last four months. College was a tough time, but right now she felt capable of handling anything.

Later that evening, Katie sat in the dorm room with Crystal and they checked their YouTube clip. Just since that afternoon, they had over 10,000 hits.

"Wow, look at his face, he's in shock," Crystal said. "I knew he was a player, but doing his homework, that's cold. So, how are you doing?"

"I feel better than I have in months. Next semester I'm concentrating on my grades. I think I might want to go to law school."

"You and your Mom are on good terms again?" Crystal asked.

"Yeah. I get now how strong she's been through this whole thing. I can learn a lot from her, you know? And she loves me. I don't need a guy like Jake to fill the hole in my life where my parents were. They're both still there – my mom more than my dad, of course. I'm spending Christmas with her."

Crystal plopped onto the bed. "Well, we have survived our first semester at college, and I can honestly say, I'm not the same person I was when I arrived here."

Katie laid back on her bed and thought about the angry young woman she'd been when she arrived. She laughed. "Definitely!"

"How about if we go to the end of semester party?"

"Let's go, but if I start appearing interested in any guys, remind me of what happened with Jake."

"You've given up boys?"

"No, but I'm bumping them down to third or fourth place in my life. Priority one is finishing college. Priority two is having fun."

"Wow, you really have had a life-changing semester."

"It's been an interesting few months. Let's go have some fun."

Katie stood and looked around the small room that had become her home. She was going to spend some time with her mother over the holidays and maybe even see her grandmother, but this was now her home until she either moved off campus or graduated. She felt at peace with that decision.

She even liked the place her life was at right now. It somehow seemed right. For the first time in months, she felt like she had the security and the stability her life had been lacking.

"Come on let's go!" Crystal said.

The two girls went out the door, looking for fun.

~

Marianne had spent most of the morning studying. She had one last test to take and then she would have completed her first semester at school. And what a time. She felt like she'd lived a lifetime during these last four months.

She glanced out the window of her apartment and watched the snowflakes pelting the ground. A blizzard warning had been issued for later this afternoon and she knew she needed to leave early to get to school on time.

Outside, she swept the snow off her car windows and started the car. It slowly cranked and the engine turned over with a grinding noise.

She'd been back from Texas for three days and had yet to see Luke. He hadn't been home when she returned, and she'd thrown herself into her studies the last few days to prepare for her final exams.

As soon as she took her final exam, she couldn't wait to see Luke and tell him about her trip to Dallas and her feelings for him. She didn't know if she loved him, but she cared about him and she wanted to see what kind of relationship they could have.

She backed out of the driveway and started down the slippery, snowy, road. The plows were out, but at the speed the snow was falling, it was hard to keep the roads clear. Residential areas were not top priority.

She carefully turned the corner and the car began to chug. It coughed, sputtered, and died.

"No," she cried. She quickly put it in park and turned the key.

"Errrr," the engine ground. "Errrr," came noise again, but the engine refused to start.

"Damn!" she cried and quickly yanked her phone out of her purse.

She dialed Paige's number. It immediately went to voice mail. She dialed Luke's cell phone reluctantly. She hadn't seen him since her trip to Texas. He answered.

"Hi," she said. "Do you have time to help me?" she asked, feeling awkward about asking him for help, but not having anyone else to depend on.

"What's wrong?" he asked.

"My car just died and I have a test in thirty minutes."

"Where are you?"

She quickly gave him her location.

"Call a wrecker. I'm on my way," he said.

"Are you sure you can do this?" she asked.

"Yes, I just finished my last class."

"Thank you," she replied.

Ten minutes later, he was there. He opened his jeep door and yelled into the swirling snow. "Leave it, I'll come back and make sure that the tow truck takes it."

Marianne grabbed her backpack and slid out of the car. Snow clung to her hair as she climbed into his jeep.

Once she was settled, she glanced over at him. The silence in the jeep was tense.

"When did you get back?" he asked. "I've seen the car, but you haven't come over."

"I'm sorry. I got back three days ago. I was going to call you once I took my exams. And now here you are coming to my rescue again." She glanced over at him. "I really appreciate you helping me."

"I'm glad you called," he said.

He stopped in front of the school. "Do you want me to pick you up?"

Marianne thought about it for a moment. "No, I can get a ride. Look, we need to talk. When I left, things were kind of tense between us, and well, I just want to talk."

"Are you dumping me?" he asked.

She laughed. "Hardly. I know we parted on uncomfortable terms, I just need to explain to you why I reacted the way I did."

He shrugged. "Then I'll see you later tonight and I'll make sure that the tow truck takes your car. Where do you want it delivered?"

"The nearest Toyota dealership."

She leaned over and kissed him on the lips, a whirl of

desire hummed through her body. "Thanks. I gotta run," she said, and jumped out of the jeep, even though all she wanted to do was finish that kiss. That was merely a peck compared to the kiss she couldn't wait to give him.

~

Two hours later, she knew she'd aced her test, and a friend in her class dropped her off at the Toyota dealership. She'd known for months that she needed a new car, but had never bought one on her own. She'd been afraid.

She was an independent woman, and she could do this. She knew how much she wanted to pay, she knew how much she wanted her payments to be, and she was determined not to go over her limit.

With snow piling up on the cars, she suddenly questioned if they were even open. She found the vehicle she'd been looking at. They had the color she wanted.

She slugged through the snow to the door of the dealership and blew in with the snow. A startled salesperson glanced in shock at her.

"I'd like to test drive that Prius sitting out on the lot," she said, shivering.

"Wow, I didn't think we'd have any customers this evening," he said, jumping up. "Which one do you want to drive?"

"The red one," she said.

"I've got a really nice Camry that I could show you."

She shook her head. "The Prius."

"Okay," he said, and went to the office to fetch the keys.

They went out into the snow and she climbed in the driver's side and pushed the button to start the hybrid engine. It purred and she smiled. She put the car in drive and drove it first around the parking lot and then onto the road. She went to the highway, because she knew it would be plowed. She did her best to make the car slide in the snow, but it handled the snowy road just fine.

When they returned to the dealership, she looked at him. "What kind of deals are you having?"

"We don't make deals on the Prius, because they are so popular."

"Okay, well I enjoyed driving it, but I'll go over to Honda."

"Wait," The salesman smiled. "How much do you want your payments to be?"

She had him. She knew she did. She was going to conquer buying her first car.

"If you'll take three thousand off the list price, I can afford the payments."

The man looked shocked. "There's no way I can come down three thousand dollars off the price of this car."

"Take that price to your manager," she said, not backing down.

He frowned at her. "Do you have a trade in?"

"Yes, it was delivered earlier this afternoon. It's not running."

"There's no way I can give you three thousand off the car," he repeated.

"Take the offer to your manager," she said, determined

"But that would mean I'd have to give you fifteen hundred for your vehicle."

Marianne got out of the car, dug out her cell phone, and pretended to make a call. "Come get me. They're not willing to deal."

"Wait," he said. "I'll take the price to my manager, but I can't guarantee he'll take it."

"Hang on, let me call you back," she said into the phone, though she'd never dialed the number. She glanced at the salesman. "All he can do is say no and then I'll call my friend to come get me. I don't have to have a car today, but I just thought your dealership would want another sale to take off your year-end inventory."

The salesperson filled out the necessary paperwork. "Sign here, showing that you will buy the car if he agrees to this price."

She signed the paper and he disappeared.

An hour later, she smiled as she pulled out of the parking lot in her new car.

She laughed. She'd done it. She'd bought her own car without anyone's help. With glee, she headed toward home and Luke. She'd overcome her last fear of being single and had made a deal on a car!

She pulled into the drive and honked the horn. The snow still fell, and the sun was setting casting an eerie glow to the world. It was silent and white and more beautiful than she could remember.

Luke hurried out in his snow boots and jacket.

She jumped out of the car and hugged him. "Look, I bought a new car."

"You went green," he said. "Cool."

"I've never bought a car all by myself, and after my other car died today, I knew I had to overcome my fear and take the plunge."

He smiled at her and noticed her shivering. "Come on, let's get you inside before you get frostbite. Tomorrow when it's warmer, you'll have to let me take it for a test drive."

Marianne fairly skipped into Luke's house.

"How did the test go?"

"No doubt in my mind that I passed it."

"Good," he said, taking her coat from her. "I made a fire in the fireplace and I cooked us some stew."

"That sounds good," she said. "Can we talk before we eat?"

"Sure."

They sank onto his sofa in front of a roaring fire. She didn't resist the excited feeling she always seem to have around this man. She didn't know if this would last forever, but she wanted to take it one day at a time.

He gazed at her expectantly, his eyes shining with enough heat to chase the chill out of her bones.

"I know that when I left the other morning, things were tense between us. And then I had to leave immediately for Texas before we could hash this out. You have to understand that I spent so long in a bad marriage and that I am extremely protective of my daughter."

He nodded his head. "I understand."

"My relationship with Katie has been strained the last six months. My relationship with my own mother has been difficult, and when you suggested that I just give it some time, it was like hearing my ex-husband telling me I worry too much. All these feelings of anger and hostility suddenly bubbled to the surface and it wasn't you I was angry at, it was Daniel."

"Do you still love him?" Luke asked.

"God, no," she responded. "In fact, the most amazing thing happened while I was in Texas. Katie learned the truth about my marriage to Daniel. My mother has found happiness and she's doing okay. I left Texas knowing I no longer hated Daniel for what he did to our marriage."

Luke smiled.

"On the plane back all I could think about was you. You're different from any man I have ever had in my life. You make me laugh. You encourage me. You entice me to try new things, and you make me a better person. I'm not ready to rush to the altar, in fact that scares the hell out of me, but if you'll have me, I would like to have a serious relationship with you."

Luke sighed "I thought I had certainly screwed things up that morning. I'm opinionated and vocal, but not controlling. We may not always agree, but I'll listen and try to see your side as well as my own. From the moment I set eyes on you, I've been attracted. You are one hell of an interesting woman. I very much want to explore this relationship with you."

The sound of stew bubbling over on the stove had him jumping from the couch and running. He turned it off and came back to the sofa. He pulled her up by the hand.

"Aren't we going to eat?" she questioned.

"Later," he said, and led her to the bedroom. "I've been waiting for a week to get you back in my bed."

She laughed. "Well, the waiting is over, and now we're starting over."

<u>Epilogue</u>

Two Years Later

Marianne sat with the other graduates waiting for them to call her name. Today she was graduating with her Bachelor of Nursing degree, and her daughter and her mother were sitting with Luke somewhere in the crowd. She kept looking for them, but had no idea where they were.

She and Luke had been together for two years now, and her mother and Katie were pushing her to marry him. She loved him with all her heart and she knew that the last two years of her life he had made her happier than she'd ever dreamed possible.

They were partners, they were lovers, they were best-friends, and someday they could be husband and wife, but she wasn't in a hurry.

If she had known this was how love was supposed to feel, she would have left Daniel sooner.

Katie would be graduating from school next May and she was already making plans to attend law school. Marianne was so proud of her. Though she often dated, there had been no one serious since Jake.

Her mother, Brenda, and Paul had been married a year ago. His wife Marjorie had died six months before they were married, and out of respect for his wife, they had waited what Paul felt was an appropriate time before marrying. It was old-fashioned, but Paul felt like he owed her that much, and Brenda respected his wishes.

Together, the two of them traveled back and forth between Texas and Colorado, spending a lot of time fishing and at the lake, and the rest of the time remodeling Paul's home.

Paige was still Paige, and her latest boyfriend was

taking her to Italy for a month. They had dinner occasionally, but Marianne didn't want the same things in life that Paige wanted and that was okay.

"Marianne Larson," her name was called, and she heard her friends and family screaming and whistling as she took her diploma from the college president and returned to her seat.

Overwhelming joy filled her. She'd done it. At forty-two years of age, she'd received her college degree.

She'd come so far, and she was incredibly happy. After taking a couple of weeks off, she'd soon start working at the hospital in the emergency room, doing what she loved. Since the night that the young woman had died, she'd known this was her calling. And now she would be one of the ER nurses.

After the ceremony, she ran to meet her family, the people who she could depend on to be there for her always.

Luke came up and gave her hug and kissed her full on the mouth. When they came up for air, he whispered in her ear, "I'm so proud of you."

"Uh, do we need to get you two a hotel room?" Katie teased.

"One with whips and chains," Luke teased her right back.

"Ew gross," she responded.

He pulled out his camera just as Brenda poked Paul. "Take a picture. I want you to take a picture of my girls."

"Honey, why don't you get in the picture with the two of them?"

"Me?"

He patted her on the butt. "Yes, you. Now get over there so I can get the three of you lovely ladies."

"Yes, Mom. Come get in the picture with me and Katie."

Marianne felt such a swell of pride as her mother stood

on one side, her daughter on the other, and both men took their pictures.

She couldn't help but smile as the love of her family surrounded her. She couldn't remember the woman she used to be and was grateful for who she was now.

The day she'd delivered Daniel's clothes to his dominatrix had been a new beginning for Marianne. Starting over had been the best thing that ever happened to her.

Thank you for reading!

Dear Reader,

Thank you so much for reading *Secrets, Lies, and Online Dating*.

Whether you loved the book or hated it, I would appreciate it if you let everyone know by leaving a few words on your favorite vendor's website.

If you enjoy western historical authors, please join the Pioneer Hearts group on Facebook. This is a fabulous group of readers and authors who enjoy westerns.

Sign up for my newsletter at sylviamcdaniel.com if you'd like to learn about my new releases as soon as possible.

Reading one of my books is like spending time with me, and I just want to say thank you from the bottom of my heart.

Yours in Drama, Divas, Bad Boys, and Romance!
Sincerely,
Sylvia McDaniel

Books by Sylvia McDaniel

Contemporary Romance

Standalones
The Reluctant Santa
My Sister's Boyfriend
The Wanted Bride
The Relationship Coach
Her Christmas Lie
Secrets, Lies, and Online
Dating
Paying for the Past
Cupid's Revenge

Anthologies
Kisses, Laughter & Love
Christmas with you

Collaborative Series

Magic, New Mexico
Touch of Decadence

Western Historicals

Standalones
A Hero's Heart
A Scarlet Bride
Second Chance Cowboy

The Cuvier Women
Wronged
Betrayed
Beguiled

Lipstick and Lead
Desperate
Deadly
Dangerous
Daring
Determined
Deceived

Scandalous Suffragettes
Abigail
Bella
Callie
Faith

The Burnett Brides
The Rancher Takes a Bride
The Outlaw Takes a Bride
The Marshal Takes a Bride
The Christmas Bride

Anthologies
Wild Western Women
Courting the West
Wild Western Women Ride
Again

Collaborative Series

The Surprise Brides
Ethan

American Mail Order Brides
Katie

About the Author

Sylvia McDaniel is a best-selling, award-winning author of historical romance and contemporary romance novels. Known for her sweet, funny, family-oriented romances, Sylvia is the author of The Burnett Brides, a western historical western series, The Cuvier Widows, a Louisiana historical series, and several short contemporary romances.

She is the former President of the Dallas Area Romance Authors, a member of the Romance Writers of America®, and a member of Novelists Inc. Her novel, A Hero's Heart, was a 1996 Golden Heart Finalist. Several other books have placed or won in the San Antonio Romance Authors Contest and the LERA Contest, and she was a Golden Network Finalist.

Married for nearly twenty years to her best friend, they have two dachshunds that are beyond spoiled and a good-looking, grown son who thinks there's no place like home. She loves gardening, shopping, knitting, and football (Cowboys and Bronco's fan), but not necessarily in that order.

Look for her the first Tuesday of every month at the Plotting Princesses blogspot, and be sure to sign up for her newsletter to learn about new releases and contests. Every month a new subscriber is entered into a drawing for a free book!

She can be found online at: www.sylviamcdaniel.com or on Facebook. You can write to Sylvia at P.O. Box 2542, Coppell, TX 75019.

Looking for a new book to read?

Sometimes exposing the truth about love can leave your own heart exposed.

Documentary filmmaker Reed Hunter is ordered by his boss to expose relationship coach, Lacey Morgan's Twelve Steps of Dating program. Discovering the matchmaker is not the swindler he thought, catches him off guard.

Lacey twists him in knots, revealing the value of relationships and shattering his bachelorhood philosophy. But when she learns the truth about the documentary, Reed must choose between reaching his career goals at the expense of Lacey's or receiving the love he never expected to find. Which will he choose?

Sneak Peek into The Relationship Coach

Relationship coaches are no more than glorified witch doctors making money off people's emotions.

Reed Hunter stepped into the back of the glitzy, hotel ballroom in Austin, Texas, to catch the last few moments of relationship coach Lacey Morgan's Twelve Steps of Dating Seminar.

Reed received a lot of satisfaction from protecting underdogs who are unable to defend themselves from the many scammers in life. Like a crime fighter, he focused his camera on swindlers and cheats, revealing how they stole hard-earned cash from innocents. Con artists like Lacey Morgan.

A beautiful, professionally attired, longhaired blonde, wearing a short skirt that exposed boundless legs, owned the stage. Despite the fact she was going down, two things impressed him. Her Miss America smile and her mystifying ability to screw with people's relationships-first his boss's and now his.

She strode to the edge of the stage. "Today, we've learned to recognize your expectations in a mate. You've learned you need to find someone who matches your lifestyle. Someone who challenges and makes you think about life differently. Someone who likes to do the same things you do, but encourages you to try new experiences."

Reed coughed to stifle the sound of laughter rumbling deep within his chest. People bought into this psychobabble crap?

Lacey Morgan, dating guru, had convinced his girlfriend, Blair, to end their convenient sexual relationship. Since he wasn't promising her a ring, a honeymoon or his last name, she'd decided to move on. And she had. Packed up, moved out, and left with a so-long-sucker text message.

"I know many of you were dragged here by a friend, coworker, or the significant other in your life. However you got here, I hope you learned something today that will help make your relationships stronger."

Waving to the crowd, she strode from the stage. The audience stood and cheered, paying homage as if she were a rock star, not a therapist.

Blair's leaving had brought Ms. Morgan to his attention. And he enjoyed nothing more than exposing shysters like Ms. Morgan who earned their often opulent lifestyles by feeding off people's emotions. After he exposed Ms. Morgan's devious ways, Blair would probably return and thank him.

Shaking his head at the number of gullible people who believed her spiel, Reed stepped into the hallway, leaned against the wall, and stared as the audience streamed out of the door. Most of the women stopped to purchase a book or CD or DVD. He watched her assistants take their money with a mobile card reader. If the cunning cheater had a cash register, the cha-chings would have echoed through the hall.

Yes, she was stealing from the lonely and vulnerable.

Ten minutes later, her assistants began packing up the merchandise while he stood waiting, waiting, waiting.

A door opened.

There she was, Lacey Morgan. Charlatan. Chiseler. Cheat. Her gorgeous face and knock-me-to-my-knees body sent the air in his lungs packing for a short vacation, leaving him gasping like a man in need of a ventilator.

Per her online bio, she was in her late twenties and only had two letters behind her name-not psychologist, psychotherapist or counselor, just a B.A. And he was living proof any dumb schmuck, that goofed off for four years, could still get a Bachelor's degree.

Reed moved away from the wall and stepped in front of Miss-I-Know-Everything. "Excuse me."

She turned and he switched on his best trust-me-I-want-to-help-you smile.

One of her assistants, a short brunette, stepped in front of him. "Can I help you?"

"I have a question for Ms. Morgan." He completely ignored her employee and averted his eyes from the swell of Lacey's breasts that were no longer hidden by her suit jacket.

Lacey laid her hand on her employee's shoulder and locked stunning blue eyes on Reed.

Any other time, those lovely blue eyes would have had him in full pursuit of the hot Ms. Morgan.

"Yes?"

He held out his hand and used a deep timbre that always scored him a woman's number. "Reed Hunter. I'd like to discuss your business over dinner."

"Sorry, I'm not available." Her response was quick, cold, concise, and held no consideration.

This could be a tough sell.

"I'm producing a film. A documentary on relationship coaches, and I'd like your business to be the main focus."

Few people could resist being on camera. Few people realized the power of film. Few people knew Reed Hunter's skills to expose imposters with a camera.

"Why would you want to include me?" she asked, her voice direct, her gaze cautious, like she might be immune to his charm.

"I want you," he said, upping the charisma. "You're the best relationship coach in the country."

Her face visibly relaxed and her scrutiny morphed into at least consideration and at last earned him a smile.

"Thank you. Who else is part of this film?"

He named two other relationship coaches he'd found on

the internet, never intending to film either of them.

"What other films have you produced?" she asked.

"I'm not as well-known as Michael Moore, but I won an IDA for my film on the Russian sex trade." He left out the other films he'd done on people who conned and cheated their way through life.

"The IDA?"

"The International Documentary Association. It's the industry's best film award."

"Nice." A soft sigh lowered her shoulders and the tiny tension filled lines around her eyes relaxed. The barriers she'd erected between them slid down a notch.

"Within the documentary film arena, the IDA's are as prestigious as the Oscars." Someday he'd win that golden statue, but not with a film on dating.

"Tonight, we return to Dallas." Lacey glanced at the woman standing beside her before she returned her attention to Reed. "Amanda is my marketing rep. Send me a DVD of one of your documentaries. Call her and make an appointment. We can discuss your offer," she paused, "after I see one of your films."

Success pumped like a narcotic through his veins, swelling his chest and head. Lacey Morgan was no different from all the other women he'd coerced over the years. Once she signed the release, Reed would reveal this scheming swindler and save men's sexual arrangements from the likes of this relationship coach.

His camera would reveal how she made a living off susceptible, defenseless women with unrealistic promises.

Amanda placed a business card in his hand. "Our office hours are on the card. Call me."

His jilted boss, Graham was right. Reed would film the lovely Ms. Morgan as a crusader for dating and then reveal her as a fake using people for their money.

"Thanks, ladies. See you soon." He strolled away, the familiar pursuit of the hunt spiking his heart rate faster than running a marathon. *Game on, baby. Game on.*